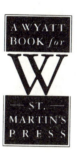

A WYATT BOOK for ST. MARTIN'S PRESS

Land O' Goshen

Charles McNair (signature)

A WYATT BOOK *FOR* ST. MARTIN'S PRESS

NEW YORK

This book and this life for you, Patricia.
And Bonnie Dreame, of course.

Design by Sara Stemen

LIBRARY OF CONGRESS CATALOGING-IN-PUBLICATION DATA

McNair, Charles.
   Land O' Goshen / Charles McNair.
      p.   cm.
   ISBN 0-312-11296-3
   1. Boys—Southern States—Fiction.   I. Title.
PS3563.C38777L36   1994
813'.54—dc20   94-19692
                                                      CIP

First Edition: November 1994
10 9 8 7 6 5 4 3 2 1

Acknowledgments

INSPIRATION FOR THIS book belongs, in important ways, to Jack Burt Bullis, the friend who was a faithful muse on my shoulder all these years.

I thank, too, all my family, friends, and teachers—especially Julia Bedsole, Lois Baker, Tom Rabbitt, and Barry Hannah. A special thanks to Sam Rainer and Tom Stoddard, who made a difference.

I am very grateful to Fred Hill and Bob Wyatt, who saved a place at the table for a long, long time.

Finally, my humble acknowledgments to all the beloved books and writers that lit the way.

$\mathscr{C}$ONTENTS

$\mathcal{S}$ACK

WE CAME HIKING into Goshen, Sack and me.

The fleahop town was just like I remembered, except for little things. Two or three more roofs fallen in. A new wildcat sneering out the window at the animal-stuffer's shop. A big plywood cross, painted gold and decked out with plastic flowers, stood in the burned place where the whiskey dealer used to have a store.

This flashy new yellow traffic light blinked over the main crossroads, so right-out-of-the-box clean it hadn't been shot with a rifle a single time yet.

That new yellow light never even slowed the army trucks down. Night and day, they tore through all the crossroad settlements in these parts—not just Goshen. Highway 27 rumbled like this since the devil soldiers blew up that train and took over the church house at Clopton. Ugly stories came out of all that new fighting.

On the axle-busting dirt roads, those trucks raised red-dust rooster tails. On the blacktops like this one, ration cans and lost helmets trailed behind. It's so hot in Alabama this time of year soldiers can't stand to wear their helmets. The throwaways lie by the road like turtles.

I reckon those trucks full of sun-burned soldiers run down all the stray dogs and turn them into those greasy spots you see in the road now and then. Believe me, bad dogs are the first thing me and Sack look out for when we get to a town.

We walked into Goshen as quiet as could be and didn't say much to the pitiful local folks left to skulk around the shot-up row houses. It's a miracle they don't get run over too.

Two or three of those old liars hunkered down in the weeds back of the tire store, eating throwed-away butter beans out of a hubcap, gone blind from all the bad white lightning they had to make in secret the last three years, since The New Times was declared and the trouble started.

One of those dudes might be my daddy, for all I know. A boy fourteen years old and on his own will worry about a thing like that.

*

One thing about Goshen hadn't changed. You could hear that tore-to-hell sheriff's car coming for a mile before it snaked around the curve down in front of Hix Hamburgers. It was the only rattletrap squad car Goshen had to offer. I knew every bruise and scrape on its hood and every rusty hole in its side. Me and Sack kept a lookout for car number seven.

Up clanked Mr. Police Car, black-and-white, with a big gold cross painted right on the side. Me and Sack hopped quick off the blacktop and got down in the weeds.

We hid for a good reason. The sheriff just might get another look at us later on. And even a sheriff like Goshen's, a sheriff with a brain the size of a rabbit pill and eyes so close together you couldn't shine a light in just one at a time, even an old boy like that can put two and two together sometimes.

Me and Sack don't take foolish chances. We got a mission in life.

Johnny Law cruised by, him and his Cadillac belly and his big mirror shades and his giant plug of Redman. His head looked like a fly head. He spit at the road and the juice hit his arm. His big hat knocked the mirror out of whack. He never saw me and Sack scrooched up in the dog fennel and Indian cane.

A hamburger stand signpost was rotted off at the ground close to me and Sack. It would have fallen over if the blackberries and wild plum trees hadn't grown so thick. You could read something real funny on that sign: EAT HIX.

"That's just what we aimin' to do ain't it, Sack?"

I gave him a good friendly shake and glanced up the road in the direction the sign pointed, at the Hix Hamburgers stand. All of a sudden, my heart felt happy and thrilled, like a day at the beach when you're four years old and you see the big green queen waves roll in for the first time ever.

We eased on down the weedy shoulder and disappeared in the tall woods. When we found the right hiding place, we laid low, snoozing, blowing gnats, biding time till good and dark.

Every now and again, when I popped up out of a catnap, I made plans for the night, drawing them out in the dirt beside Sack. The dirt is a good place to draw. If your plans don't work out, you just wipe and start over. Nothing's right. Nothing's wrong. Nothing's there forever.

Gradually, things dimmed down and the cool breezes

came, jerking the tops of the pine trees and showering us with little twirlybird pinecone seeds in the dark. Hix already sounded louder than you could believe, like a place where people skinned tomcats alive with rusty forks.

I shook Sack once to wake him up good.

"Come on, Sack. Hit's the promised land!" I whispered. "Hix is the promised land for sure!"

That was the blessing. Then me and Sack went off to the feast.

*

We tricked our way out of the dark woods and eased back onto Highway 27. We strolled along through the potholes on the two-lane, like it was the most natural thing in life. Still, my nerves buzzed and jangled. Me and Sack stayed ready to duck out of sight if even a lightning bug flashed the wrong way.

Hix Hamburgers stood in the ugly yellow light of its own sign. A big Bluebird church bus slumbered in the parking lot. The letters on the side of the bus said THE LARKS OF THE LORD. Black smoke boiled up from under the front, and down in the smoke these soldiers in dress uniform turned wrenches with oily hands. Ladies dressed in church clothes stood all around the bus, admiring the soldier boys while they worked. The ladies sang to them—"Do Lord, Oh Do Lord"—and when a soldier asked for a greasy tool, they clapped like he'd just won a trip to Heaven.

I knew what that fuss meant. These ladies made up one of those jubilee singing groups headed for Chippalee, just down the highway. Soldiers escorted groups like this to keep them safe nowadays.

Chippalee, long before the trouble, was world-famous for all-night gospel shows. Now, it's a jubilee forever down in those parts. Chippalee is like a singing Jerusalem. Folks flock there to see the tar-paper shack where The Father was born. And they gather seven nights a week down on the banks of Old Mercy River, to sing supper-on-the-ground songs like "Peas in the Valley" and "Corn Bayou, My Lord, Corn Bayou."

A boy like me sees a lot. I know a few things about those holy rollings. They might not always fit the government's idea of what a sweet-and-light church get-together ought to be. Sometimes the younguns go feelin' titties and toolies out in the woods. I don't reckon there's enough preachers anywhere to stop that. Most of the old folks, and that's most everybody, since folks that can walk and see and shoot straight are off fighting, they gobble food off paper plates and talk real loud about Jesus when somebody they don't know gets too close.

You see the government men too, with their white shoes and polyester suits and blood-red pocket Bibles. Shot-up soldiers come here too, sent for the right kind of R&R. When a boy my age doesn't have arms or legs in his uniform, and he wades out in the river for a blessing, nobody says much.

Anyway, after folks get healed or baptized in the river, they almost always come on up to Hix to get the same thing done to their bellies.

Oh, Hix is the place. On Friday nights like this one, Noah's flood couldn't wash away the awful fun. Inside that yellow-lighted place, Johnny Cash walked the line for the Lord and old lonesome Hank squawled about how he saw the light. Easing down the road out front, me and Sack just shook our heads at that church bunch shoveling down the ninety-nine-cent hamburgers and clapping their hands to those old gutbuster songs.

Just then, my bare feet felt a rumble in the asphalt.

"Sack! Hit's a truck! Git it!"

A troop truck gunned the curve and raced toward us. Two steps, a dive, and a short roll got us clear of the headlights. We tunneled under a honeysuckle wave that dogged down an old barbed-wire fence.

The truck ripped closer.

I never heard anything so loud as that one truck engine. A streetlight, hung on a wire over the road, swung back and forth in the pure noise like a bell. When the headlights lit my hiding place, I saw strange stuff shining in the bushes all around me. Little red eyes and broke bottles and diamond rings.

But after the truck tore past, dragging off its commotion, the world got right again.

Wild. Wild and true.

Except for Hix, with its fake yellow lights and all them sick, self-righteous souls.

*

"Come on, Sack," I growled. I was mad now. "We got a job to do."

Sack and me, we ran fast as little foxes. We kept under a row of mimosa trees with our eyes on a tumbledown outdoor bathroom in the weeds back of Hix. That's where me and Sack would get ready for business.

I had to bust down the sheet of plywood nailed over the outhouse door. It was a sight to chill your blood inside. You would have sworn that poison wild animals blinked up from the swamp of brown puddles spread in the floor and caked on the walls.

"Sack," I whispered to that evil room, unbuckling my pants and taking them down. "Sack, git ready. It's clobbering time."

That's when I pulled Sack out of his brown paper bag.

I unrolled Sack and held him up in front of me.

I clutched the broken plywood door with one hand and balanced on one leg. I got Sack around my shoes, and hauled Sack up my legs. I tied Sack's deerskin thongs together in one piece across my chest.

Then I took and put my clothes in the croker sack where Sack lived.

I was Sack now, and he was me.

*

This old spotted mirror with a broke spiderweb in it hung in the dark above the bathroom dookey hole. That mirror showed just how fine we looked. Scarier than the scariest thing you ever saw.

If you never imagined what a fellow can make out of cottonmouth moccasins and runover possums and a horse's tail and a passel of dried black squirrel guts, then you ain't really imagined yet.

"They ought to dress the TV preachers like this," I told Sack, working my mouth fangs. "They could save all their fancy words, and just *scare* the hell out of folks."

I left the outhouse, feeling fine.

My heart beat a big drum. I could smell the red dirt in one of the peanut fields close by. I smelled a skunk too; he was out there tonight, turning loose the juice. I closed my eyes, took a deep breath.

I saw Hix Hamburgers, Friday night, Goshen, Alabama, U.S.A., on a big screen inside my head. It felt like the spooky show on a giant TV late at night.

A clucking teen-age girl in her best blue Sunday dress sat in a front window. She wore a head full of yellow hair curlers and held a wilted napkin in one hand. With it, she dabbed the cowlicks back off her dumb soldier boyfriend's face. He'd bit into a corn dog that was way too hot, then spit this pink mess back out on a paper plate.

A sad old man sat at a counter on a red swivel stool. It was a miracle they let him in. You could see he wasn't a New Times Christian, but even now folks around here let things slide sometimes. He dribbled a brown creek of snuff juice off his chin, down into a milk-shake cup. He trembled with these permanent hiccups. Under a dirty white shirt, his chest jerk-jerked. He shook his oily houndstooth hat right off his head, he got to knocking so. He kept glancing around, the white of one eye showing. He looked like he was waiting on somebody that should have been there twenty years ago.

That wasn't all. This whole string of cotton-mill mamas came and went at the curb-service window. They weren't allowed inside, since they didn't have a man with them. They toted foot-long hot dogs in wax paper back to cars that bounced up and down on their axles under loads of fighting, squawling kids. Chili ran down both fat arms of those women, like baby job out of dirty diapers.

I saw one old gal in a pickup truck. She had this sassy nose up on high heels and her shirt unbuttoned down to her navel. If you don't think that was a double-dog dare of a thing to do, then you haven't lived around here. Some places, she'd be dragged away for an operation, and who-ever looked at her might be blinded in one eye.

A farm boy had bought this hot-to-trot girl a cherry Coke, and he was waiting for change from his paycheck by the service window. He grinned at her with all eight teeth showing. He had it made, dollars in his pocket and a Friday night out with this living bouffant. Her hairdo looked like it needed a rabies shot.

The Larks of the Lord twittered around inside Hix, pointing at the little Jezebel with their sharp fingers. And sure enough, a man with a face like he'd farmed hogs all his life came out of Hix, saw what the fuss was about, and went straight back to the phone. Those Larks all joined hands to pray. They launched another round of "Do Lord" too, clapping together and acting for all the world like they were just plain too good to ever even sit naked in a bathtub, much less pass gas in one.

It was more than me and Sack could stand.

I opened my eyes. Here I stood, by the outhouse. The cool full moon floated there, big as a big white owl on a limb. I smelled wild plums in a tree. And look: I was Sack, and Sack was me.

"I know it's the right thing to do, Sack," I said out loud. "Hix Hamburgers ain't no good place."

*

The back screen door of Hix screeped open. Out of it stepped a white-trash cook, free for a Picayune and a breath of fresh air. I could smell the chopped onions and boiled weenies on him all the way over here.

He sat down, bone-tired, on a cement block behind the door, hid good from the boss. He snugged up to the back wall and rolled a Prince Albert. No wonder he hid. Cigarettes were still allowed, but people who smoked them were lucky to have jobs in eating joints nowadays.

A match flared, and I saw little shoe-peg corn teeth stuck all out of his gums. Black hair sprouted in wild spears from the edges of his chef hat. He wore a big gold cross pinned on his chest, like everybody with a job wears now. He dragged on his cigarette and closed his eyes and blew out the blue-white smoke.

I saw that boy and Hix and all this halo-lighted world. And some kind of hot red juice shot through me.

I stalked straight across the lot. I passed Coke bottle crates and throwed-away lettuce heads and soggy cardboard boxes. I stepped over piles of car fenders and railroad ties and rotted newspapers.

The cook sat by a rackety air conditioner. It buzzed and

whistled and spit out sparks of blue fire. There wasn't a prayer he could hear me coming.

I stomped right up. I leaned over close enough to count the beads of sweat on his forehead. Something else played on his scalp too—cooties. I saw a dozen. They looked like fat white birds grubbing for food in a scorched pasture.

It got my goat to see something like that on a cook's head. No matter who he cooked for. My toleration plugged up, it made me so mad.

I grabbed his ears like two jug handles. His eyes popped open, and I pushed my awful looker down in his face. His jaw dropped like a car bumper falling off, and his pink tongue tangled out.

"Mama dog!" he said. "This the end of me, ain't it?"

"It is," I said. "Git ready!"

"Mama dog," he whispered again. "Wait. *Please!* I got a daddy sick." Sweat drops hopped off his head like fleas. He swallowed again. His throat lump went up and down, like an elevator. "I got a beagle hound."

"I might let you live," I told him.

"I dig a gully leaving this place," he swore. "Please, devil thang!"

"You git from here tonight, right now, and leave this awful joint and don't ever, never, come back. Not to cook for people in a place like this. You got that?"

"I'm gone. Lawd God have a'mercy."

I let go of his ears. His cement block teetered and fell. His two long snaky hands shot for the sky and he flopped back with one foot kicking, hung up in a mop bucket.

"GO!" I growled. I showed him all ten of Sack's awful claws. "Git! Git out! Before it's *too late!*"

I mean to tell you that short-order cook took his chance when it came. He sprung up high like a fly and sailed through the Alabama sky. He flew slam over a pile of cor- rugated tin sheets, two rows of tomato stakes, a throwed-away refrigerator, some garbage cans, a fifty-gallon drum of lard, five rolls of chicken wire, a broke-up bunch of cement blocks, three-dozen car batteries stacked high as his waist, and most of a blackberry patch. He lit down on that bucket that had him by the foot and took off, clankety-clank.

He never looked back once.

*

The rest I did to Hix Hamburgers, I did quick.

I first took and wrenched off the rickety back screen door. Then I stomped in on top of it, banging and slamming my arms on the cooking equipment. I gave out my most awful wild screeches.

In that kitchen, full pots and pans jumped right off the stove, they were so scared with fright. Hot lakes of sizzling french-fry grease and logjams of spilled weenies and sumpholes of chili and floods of cheese grits poured all over the dirty floor.

The busboy and a dishwasher, up to his elbows in suds, and the 300-pound waitress, plus the skinny redheaded one too, all fainted in one big pile.

You just don't know how it feels if it ain't happened to you. I mean, when you come into a room and such a thing occurs. The Father—or St. Elvis his own self—couldn't feel what I felt right that second.

"Arrrrgh!" I screamed. "It's clobberin' time!"

I stopped at the swinging doors of that hot kitchen. Through the steamy porthole, I could see confused customers out there at the cafe tables. All those girls with bows in their hair and flirty eyes, they stopped what they were doing. The soldier boys all put their hot dogs down on their plates at the same time, with one last chew halfway down their throats.

A woman yipped like a mashed dog. Then it got quiet.

Quiet as the bottom of a deep hole in the deep woods in the deepest holler of the night.

That's when I opened the kitchen door.

Everybody went pure crazy. A hundred blind dogs with their feet nailed to the floor in a burning slaughterhouse wouldn't have made one bit more noise.

"Wild Thang!" they screamed. "Wild Thang!"

It made my skin goose up with glory.

"Run! It's the Wild Thang!"

Women shimmied up the legs and clear to the shoulders of their froze-up husbands. Scared boys came racing out of the freezer room, their aprons flapping behind them like white haints. Tall buildings of hot dog buns caved in on the grill. Pigs' feet, whole twenty-gallon jars of them, pitched down and crashed and the feet galloped through the crowd in a red vinegar flood. Chocolate milk-shakes splattered windows, like dookey in stalls where scared wild cows were kicking.

Sack has a power stronger than guns or knives. Sack has a power stronger than steel or iron. I know, because I'm Sack, and Sack is me.

When the last Christian Soldier boy crashed right through the front window, he ran off with three sets of venetian blinds all over him like mad skeletons.

Out that hole in the window, I could see the full clean rising moon, bright as God's best angel. I stood still a minute, and let the good white light soak right down to my bones. I felt like I had a kind of light on inside myself.

Sack showed them. One minute life had on Sunday-school ribbons and shoes and a starched uniform. The next minute, it got blue-in-the-face scary and everything changed.

That's how God made the world. Full of good miracles. And full of bad ones too.

Me and Sack, we knew both kinds.

The cash register got left with its mouth standing open. Through Sack's eyeholes, I could see money in it. Chocolate syrup snaked down one side of the register and more of it stood glopped in a black pool in one of the silver change drawers.

I reckon I got two hundred dollars—easy. Candy from a real dumb baby.

But then I took and flung that bad money all over the place. Dollar bills fluttered down like shot birds. The Father's face landed everywhere. His crispy new money wasn't why I came here.

I heard a fussy whining, like a giant mosquito.

I picked my way over to what was left of the front door for a look. I had to be careful. Glass from busted Daddy Bucks syrup bottles stuck up out of sweet golden puddles. There were more mushy grit slicks too, and ponds of smoking chili chunked with beans and weenies. Whole packs of raw chicken necks laid out with tore-open bags of cornmeal dumped over them. The spilled forks and sharp knives silvered up that mess real pretty.

Out the window, I could see a bunch of the Larks down in the parking lot. The church bus was gone now, and so were all those yellow-bellied soldiers. A few desperate women stayed behind in a cloud of smoke, and they clawed and spit and took the Lord's name in vain and pulled hair, all six or seven at once trying to wiggle through one broke-out window of a white Cadillac.

I saw another sight. This little tiny girl with yellow hair, standing right in the middle of the parking lot. She looked about four years old. She was all of a sudden left alone in the big empty world.

Just like me.

This plain white dress she wore, the one all little girls

have to wear now, was just covered with chili and dirt where she'd got knocked flat. Stray yellow hair caught in the corner of one eye. She squawled black streaks and crammed four dirty fingers in her mouth.

"Girl!" I called, nice and soft.

She hushed right in the middle of her loudest holler yet.

"Girl, go on now! Hix ain't no place for you!"

That poor, spooked, left-alone child turned and ran off toward the white Cadillac like a toy doll you wind up. By then, one of the Larks wearing a fancy green silk robe had missed little Velveeta, or whoever she was, and hustled back for her.

Those two girls met in the middle of the parking lot. The green mama swooped down and got her little baby and she was saved.

My heart almost broke right in two when I saw that. I reckon my own mama would have been that brave, if she'd made it this far.

The Cadillac wheeled up, and a door flew open and swallowed those two. The car jerked toward the highway in a red-dirt hurricane, and burned off a hundred yards of rubber when it hit the paved road.

My eyes started to burn too. I couldn't see a durn thing, not for a whole minute.

A fellow's got to do what a fellow's got to do. Someday, maybe years and years from now, people around Goshen might be glad for one night when life went wild.

They might sit around the fireplace, or whatever folks sit around in those times, and tell how, just once, things in The New Times weren't just exactly the same as every other oh-so-holy night, forever and ever amen.

They might talk about how Sack came. They might talk about what Sack did to remind them how the world really was. They might remember something way different from

TV preachers and church buses and Christian Soldiers and a bunch of hypocrites in black robes promising how good life would be after decent folks gave everything to the church and then died.

I swam out of those salty tears thinking about that.

I eased on outside, right up under the ugly sign in front of the hamburger joint. Moths bumped their heads against the giant plastic hamburgers. A horrible-looking root beer overflowed its glass and dripped poison down the side.

I spotted a chunk of wood in the parking lot. I busted the sign with the wood. Then I found a mop stick lying somewhere and knocked out every other light in the whole durn joint. I ran a little wild, I reckon. I don't really remember every particular thing.

*

I changed back in the outhouse, and me and Sack stumbled off to the east, toward our secret place.

I watched the rising of the total moon, higher and higher. That glorious sight. The moon gets as perfect as a thing can get. I bet there ain't a church steeple on it.

Tomorrow, it rises full one more night. Me and Sack go to Bob-A-Lu, the next place to save. It's over the river and through the woods.

Hallelujah!

There's something I believe in. This is it: We all been losing ground since the Garden of Eden.

But now, me and Sack, we're making up for it.

HARD BY Old Mercy River, way back in the deep woods, stands this Indian mound.

It's the spot me and Sack call home.

One time, I dug a hole in the mound and turned out enough Indian bones to fill up a cigar box. I found a big clay pot that crumbled to pieces. There were some arrowheads and a wolf skull so old you can't count back that far in years. That's what folks buried once upon a time, instead of burned jeeps and shot-up trucks and soldiers.

This mound stands higher than a house, but it's a pure midget compared to Big Temple. That's the mound they pushed up over all those shot-dead boys last year at Kolomoki.

Big Temple is flat on top, with prickly pears and short yellow grass up the sides. You can see falling stars all night long if you stand on top. But you ain't allowed. Up on top is a statue of The Father. Only the most important people in the world can go visit that statue. Anybody else gets shot down like a dog.

Out here, on my little mound, there ain't no scary bronze thing draped in black preacher robes like a scarecrow on a cross. Nobody but Sack and me climbs here, and the wind doesn't blow all sad and mournful like it does around Big Temple. On a night like this, the full moon shines bright as day. You can see out in the woods where the animals come and go. You'd think it was the only peaceful place left in the whole world.

Maybe it is.

It's The Secret Place, and it's mine and Sack's.

These big red trees grow in a circle right around our Indian mound. They're different from the tulip poplars and blackjack oaks and other trees that took over this bottomland. I can't begin to guess how that red ring of giants got there, or who planted them. I know the little black fruits on the limbs smell sweet in the spring when the wind blows, and the needles grow as thick as needles on a porcupine's back. But who put these trees here? I can't say.

I can tell you this, though.

This place makes a happy noise in your heart when you get here after a long scary night.

*

My brother Randy and me, while he was still alive, found this spot together. Randy liked to hunt, and I was his little hunting brother. We'd find a new piece of woods every trip out, a spot where Randy could pick off a half-dozen squirrels before the come-up sun pinked the tops of the trees.

Randy could do everything. Shoot that rifle. Play football. He got picked president by the boys in the orphans' home. He always won prizes at the fair for knocking off the stuffed cats with baseballs. He could strip the net five out of five from the big hole in the playground. Good at girls too. He was a pure legend around Goshen.

He didn't turn all high and mighty, though, the way you might think. He was a good brother. Whenever we went to the trees and fields, he took care to teach me. That's how I know everything I know about the deep woods.

Randy showed me how to creep so quiet I could come up on a scared bobwhite and touch it with my finger before it flew. He gave me lessons on all the animals and rivers and the skies. Stuff you can't learn anymore. He said in the olden days people used to get down on their knees and pray to nature, and the trees and fields gave them what they asked for.

You won't read *that* in a history book anymore. They burn books for having stories like those.

Anyway, my brother Randy watched over me in the woods. I never once got hung in a barbed-wire fence or slapped in the face by a limb. One time, Randy saved me from stepping in a steel bear trap somebody set out at the edge of a sweet-corn field. This was back when a bear was the worst thing in the woods anybody around here ever had to worry about.

My brother always got this look in his eye when we set out on a hunt. He forever wanted one thing. To go farther and farther back in the wild places, farther than anybody ever went before.

No swamp was too wild, and no woods too thick. If the next hill was a mystery, Randy wanted to go over it.

The summer he got out of high school, we set off on a seven-day hunt. Me and him started one morning way before the sun got out of bed, and we blazed a trail in the woods that day till the sun tuckered out and just sunk down cold and tired to a soft spot on the ground. We traveled hard for a solid week, back to the rough-and-ready land, living off the bounty of Alabama. The woods in some places got so thick I believe even the mosquitoes had to land on the ground and walk to get through.

In the very deepest part of the woods, we made a camp. Randy pitched our tent and sparked a fire, and we cooked four wood doves he shot, with rings of swamp pineapple crisped into the breasts.

From there, we just explored all next day, slipping through the trees and little gullies, always watching the limbs jump just up ahead. When we came to a meadow, me and Randy walked through, and it seemed like all those yellow flowers bowed down their heads.

Before we slept at night, sitting by the campfire, Randy would explain and explain, like a river running, about what me and him might have to do soon. The fighting was already started, he said. Folks like me and him, we had to have a plan.

Next morning, the sun turned the woods silver. I saw a teen-age deer walk up to a hickory tree and scratch the shaggy bark against the place where his horns would grow.

Something itched inside of me too, but I didn't know what it was then.

*

Me and Randy found The Secret Place on that trip, way out in the woods, miles and miles and still more miles past the last rusty potted-meat can and lost shoe and empty shotgun shell left by people.

When we saw the Indian mound, both of us stood there with our mouths open. It was like finding some lost old city.

We took in the mound and the ring of big old red trees. The Secret Place just soaked up the peaceful quiet. You could believe important things happened here one time.

Things that nobody left alive anywhere remembered. You could just feel old, serious thoughts and doings in the air.

We made camp right on top of the Indian mound that night. It rained to beat the band, but some kind of strange thing happened. A good thing. Our fire never went out. Our sleeping bags didn't get wet. Randy said he had a dream about people made out of fire that danced around us with colored animal skins and kept the rain off.

My brother could have used a few more friends like that. In three more months, he was dead and gone. He got shot and killed when the government men, the Christian Soldiers, came to take our town.

Now Randy lies with all the other boys under Big Temple.

*

It got to be first light of the morning just about the time me and Sack settled in from our long night's work.

I lay flat on my back on top of the mound, plumb in the middle of the world. The grass smelled sweet, and grasshoppers zinged every which way, and a hawk stretched its arms out trying to grab hold of everything below it at once. Way high, the clouds in the sky piled up.

I thought about Hix Hamburgers, just once, then forgot that Hix ever happened.

I slept so hard that I dreamed about sleeping. There I was, in a dream, watching my own self take a nap. I jerked one foot, the way a cat does sometimes when it dreams about chasing a mouse.

On up in the morning, I stirred. I caught a fat bream and cooked it over the hot coals I kept. The meat was white, like the fast parts of Old Mercy River where the fish came from. I ate sweet wild grapes off a vine too.

After food, I lifted Sack down out of a tree limb where

he swung like yesterday's laundry, drying out. Out spook-
ing, I always sweat him up fierce. I don't ever wash him
either. He smells to high heaven, but in these times, that's
extra scare power.

I took and stuffed Sack back into his croker sack. I
found that sack in the river. It's the best river thing I ever
found, unless you count a box of canned pork 'n beans that
floated down from the sky on a dirty white parachute one
afternoon last summer and snagged in a tree by the river.

You could hear guns almost every night in those days. I
was fishing and caught a soldier's boot out of the river not
long after that. His foot was still inside, blown right off. I
knew the trouble was bad upriver when that happened.

Down in the croker sack, Sack played sound asleep. His
little furry arms crossed under his chinny chin chin. He
wore this smile.

I wished him sweet dreams.

Sack was safe. Sack was good.

As long as I lived, nothing would happen to Sack. Not if
I could help it.

See, I lost every other person I ever loved. Mama.
Daddy. Randy most of all.

I'm tired of losing love like that.

*

Sack went on to dreamland, and I patted down the grass
over his hiding place so good you couldn't tell a soul had
stepped there for a hundred years.

Sack slept in the side of the Indian mound, a secret place
like the door to a storm cellar. I found this hole by accident, after a gopher tortoise popped out of it one afternoon. The passageway wormed all the way, deep, deep
inside the Indian mound. There's no telling how long that
hole lived there, or what all went in and out of it all those

years ago. I got a little shiver thinking about what might come out of a hole you didn't know.

After bedtime for Sack, it was my turn.

The sun scorched down, mid-morning now, blinding white all around. My hammock, made out of soft green wisteria vines, begged to me from the shade of those red trees, and I crawled in. The breeze got pushy and blew my cradle rock-a-bye. I was a happy red-haired baby in a birthday suit.

Life seemed simple as pie. In the day, I snoozed and rested up. At night, I strutted loose out in the world with my shoulders square, a fourteen-year-old cock o' the walk.

I wanted to be great one day. As great as Randy, if I ever could.

I wanted to be a legend too.

Me and Sack.

*

In the afternoon, I woke up hungry and checked my willow traps in the river. This big fat catfish wiggled inside one.

I saved him for later. The longer you leave a catfish in fast water these days, the safer. A catfish will eat anything, and you never know what settles to the bottom in the slow, deep part of a river when there's a war.

No more fish in the other traps, so I waded out onto the bank and picked some huckleberries for a snack. My fingers turned purple as a cow's liver. Then I wrapped a trumpet vine around my head to keep the mama bird away while I climbed a tree. I got down a handful of bluejay eggs and sucked the middles out of them. If you never tried that, you ought to. Bluejay eggs taste sweet as jelly.

When I eased back down in the hammock, careful not to flip, my stomach looked as big as the Indian mound, if an Indian mound had freckles all over it.

Oh me. Life felt good that minute.

Legends down here start the way little sparks jump off a burn in a pasture. The wind picks up and the sparks take off like a flock of spooked cardinals. Soon you got a legend that burns ten-thousand acres.

Me and Sack want to blaze up so fierce and pure and good that none of these bad folks with bad ideas taking over the world nowadays can stand up next to us. We want to wake up those tired, beat-down old souls in every place where folks just gave up to being stupid and bored and commanded.

We want to do right by Randy, and honor what he believed.

It might take the rest of our lives, me and Sack.

Maybe some folks think it's crazy. They might say living out in the woods all alone and plotting to scare all the bad out of folks ain't for any boy in his right mind.

Well, there's worse things than being in your wrong mind, if that's what they think.

You could be old and lying up in a sickbed somewhere, watching The Father on every TV channel, his eyes burning holes in you and his tongue blacker than a musk turtle's.

You could be in some jail, waiting for the ship to come haul you off to some miserable prison island. That's where they send people now who walk swishy or throw a ball funny or get pregnant when they're not married. Those that can't get to sleep at night without a drink of alcohol.

You could have a tattoo. Then you'd be rotting in jail for sure. Marking your flesh is a big sin.

No sir, the world ain't right. But I'm Sack, and Sack is me, and we're doing something about it.

Oh, we get lonely now and again. Sometimes I wish a girl lived here. Some sweet little something whose eyes got big when I tell her about the woods. Somebody to sing when she takes a bath in the river.

But a girl, she could go away. Mama and Randy and everybody I ever cared about, they all went away like that.

Sack won't. I know.

It's me for him and him for me.

Forever and ever amen.

$\mathcal{T}$HE WILD THING

WHEN I FOUND Sack, it was the fall time of the year. The weather was cold, and ice hung on telephone wires. Fires burned all up and down the streets. The tore-out pages of outlaw schoolbooks went into the fires, thick as leaves, dumped box after box by square-jawed soldiers.

I still went to junior high school all day. That was before I couldn't go to school, because I was Randy's brother and all. At night, I lived in that horrible orphans' home.

A sad story just came in the newspaper.

It told how Randy, Mr. Hometown Hero, got killed. The article said he broke in on a poor grieving widow woman out at Ardillo. It said he shot her and did even worse than that to her. It claimed Randy killed a policeman too, a man with a wife and two babies, before he shot himself in the stomach like a coward and died before he made it to the hospital.

Well, I played along. You didn't have to be too smart to

see why. The Christian Soldiers brought a string of prisoners marching past the school every day, men with their eyes put out, women with their lips cut off, you name it.

So I pretended to believe that story in the *Goshen Reaper* like it was the Gospel. I just went on like always, wondering what my dead brother would want poor old Buddy to do now. Oh, the boys at school hated me after that article. Somebody would bully me every day. Sometimes three or four together. To be honest, the teachers didn't act much different.

One day at school, a colored man raked leaves on the playground. Just like every other day, I kept to myself, daydreaming, hanging my feet off the monkey bars. Oh, I was sad.

Well, this colored man, he came over close to me. *Sweep, sweep, sweep* went his rake. Then the sound stopped, and, like magic, a note appeared in my lap, folded careful.

I never saw that yardman before that day, and to this day, not since.

But his note told me how Randy really got killed. He died fighting off some Christian Soldiers that came in to round up country kids with mamas that weren't married. He got shot in the heart in a big battle. He was really brave. But the government bulldozers pushed dirt over him and four hundred other dead rebel boys at Big Temple.

That's what the note said.

*

Three years back, right after that sad note, I walked to the fair one night, from the big white orphans' home up the long Cottonwood Road to the fairgrounds. Everybody said this would be the last year fairs would be allowed. So I figured I better get one last look.

Miles away, you could see midway rides light up the sky.

Neon green and yellow smeared the sides of a big double-decker Ferris wheel. It flashed and twirled and loop-de-looped in the air, way taller than the chimneys on fifty-year-old houses. You could hear music and scratchy amplifiers and screaming girls and the sound of generators revving up.

My windbreaker kept off some of the freezing cold that night. But gradually my nose and my lips felt like they belonged to somebody else. The stars looked like busted ice. It got cold even down in the bottom of my pockets.

But when I got close to all that excitement, the cold didn't matter so much.

A roller coaster zoomed around its track like a crazy June bug tied to a string. Somebody pounded a giant wooden hammer on a lever and sent a shiny ball up a tower and donged a bell at the top. Up and up and up clanked the double-decker Ferris wheel, and this drunk-man's music googled a tune. Then . . . over it twisted, a giant steel train wheel of a ride, rolling out of sight behind the black limbs of pecan trees.

In the parking lot outside, a huge army tank aimed its long gun at the highway. Another year, it might have been a fun display for the National Guard or the Shriners or somebody. But the hard-eyed men perched in the top of that thing told a lot about the times. They wore three-day beards and kept their fingers on the triggers of their guns.

I walked all the way around to the far side of the fairgrounds. In the darkest dark spot I could find, I climbed a swayback chain-link fence, perched on top, and squinted till I saw a place to land. When I dropped on over, the whole fence shimmied and clanked for a quarter mile.

I was extra careful about that fence. One of the boys in the orphans' home told how his aunt snuck into the fair one time. Her diamond ring hung in the top of a chain-link fence when she jumped, and her finger snapped right off like a wax bean.

I ain't bad. I only snuck in the parking compound because I didn't have the money to pay. Money don't grow on trees if you're an orphan.

All between the parked cars, me and a few other stragglers tromped the dirty peanut hay spread out for the fair. They had the county convicts lay in that straw for a solid week. Those convicts were folks that couldn't pay their Bible taxes, or who wrote to the newspapers and said the wrong things the year before The Father got elected. I reckon they just graduated those convicts straight from their shovel handles to the sideshow booths on the midway. You just had to look at any carnie, just once, to know he'd done some time. There might be a notch out of his ear. Or one eyelid missing.

A heavy, red-faced man was in charge of taking tickets, and he shook like an old cold dog. He had a nose the size of an Irish potato. I took a chance and handed him a green half-ticket I picked up off the ground, and he never even looked at it, just groaned a little when I went by.

Just by the entrance, two more soldiers huddled together over a trash drum with a fire in it. You could see bandages on one soldier, wrapped tight just below the cross-and-halo shoulder patch. You wouldn't expect to see a man shot in the arm on duty at a county fair.

Maybe every able-bodied man the government could spare was down in Florida, where folks said the fighting went hard night and day.

There was another fifty-gallon garbage barrel by the first tent I came to. Out of it, a box of Goshen Fried Chicken called my name. It wasn't chewed all the way when I picked it up. But pretty soon it was. I found a piece of corn dog and half a candy apple and ate that too.

Out on the midway, it was a fair like you never saw. The

barkers blared and hollered at all of us through their bull-horns. They called us poor dumb hicks and played scratchy music and smoked whole home-rolled cigarettes in just two drags.

Boom! Boom! Pow! Pow! Balloons popped, and cap pistols fired. The bumper cars spit white sparks where they touched the ceiling. Two dozen loudspeakers squawled and whistled. Beside every fast ride, big oily gears turned and churned, just itching to snatch little boys in and mash them to potted meat.

Some of the weird faces painted on the freak-show tents looked better than the people who stood in line. Other places, men too tall and skinny to be alive dragged their bones in baggy overalls from quarter game to quarter game. The bright glittery little eyes of the carnies who waited for them looked like they never closed, even when they were sound asleep. Oh, it was something. I even saw a harelipped fellow. He ran the four-photos-for-a-dollar booth. You could see all his rotted front teeth, black and yellow like old dice, under his split top lip.

Oh, they knew how to get you right in the heart, though.

"Hey, Red," a little guinea-wasp woman at the throwing gallery said. "Where's your handsome brother this year?"

I just walked right by. All the knock-'em-over cats lined up behind her stuck out their pink tongues at me.

"How 'bout it, Little Rooster? *You* feelin' lucky?"

I didn't have an answer to that one.

Bad as it was, I saw quick that more folks than me have problems in this world.

"Hey, Hippo Lady!" a carnie on down the way yelled. He sat in a cage, perched on a little platform over a giant bucket of water. A dunking booth. This was what he did, even on a night this cold. He *dared* folks to hit a bull's-eye that would pitch him in.

His sassy mouth picked out a pitiful fat woman, so big

she had scabs where her legs rubbed together. "Hey, fatso lady!" old carnie hooted, through a bullhorn so everybody could hear. "Wooo-eee! You fat as a *hog!* You ever pass up a potato, gal? Hey! What's that on your arm . . . that a midget?"

Oh, it got off so bad with this little bristly Chihuahua of a man who was escorting that woman. Poor fellow throwed his arm out trying to knock Mr. Carnie in the water. Trouble was, he couldn't hit a bull in the butt with a bass fiddle. He spent thirteen dollars in dimes and nickels just while I watched. It finally got to where he was all in tears, his arm hurt him so.

That carnie ragged him the whole time. "Hey, Nolan Ryan. Missed a mile, Nolan Ryan. Hey, Nolan, that your fastball?"

Most people turned and walked away, it got so bad.

*

I saw these other pitiful folks play Oscar the Mouse and lose all their money. Oscar was a gambling game. A betting man put his hard-earned dollar down on a spot of color—green or blue or red or something—on this countertop. Back of it, a carnie in a black bathrobe spun a big gambling wheel, then jerked a lever.

A box dropped its bottom out. This plain old gray house mouse bombs-awayed onto the spinning roulette wheel. Naturally, it ran like Old Nick was after it, dizzy and scared to death, staggering right out to the edge of the turning wheel. It faced a choice then. All around the outside edge were getaway holes. Oscar the mouse either ducked down a hole with a little plastic flag or ducked down a hole without one.

If Oscar picked a hole with a flag, and the flag was the color of the spot where you bet your dollar, you won BIG.

Everybody's money on the whole countertop. But if that mouse went down a hole without a flag, the carnie grinned like the grille of a '56 Chevy . . . and scooped in all the dough himself.

You know, I believe that mouse was scared to death of a little plastic colored flag. You'd think so too, if you saw how many times that booger ran down a hole without one. Old carnie must have raked a thousand dollars off the counter, and I saw some poor gambling man limp off with his pockets turned inside out and his head hanging like it was full of rocks.

I made one whole turn of the midway, just checking out the sideshows. This year's crop was scary: the Pitiful Little Crawfish Boy, born in Lester, Arkansas, guaranteed half red, half white, pinchers big as baseball gloves. Marie O'Dey, The Mummy Mommy, a woman in the family way who drowned in some weird lake out west and got changed to a pregnant block of gray salt. Smokey Hoke, a colored fellow who could puff on a pipe and make the exhaust come out his ears or his eyes or, according to two men that paid extra to see it, even out his behind.

One tent held a live squirrel with two heads. It ate two pecans at once. And I saw another tent that held a "bul-lis"—a sheep baby. It was half-human and half-sheep, floating in a jar full of watery mayonnaise stuff.

*

The best of all came late. I must have circled the midway twenty times, still not tired of it, before this barker set up a racket from a trailer-truck flatbed. It was off the main mid-way, through a gate you had to pay extra to pass. I ducked below the ticket window and dog-walked right in.

The barker beat a snare drum to draw the folks, and

when enough of a crowd showed, he introduced his big surprise.

"Ladies and gentlemen!" screeched his bullhorn. "Danny Dynamite, The Hu-man-n-n-n-n Dynamooooo!"

A big sparkly red curtain parted. Danny Dynamite turned out to be this gray old man, who sat on a milking stool and rubbed his flabby arm muscles without smiling. This fellow was so skinny you could probably read through him. He wore a floppy black cowboy hat, a pair of bright yellow wrestling trunks that fit him tight as a shower cap, and a pair of green plastic flip-flops. That was all.

He was a pure surprise on that stage, after what *had* been prissing around all night up there. The crowd just worshipped this big bleached-blond colored woman, who called herself Miss Abunda. She sang a song she wrote herself, called "Fluffy Oyster." It looked like she was a threat to take off her clothes. She probably did, a year before, ere The Father got in and started to meddle. Tonight, she just sang and scratched sort of dirty.

Most of us glanced around, real nervous, at the two Christian Soldiers patrolling the midway. They all seemed to be looking somewhere else, though, while that nasty dance went on.

Later, I saw one pocket an envelope from Miss Abunda herself. Then I knew how it worked.

After her show, Miss Abunda signed autographs and milled around in the audience, while this old fellow on her stage rocked his stool and shivered, blue in the cold. He hugged himself and squinched his eyes like his head ached with the worst hangover of all time. And his stage manager shilled a mighty shill.

"Danny Dynamite! Ladies and gentlemen, he'll do the most dangerous trick of ALL TIME! You'll tell your grandchildren! Mighty Danny Dynamite! The man that a whole stick of dynamite can't blow to kingdom come!"

Dynamite!

That magic word even got the attention of the men crowded around Miss Abunda. She pouted when they forgot about her and stared at the platform.

"That's right!" blared the barker, pointing with his drumstick at the old fellow onstage. "Dynamite! Yes-N-deed! T-N-T! One of the most destructive forces known to man! Better get your earplugs ready, gentlemen, and you ladies hide your eyes. This trick has always worked before . . . but we *are* playing with dynamite!!!"

Mighty Danny gave a nervous cough then. It probably tore out a piece of his lung.

"Ladies and gentlemen . . . without further ado, I give you . . . Mighty Danny Dynamite!"

Well, it turned out to be the one thing at the fair that was really worth it. There's always one thing. I remember a mule once that dove off a diving board into a giant sponge. Another time, a man worked magic and made a live boar hog appear inside a refrigerator packing crate.

From his tights, right in front, Danny Dynamite pulled out a stick of dynamite. That crowd oohed and aahed. I didn't count, but you could bet a hundred people stood around there. They could see it was real dynamite. The letters *TNT* showed plain.

Old Danny waved his other hand in the air and *presto!* A Cricket lighter twinkled between his fingers. It lit up his floppy hat and scabby grinning old turkey head.

The crowd got quiet.

Over Danny Dynamite's head, the lighter moved, slow, so slow . . . till it touched the dynamite fuse. And lit.

Sssssssssssss!

Somebody hollered a warning.

The old man on the platform stared straight at the man who yelled and gave this big old toothless smile, nothing but black air behind it. The fuse of the dynamite sizzled on.

"Look out!" the farmer yelled again, up on his toes. "Danny, it's gonna blow!"

The fuse burned like a Christmas light, merry and bright . . . right down to the end. The old man still had that crazy smile on his face when he folded his arms and coddled that stick to his wrinkly old bosom like a nursing little baby.

For just a second, everybody froze, like we all posed for a picture and we knew the flash would blind us.

A quick bright white light hurt our eyes, sure enough. Then—

KA-BOOOOOOOOOOOOOOOOOOOOOM!

Oh, it was really dynamite, I can promise you. The blast knocked down half the people in that crowd. Smoke hid the cowards, who crawled for their lives on all fours. A big old corn-fed boy tried to hide behind me like a tree. You never heard such a carrying on, squawling and bawling. My own ears went out for a second and I heard the sound a TV makes when you lose the picture and all you have is snow.

After a minute, I could see again. And plain as day, it *was* a miracle.

The trailer appeared out of the smoke, then disappeared, then came back into sight and you could make out old skin-and-bones sprawled on top. That was the miracle. Mighty Danny Dynamite still had all his arms and legs. The floppy hat was blown to shreds. One of the flip-flops was gone forever. But all the rest of Danny hung together.

Now the two soldiers rattled up, submachine guns ready, their eyes scary to see.

The barker hustled back up the steps of the flatbed with a wooden bucket of water. He sloshed it right in Danny's face. One leg kicked, the way a frog leg kicks when you drop it in hot grease.

Not two minutes later, Mighty Danny smiled that big empty smile and threw up a skinny hand and walked down off the trailer, alive as you and me. Maybe he went a little bit rubber-legged on the steps, but he was, for sure, alive. He made a point to pass through the crowd, so folks would know it wasn't faked. He came so close I could smell his singed hair.

The crowd parted like Jesus had come down the steps of a bus. Folks clapped, and it caught on and a couple of fellows even threw in a cheer or two. Mighty Danny staggered right past the two soldiers, who looked hot and bothered but said not a word.

Up the midway, the old guy ducked into a tent and was gone.

I puzzled on what I saw, walking the midway myself one more time. I heard folks chattering like squirrels about that old man and his dynamite trick. One fellow in a big proud cowboy hat told his boy, " . . . I've heard about it. A man can put it just in the right place and set it off and the concussions will go every way but toward you. But I be damned if *I'm* gonna take a fool chance . . ."

Danny Dynamite would make a legend, I reckon.

That was when I decided I would be a legend too.

I'd be a legend like Randy on the football field. Somebody that nobody would ever forget. Somebody that nobody would ever leave with mean relatives or abandon in some orphans' home that was worse than any freak house on earth.

The night got breezier, out away from that crush of folks. I put my hands way down in my cold pockets.

I hung out under the rides, the fast, upside-down ones like The Bullet and The Zipper, and caught money when it fell out of people's pockets.

I got a dollar and twenty-seven cents, and I won a prize with it at the weight-and-height guesser's booth. He thought I was fatter than I really am. He said 140 pounds.

I picked my prize. It was just the thing to cheer me up, a two-foot-tall ceramic Wild Man from Borneo. His lips dripped blood-red, his chest sparkled with gold glitter, and a screaming girl reared back in his hand.

I went and sat on a warm electric generator and looked at what I'd won for ten or fifteen minutes. Old Borneo's mouth could have been the gate to a barn. His giant fist thumped that shiny chest. It thrilled me so big.

But it didn't last long. This nasty dried-up man came out of nowhere and ran me off the generator. He said I might hurt it. Then the world around me was just a sad old mud-show fair again. It smelled like cotton candy and pigs. It made me dizzy like the House of Mirrors. It felt stupid.

I saw some kids I knew at school, but I wouldn't talk to them. I knew they'd break Old Borneo and make fun of me.

I handed over a dime and ducked into one of the side-shows without even looking at what was inside.

*

I finally found a place that wasn't cold.

The tent was roasting with people, in fact, and crammed to the flap. Men and women and big-eyed children, too, stood on their tiptoes or climbed bales of hay to see. They all stared like they were hypnotized at this unbelievable thing.

When I looked, I couldn't believe my eyes either.

I reckon Sack at first glance wasn't exactly scary, if you've seen much at all in this scary world. He fit over the face and arms and legs of some poor carnie. On this plank stage, the carnie seemed too tired to do much but just stand there.

Anybody with eyes in his head could tell Sack was a costume made from a bunch of junk. You could see it so plain,

the little pieces of steel wool and tufts of horsetail and bal-
ing wire.

But, all of a sudden, Sack staggered around the stage so
the audience could see him. He grunted and woofed and
slobbered. He roared and hissed and barked. He carried
on like a man in pain. And I declare somebody must have
hexed some powerful juju into those rags and tags.

Sack just scared the pee-dog daylights out of those folks.

You would have thought the scariest wolfman that ever
lived was loose under that big top. People screamed and
the whole front row teetered back on its bench and almost
turned over. One woman, just up ahead of me, wet her
dress and shoes. I had to jump back to keep dry. Away
across the tent, I saw a colored man fall on his knees and
raise his arms, speaking in tongues, the whites of his eyes
shining.

The power of that getup was something, something to
see. The people who saw it were fundamentally all shook
up.

I knew something right then, that night. I knew who that
outfit was meant to belong to.

I knew Sack would be me, and me Sack.

I didn't know how.

But I would figure something out.

*

After scaring the daylights out of folks, Sack stumbled to
the back corner of the big orange tent. A tarpaulin Indian
tepee waited for him.

Sack passed gas when he squatted to crawl through the
flap and retire for the night. It was so loud you could hear it
over the high screams.

Another carnie, this burly black-haired woman, leaped
up onstage. She wore gold pirate earrings and a half-inch of

makeup. This big pink painted hunk of woman looked like what's left after you skin a buffalo.

She crossed her arms and stood big and mean in front of the crowd. It was a good thing too. Some of the folks had got so worked up that they wanted to set fire to the place.

"It ain't no Wild Man from Borneo!" screamed one farmer, all his neck veins poking out. "It's a damned devil thang! It's got loose from Hell!"

"Yo! Yo!" A pack of voices howled together. "Got to put a stop to that!"

It was magnificent. I'm glad I got to see that in my life. I might understand the whole world around here if I saw enough things like Sack and what happened in that tent.

The buffalo gal got into gear, though, before the mob got ugly. She set out to clear the tent, and that was something to see too. She did it mostly by shoving grown men's faces down into the sawdust, then kicking their kidneys till they squirmed right out under the sides of the tent. She clobbered one old sodbuster and knocked his glass eye out of his head. Oh, she fought 'em. While she did, I wiggled up under a stack of hay bales and hid.

The buffalo gal won. She ran every last customer out, and then she plopped her huge self down by a water bucket.

The quiet in the tent felt weirder than the crowd. It was spookier than ever when you could hear every little sound carnies made.

The woman snorted out a big tired worn-down-to-the-nub sigh. She blew her nose hard, one finger on the side. Then she took out her teeth and flung them in the water bucket.

"Thamnation," she gruffed, shaking her big hair. "Thay goth da be a better way."

The tarpaulin flap on the Indian tent slipped to the side just the tiniest bit. This skittish eye white showed through.

"Sugarbump?"

"Um-hm," she said.

"Is they gone?"

" 'Mon out, thughah. Theth gone on homb."

The flap opened a little more.

Squinting through the straw, I could just make him out. He had a big smutty mess all over a skinny white chest, and more ribs than a runover snake. His nipples were as black as charcoal.

Out of the costume, he seemed one hundred years old and kind of pitiful. About what you'd expect from a man who blew himself up with dynamite in every mudshow town in Alabama for a living.

Sack turned out to be Mighty Danny Dynamite. Working his second job of the night, I reckon. One way or another, that white little grub of a man had scared half the folks in Goshen out of their wits in one night.

In a minute, he got brave enough to come out of the tarpaulin tepee. Sure enough, it was Danny Dynamite. He still wore those skintight yellow trunks and one green flip-flop. A little knot showed in front of his bathing suit. It looked like he was hiding a crookneck squash.

He shouldn't have shown off that squash.

The buffalo gal got a look, and her eyes turned into big red valentines.

"Heth, heth, heth," she grinned, without a tooth showing. "Whadda we hab here?"

The old man realized what was up, and all of a sudden looked the way he did just before that dynamite blew up. His eyes rolled like boiling eggs in a pot.

I ducked. He didn't spot me.

"Aw, honey," I heard him whine. "Now I done put in a full whole day. I done been blown up, and that kinda work wears on a feller. I been stuck in that danged night-crawling low-rent wild man getup in this hot tent with eighty people breathing at me, and I just don't hardly feel much like . . ."

She was on him like a snake on a rat. She wallowed him down.

"Oww, oh please, honey . . ."

It was useless. He hollered. He grunted. But he couldn't stop what nature turned loose.

I heard the wet sound of swim trunks stripped off in one motion.

"Oh, thet me looth, Thpooky!" she yelled.

Right then, I did the bravest thing I ever did. Up till that night, anyway.

I crept around to the tarpaulin tepee in back of those two, slipping from one bale of hay to the next.

I eased my hand under the back of the little Indian tent, up into Lord knows what. I reckon it would be like reaching up under the Buffalo Gal's dress. You just didn't know what might be waiting.

Tonight, Sack was. Ready for me. He purely leaped into my arms. I think he even made a little squeaking noise. I knew right then that a new life lay in store for us.

I left my ceramic Wild Man from Borneo in the tepee as a swap. It grinned at me with its big red mouth, and that girl captured in his hand waved bye-bye. And I dashed for the door, past that sweaty mountain of a woman and that rattling little sack of bird bones.

I needn't have run. I don't think they'd have noticed right then if the whole tent blew away and left just the cold clear stars blinking down.

Something happened when I hit the icy air outside. Maybe it was Sack, speaking for the first time. Maybe it was just pure chance, like the falling star that hit some lady while she watched TV on her couch up in Sylacauga.

All I know is this: I heard a bugle blowing. Only it blew in my brain. A great idea.

I turned around and raced back into the tent. I ran right up beside those heaving fairpeople.

I snatched her false teeth out of that bucket by the stage. It wasn't a bit harder than snatching a crawfish out of a ditch without getting pinched.

Those would be Sack's teeth. Some of them anyway. Along with the things I added from the deep woods to make Sack *really* scary.

Then we tore out for good.

I can run like a hot wind. Randy was the only person I ever knew that could run me down, and even he couldn't catch me if the race was longer than a football field.

Let 'em run and run as fast as they can.

They can't catch me.

I'm the Wild Thing.

OVER THE RIVER, through the woods, me and Sack rolled on toward the Bob-A-Lu.

Mr. Moon shined up there in the middle of the sky. He looked to me like a silver river rock. Fat black clouds slid on and off like dirty beavers, but the way was clear and bright.

We walked and trotted and walked and trotted. Too many miles to count passed under our feet. We climbed through haunted Bighead Gully, slipped around the edge of Soggyboggy Swamp, tiptoed through maybe another seven miles of thick woods, prickly pears, and thistle fields, and finally took a deep breath at the top of a pine-headed hill looking down on Highway 31.

And there she blowed—the Bob-A-Lu.

At night, Bob-A-Lu shined bright. Some folks say it fell off the back edge of honky-tonk heaven a few years back and crash-landed in the middle of this hundred-acre field of kudzu. Drunks used to tell about white doves and angels flying over, instead of pink elephants.

Bob-A-Lu is a legend too, in its own way.

But not even Bob-A-Lu, mighty as it is, has stayed the same as before The New Times.

A few years back, cars packed the parking lot every Friday at quitting time, and a pure flood of good old boys slopped their way through the mudholes and beer bottle caps toward the crooked front door. When the house band kicked in after dark, the roof of the place purely jumped up and down, like in a cartoon. The Bob-A-Lu was like that, a drinking and fighting and caterwauling and picking-up-a-one-night-wildcat kind of hangout.

I mean, the cars and pickup trucks used to just stampede here, before the trouble and the new laws. They slid up to Bob-A-Lu on scrunchy oyster shells, and the doors flew open and out hopped wild-as-the-wind country boys who dashed in so fast they were at the bar with half their first cold one glugged down before the screen door whacked shut behind them. That Bob-A-Lu parking lot didn't get empty till Monday morning, either, just an hour before the pipe fitters and ditch diggers and peanut mill workers and tractor drivers all had to be back on the job.

The government took the place, naturally. The Father came in, and every roadhouse in the land got scrubbed pink-behind-the-ears clean. No beer. No booze. No way.

So Bob-A-Lu was different now. Not as many cars. Not so many good times. A lot of the meanest customers got disgusted and went off to fight in the war. It didn't matter which side, long as it was fighting.

Bob-A-Lu just watered mostly the dumb ones and the shot ones and the crippled ones now.

Still, local folks came and had the best time they could.

What else were they going to do?

*

Me and Sack picked our way down the hill. We didn't see a single wild animal that whole last mile. It seemed peculiar after a night in the woods. On a walk out there, you spooked up every kind of four-legged thing you can think of . . . and one or two you probably can't. Like a green Snapping Skankdog. Me and Sack saw one tonight, and its tail broke off when we chased it.

I took and tied that tail to Sack with forty-pound-test fishing line. Along with the possum and armadillo and fox and coon tails and even worse stuff, it made him a sight to see. Sometimes, I admit, Sack scared even me.

Me and Sack crossed Highway 31 and got into the parking lot. We zigged and zagged through a few bomb holes and around some burned-up cars. I slung the croker sack over my shoulder when we got close enough to smell the joint. French-fry and hamburger grease coated the screens, so me and Sack stopped to take a deep breath of fresh air before we went in.

Out front of Bob-A-Lu a couple of palm trees scraggled, dead as palm trees could be. They'd been trucked in from Panama City, or some such place, and spray-painted white halfway up the trunks.

Country people around Goshen whitewash their pecan trees to keep beetles out of the bark. I reckon the owners of Bob-A-Lu hoped it would keep their palm trees safe and sound too.

You could see, though, that bugs didn't make the holes that killed these trees. Bullets fired in a skirmish about a year ago chewed up every trunk. It killed those palm trees dead as if a man took and girdled each one with a sharp ax.

The front of the joint looked like every cinder-block roadhouse you ever saw . . . if you didn't count three or four hundred bullet holes. Some joker had circled the big ones with red paint and written "OUCH!" by them.

Bob-A-Lu's idea of a red carpet rolled out from the front door. It was a walkway of heavy roofing felts, black, red, blue, green, one color piled on top of another. It looked like a stuck-out tongue. Rainwater stood every few feet along the walk, and every now and then you could see a wharf rat ten times bigger than Oscar the Mouse creep out from the shadows and nibble a drink.

Cut-in-half rubber tires—some white sidewalls, some not—bordered a beat-up flower bed next to the building. In with the dried brown camellias and shriveled azaleas and leaned-over tomato stakes grew a few sad cotton plants, just begging for a boll weevil to come and take them away from this vale of tears.

Over the screen front door burned a horrible yellow bug light. Under that, plain for the world to see, hung a gold plywood cross six feet high, with these words: BELIEVE THE FATHER. OR GO TO HELL

That was almost too much. I felt my tolerance clog up, but me and Sack bustled on in through the door.

*

Around the tables sat a bunch of burned-up-looking rednecks. They'd been picking melons all week. Most everybody wore a feed cap and boots, and maybe two or three wore overalls filthy enough to be the cause of that joint's bad smell all by themselves.

Some greasers dragged on cigarettes, still legal indoors at throwaway places like this. Others spit tobacco at roaches that ran around with whole parched peanuts hoisted over their heads. Telephone-cable spools did for tables, and packs of eight or ten boys sat at each spool, right where you walked in the door.

In front of every boy at those two tables foamed a giant glass of milk. I almost couldn't believe it. Cold fresh milk in a tall glass.

The Bob-A-Lu was a changed place, sure enough.

Christian Soldiers stood around inside, too. Three bored ones in their green fatigues leaned against a wall in the poolroom. They toted big guns in black holsters. It stayed really quiet back where they were. You could hear the balls clicking over and over again at the pool tables. It sounded like somebody really bored, cracking his knuckles.

Somebody made the jukebox swallow a quarter, and it gave a chokey noise, then started to play a Gomer record.

This was the new Bob-A-Lu.

This was what me and Sack had to change.

We found a chair off to one corner. A waitress with "Poochie" on her name tag brought me some milk. Poochie wore a white dress down to her ankles. She looked pure disgusted when she set the glass down on the napkin.

Me and Sack ignored her and scoped out the joint.

At the closest table, a boy with this head of hair like a runover orange cat's was raising a ruckus. He was one of those cigarette-skinny kinds that fight all summer out behind garages and back of skating rinks. A snake in a bucket.

Across from him sat another boy, a big strapping deep-chested thing with a shiny crew cut. This boy listened and made an unbelievable face, like his milk was sour.

"Durn it, Harvey Lee, they *was!*" that snaky boy, name of Lester, said. "Tracks in the hard ground. Big around as a durn garbage can lid! You could near 'bout catch a pig in one!"

"Right." That big boy, Harvey Lee, rolled his eyes. "We talkin' about some *big* old tracks in your old man's yard, now ain't we, Lester?"

"If I'm lyin', I'm dyin', Harvey Lee." Lester gave the old boys around the table this serious-as-a-heart-attack look. "Them big tracks come up out of the woods and straight to the chicken pen. It wasn't a gizzard left when that thing finished up. It strowed feathers all over the yard. Feet laying everwhere." Lester paused, swiveled his head around, got a nod or two from some of the sun-burned faces. "I believe—I believe it was that durned Wild Thang, myself! That's what I think!"

This loud *ooh* rose up in the air, and then the tongues set to wagging.

I held Sack real tight and slid him around to one side of my chair. He was getting all worked up down in the bag.

I watched Harvey Lee, the clean-cut boy, consider this Lester and his wild story. You could see him working it out. He brushed his hand back over his spit-shined haircut and started to say something, stopped, then put his nose down in his milk glass to get a swig.

Finally, he couldn't hold back. He busted out laughing. Milk shot out his nose halfway across the room. And while Harvey Lee laughed and strangled and foamed over, a bunch of boys on his side of the table went to whooping it up too, beating the tables and scraping their chairs and falling all over one another.

Lester turned red as a boiled Indian. He jumped right up and grabbed a pool stick, making a big show.

"Durn you, Harvey Lee Lipp! Nobody laughs at me! You got you that New Times haircut and you a big football star and your daddy's got a lot of money and he signed you up in the Christian Soldiers so you can tell later what a big old hometown war hero you were. But now don't think any of that gives you a right to practically call Lester Dismukes a damn liar right to his face! Cause, brother, it sho-buddy *don't*."

The whole crowd of folks went *whoa!* when Lester bowed up like that. Folks giggled and looked over to see what Harvey Lee would say. Poochie was working on him with an apron to get the milk off, when somebody else piped up.

"Yo! Lester Dismukes!"

Every head swung away toward this other boy, out of the clear blue, who stood up three tables across the room.

"Lester Dismukes, you just better hold yore waggin' tongue! I'm Spittin' Martin from over at Rehobeth and I'm Harvey Lee Lipp's blood family as a New Christian and I'll kick your little bang-tail butt slam to the middle of next week, you keep that talk up!"

A cheer went up from all around that first table.

Lester waved his cue, stiff as a fighting dog's tail. Before he could yell again, though, one of his own boys, this freckled pine stump of a farm kid, rared to his feet.

"Martin, I'm Pure Hell Baker. That mean anything to you?"

Spittin' Martin went plum-colored and his neck veins stuck out.

"Maybe."

"I owe you one for what you done to my sister last year," gritted Baker. "I reckon them high-and-almighty New Christian folks don't know all about that little business, do they, boy? Sister's asked me to lay you open for that. And tonight might just be the night, good buddy, you go on making big talk that way . . ."

Good *buddy,* he said.

It made me nervous to hear my name pop up.

Still, I couldn't help but thrill over this place. Here me and Sack sat all fidgety, just barely through the front door and already witness to a brewing hurricane. People actually *feeling* things, saying things.

One of the most famous Bob-A-Lu girls, Mona Lisa Mayhew, sashayed through about then. I couldn't hardly believe it. I almost didn't recognize her. She looked like a nurse in all that white.

In the olden days, Mona Lisa always needed another half a foot of red miniskirt to cover up her behind. It always showed plain, and so did the purple pinch marks all over it.

Now Mona Lisa toted a little tray covered with squashed wet dollars and napkins and milk glasses full of cigarette butts. When she got as far as that Harvey Lee, she stopped and caught her balance up on top of those high-heel shoes of hers. Then she cut loose in this voice that would take the paint right off a car.

"Kin I git y'all big boys any thang?" she yowled, all crazy-eyed. "Maybe y'all need a cool drank . . ."

That's when I reached down, hid over in my little corner, and gave Sack a little secret pat, the way you pat a nervous highbred horse that's about to run a big race.

You could see it coming hard. Mona Lisa was doing her best to keep the peace at Bob-A-Lu.

About then, out of the smoky poolroom chugged the three Christian Soldiers on duty. Ahead of them they pushed Dondi Fondren, the man that owned the Bob-A-Lu. Dondi was drying out a milk glass with a towel. He was a big old boy, arms like a pipe fitter. He looked like a man just itching to rip your telephone book in two.

Dondi would have scared most folks, most places, most times. Trouble was, he got injured when the fighting came through. He had this bad thing wrong with him.

The top of his face, I mean the whole forehead, just changed color where he'd been shot or burned or dragged on pavement or something. A permanent scab hung two inches out over his eyes like a granite cliff. A strip of hair grew above that, rising on up to a bald spot, pink as a baby butt, with a little crown of curly black at the tip-top. His chin poked forward too far too, and his tongue always hung out.

Lester spotted him.

"Shoehead!" he started in. "Now you listen here, Shoe—"

Shoehead stabbed an iron finger right into Lester's bony chest. "My name is Dondi, son. Now buy some more milk and drink it, or git gone. Lester, you and your boys know the rules. You ain't gonna fight or cross words with my customers in here."

Lester got all huffy. "Harvey Lee's done called me a goddamn liar right here in front of everybody, Shoe. I can't—"

"WHOA! HOLD IT RIGHT THERE!"

Harvey Lee yelled it, so loud the windows shook.

Everything stopped. You'd think the king of Goshen stepped down off his cloud and pulled the big lever that jerked this whole part of the state to a halt.

"Did you say what I thought you said?" Harvey Lee asked, in his I-can't-believe-it voice. "Did you mention the name of almight GOD in your ugly curse, Lester Dismukes?"

Well that changed everything. I saw right then that me and Sack better get changed and do our thing pretty quick. Religion killed more folks than germs in these times.

Harvey Lee went on, with flecks of milk at the corners of his mouth. It looked like saliva on a mad dog.

"Hey, I asked you a direct question, Lester Dismukes. Did you or did you not illegally mention the name of our Father who art in heaven, hallowed be his name?"

Harvey Lee's eyes burned now, and Lester stole a glance toward the door.

One of the soldiers blurted out. "I hope you got an occupational license to say what you said, Dismukes!"

The lieutenant of the soldiers wheeled on the one who said that and screamed right at his face. "Private Ezekiel, I'm in charge of this truth-seeking unit! I'll ask all the questions here and I'll do your talking for you! You got that clear?"

The private turned a shameful color and backed off. "Yes, sir," he barked. "Clear, sir!"

Harvey Lee stared across at Lester. He looked like he could kill a man. Somebody *might* get killed too. The Christian Soldiers all of a sudden had their guns out.

"Now y'all!" wailed Mona Lisa. "Don't do that!"

She batted her eyes with the best intentions, but Lester all of a sudden looked up, like he remembered something, and stared right through her. He studied the three soldiers and Harvey Lee, working up his answer.

I heard Sack growl down low, and I put my foot against the bag.

"Harvey Lee Lipp," Lester sneered. "I say to you whatever I want, whenever I want. There ain't no law on this world nowhere that can keep me from it. No law from no man that keeps me from saying what I think."

Shoehead, who looked so big and strong, was a nervous wreck by now. He stood to lose everything if a fight broke out. It was pitiful in a way. You could see how much he loved the Bob-A-Lu.

"Y'all boys ought to be pure ashamed!" he cried out. He shook his towel at Lester. "Them fighters is in the streets burning up whole cities in some places, and all them boys shooting each other to pieces down south of here. Why, the Devil would just be durn proud to see fine young people at one another thisaway. It's just what he wants to happen. Why, if the Devil can git all the peaceful folks fightin' among themselves—"

"Aw shut up, Shoehead!"

Harvey Lee screamed it. Milky snot jumped out on his top lip, and his face went black. I mean that Harvey Lee Lipp could give a man a bad look.

Shoehead shut up too. Right that second. No questions asked.

The room got so quiet I heard somebody's pocket watch.

Then Harvey Lee spoke to a waitress without taking his eyes off Lester.

"Poochie, real quick, darlin'. Go bring Lester here a fresh big glass of milk."

While she hustled off, Harvey Lee turned to the rest of his gang. He gave a weird little laugh.

"The boss is always right, Lester," Harvey Lee told them all. "Shoehead said we ain't gonna have no fights in here, and we ain't. Especially not over some fairy tale you made up about a boogerman that stole your paw's chickens. Heck, it was probably one of your demon-possessed friends."

Lester's eyes about popped out, but he managed to keep his tongue on a bridle. His hands gripped that pool cue so hard, though, I thought sawdust might come out between his fingers. Now and again, he snuck a look at the big hog-leg pistols the Christian Soldiers pointed in his general direction.

Harvey Lee got his milk. He stood straight and held the glass up to the light like a toast.

"Now, Shoehead," Harvey Lee announced to the whole room, "here's what our friend Lester Dismukes is going to do . . ."

He turned around to Lester. "Since I'm back on active duty next week, making this country safe for floorwipes like Lester, and since I'll be away from home and missing this old Bob-A-Lu something fierce, I'll tell you what. I'm feeling a little sentimental.

"As a special good-bye, tonight Lester Dismukes here is gonna make a toast to his old friend Harvey Lee Lipp. And to *my* special friend, The Father."

Nobody spoke. Some chairs scraped real nervous. Lester seemed to be estimating the distance to the front door. Too far, I knew.

"Yes, sir!" Harvey Lee said loud, like he really was on-stage. "I got me a mission in life, Lester. I shoot Devils and shine boots. I'm in the army now. The Christian Army. And Lester, since I know you gonna miss me . . ."

Harvey Lee moved fast, like an athlete. He just seemed to appear in front of Lester all of a sudden, a head taller and now a whole lot crazier. The milk spilled a little on his big hand.

" . . . I want you to repeat this real easy little toast. All you got to do, Lester boy, is raise this glass and say three little words, and mine and The Father's sweet little names . . . just 'I love you, Harvey Lee and Precious Father.' You got that, Lester? You can walk out of here with both your ears still on if you say that."

"Whoooooeeey!" catcalled Harvey Lee's crowd, with whistles and hand claps for good measure.

Sack gave another growl, and I felt the bag quiver.

Harvey Lee breathed down into Lester's face. "You heard me, sweet little Lester. C'mon and say it like you mean it. Say 'I love you. I love you, Harvey Lee and Precious Father.' "

Lester might have been carved out of wood.

"C'mon, puke!" Harvey Lee screamed. The glasses rattled on the tables, and everybody in the place jumped. "C'mon! Where's my toast?"

Lester staggered, twisting like a worm on a hook. But the boy had guts, give him that.

"I reckon your toast is back in the kitchen," he said.

"Maybe they putting The Father's shit on it for you to eat. Why don't you go see?"

Harvey Lee squinted his eyes down to penny slits.

"Oh, Lester, sugar, you breaking my heart. Now listen. I'll say it just one more time. If I was you, boy, I'd take this milk and make that little toast. Cause if you don't, one of these soldier boys here just might take you outside and drag you off in the kudzu and cram the barrel of a forty-five pistol up your butt and *boom, boom, boom.*"

Everybody in the room heard it, and I honestly think it scared us all. But Lester Dismukes gave back the snakiest look you ever saw and hissed out of some of the worst teeth.

"Go to hell, you goddamned hypocrite. That's all I'll say to you! And all of you that get down on your knees to lick The Father's holy behind can go there too—"

It set off a pure war dance. All over Bob-A-Lu, Harvey Lee's muscled-over melon-pickers rose out of their chairs and rolled up their T-shirt sleeves, slow and serious, and spit on the floor. That's the kind of night it had gotten to be at Bob-A-Lu.

Again Harvey Lee surprised me. He reached up and put his right hand over his heart and closed his eyes with a soulful look. The milk in his big hand trembled a little.

"Lester, Lester, Lester—"

FFRRBBPPPAPPBBSSSHH!

I swore the noise was a frog stomped hard by a Wolverine boot. A sour cloud of yellow gas rose out of the pants of this skinny half-breed Rehobeth boy. He hunkered down at Lester's table, blinking his little scared eyes.

"I'm sorry, Harvey Lee!" that boy stammered. "It happens when I get nervous."

"Whoo! Damn!" hollered the whole table. They jumped up and scattered, waving their hands to fan off the perfume. The soldiers acted a little confused and waved their pistols.

Harvey Lee put up a quick hand one more time. His boys were ready to slaughter, but he stopped 'em cold.

"Wait!" Harvey Lee whispered, kind of throaty, his eyes clinched tight. "Lester ain't done right by us yet."

It got quiet as a dead mouse, one more time.

"Lieutenant Japheth," Harvey Lee said. "What's the penalty for taking the Lord God Almighty's name in vain in a public place, the way Lester Dismukes done here to-night?"

As the soldier answered, Harvey Lee Lipp oh so slow moved the glass of milk in his hand right up to Lester's thin lips. The white foamy surface stopped just an inch from his mouth.

Lieutenant Japheth's face didn't have a wrinkle on it, and his eyes were so blue you'd think there was sky inside his head. His memory seemed perfect. He rattled off a speech:

"Article five, verse four of the New Constitution: Thou shalt not take the name of The Father in vain in any public place or dwelling or that which may be conceptualized as a public place or dwelling. Those so doing shall be delivered unto the Holy Forces for penance and absolution, accomplished by scourging and confinement with mercy accorded only for the contingency of the vain-speaking."

"I hope the devil boys," Lester hissed, "make you *eat* a damn Bible one day, Harvey Lee Lipp . . ."

Harvey Lee smashed the glass into Lester's teeth.

White milk and red blood spilled all over the floor. But Lester fought back.

Harvey Lee didn't have to move far to duck Lester's whistling pool cue. He just tilted his head the tiniest little bit and that wild swing missed a country mile and smacked the table instead. Lester dropped the stick and made a face like every bone in his hands was broke. And his face. You never saw such a mess.

Harvey Lee's nod gave permission, and the war came back to Bob-A-Lu.

*

The knocked-out teeth hitting the floor sounded like rain on dry leaves.

Boys jitterbugged with their foreheads stuck together and tore-out hair in both hands.

The mad fighters screamed louder than a freight train loaded with pigs putting on rusty brakes in the middle of a lightning storm.

Harvey Lee, though, he didn't sweat it. He found a good seat and sat himself down with a big smile on his face. He stretched his size-fifty feet under a plywood table. He brushed pool-cue chalk off his new overalls with his wet thumb. I even saw him drum his fingers once.

Somebody rolled that gassy boy right across the table; Harvey Lee just gave a yawn. Somebody else, right beside him, broke a heavy glass milk jug over a boy's head. Harvey Lee just made a huge gristly muscle with his arm and counted the girlfriend-marks under his fingernails.

Pretty soon that waitress named Mona Lisa brought him a Coke, right through the fighting. She flirted up in his face, like she did back when she wore her little sass of a skirt.

"Hey Harvey Lee!" she said, just wiggling all over. "When we goin' to see them charity dog races like you promised?"

Look at that boy, I told Sack. Harvey Lee might be some kind of a legend around here one day too. Maybe he already was.

I saw Lester getting stomped. He was cornered like a black roach by seven Goshen boys and all three soldiers. Most of the rest of his sorry gang was lying around on the floor of the joint like wet garbage now.

That was when Harvey Lee noticed me.

Before I paid any attention, he had me cornered. He was big and strong, all pumped up from army training. It was a surprise attack.

"Hey, fence-post sitter. I ain't seen you in Bob-A-Lu before," he said.

Sack growled by my foot, so I talked fast. Nervous. I didn't want trouble like this.

My heart thumped hard. "I'm Buddy."

Harvey Lee Lipp sneered the next question. "Buddy who?"

"I ain't got no last name," I told him, and it was the truth. "I'm a orphan."

Harvey Lee stood up straight and folded his arms. He had this expression on his face.

"I don't reckon you happened to see the sign on the front door, did you, Buddy? Or do they teach orphans to read these days?"

I told him I didn't see a sign, or I would have read it. I could read good.

"Oh yeah. There's a sign," Harvey Lee said, real ugly. "It says 'No Orphans,' plain as day. You *sure* you didn't see that?"

I took his hint. The noise picked up—somebody knocked over the Coke machine—but I gave a shrug and spoke a little louder, so he'd be sure to hear.

"I reckon I missed that sign."

Harvey Lee cupped his hand to his ear. "How's that?"

I picked up Sack. "I reckon I missed that sign," I told him. "I reckon I'll be going."

"Damn right you will," Harvey Lee whispered, his stone-hard hand on my shoulder all of a sudden. "Get outta here. Fuckin' orphan."

Me and Sack gladly started for the door.

"Hey!" Harvey Lee growled. "You got a last name now, Buddy. It's Butthole. Buddy Butthole. I ever see you in here again and you're sitting by like some sissy girl while good men fight for The Father, I'll write that last name on your face with a knife. We'll see can you read *that*."

I jumped over two eye-gouging fighters and made for the door.

But Harvey Lee still wasn't through. A bully can't get enough of a bad thing.

"Oh, Butthole. One more thing. What's in that croker sack?"

Truth or dare.

I opened the top of the bag, looked down and checked. I didn't want Harvey Lee to see my eyes when I told my lie.

"It's fish," I hollered, over the noise.

Harvey Lee looked disgusted. "There's another sign on the door you missed," he said. " 'No Fish.' We hate fish at the Bob-A-Lu. Especially fish that smell like *that* fish. You understand?"

"Yes, sir. It won't happen again."

Harvey Lee smiled, real smug.

"It sure to hell better not," he said.

Just that second, somebody flying backwards through the air broke out the hanging lightbulb by Harvey Lee. It knocked out all the lights inside Bob-A-Lu.

Me and Sack found our chance, and we dashed away.

*

Grrrrr.

I was so mad I thought a blood blister might pop up on both sides of my neck.

Buddy Butthole. Grrrr.

It was easy to change out back. We did it behind somebody's abandoned tractor. Just a few feet behind us, that field of kudzu made like a slow green fire, drifting up the moonbeams toward the full moon.

Sack felt hot and heavy, full of old sweat and scary juju. Powerful and mighty and good. I jumped up and down, just feeling the blood howl in my ears so fine.

I was Sack now, and Sack was me!

We ran straight to the back of the joint. We could see through the eyeholes into one back Bob-A-Lu window. Shoehead was mixing it up in there now. In one hand he held the broken neck of a guitar, trailing the strings like a cat-o'-nine-tails. The other hand was a mighty fist as big as a baseball glove. He was knuckling away at any teeth he saw in the dark. Noisy whoops and scraping chairs swamped out the Amy Grant record on the jukebox, knocked on its side but still playing.

If you ever looked down in the middle of a rotted black cabbage where the naked white worms were working alive, you'd know what it looked like inside Bob-A-Lu.

All of a sudden, the lights blazed back on, bright as Montgomery, I reckon.

"Sack," I whispered out loud. "It's clobberin' time!"

That wonderful hot wild stuff squirted through our blood. We counted to three and said that Indian's name, Geronimo, and leaped in through the window on a flying-fisted storm.

Some storms, no matter how fierce, don't last too long.

*

Stand at the front door of Hell during an ice-water break. You'll see people running like they did out of Bob-A-Lu.

The barroom windows splattered, and desperate boys just poured out, crashing and crawling one over the next through the broken glass to get away. Screams and lost shoes filled up that joint.

"It's The Wild Thing! Lordy, it's The Wild Thing!" they hollered.

Oh, we scared them so bad. Folks butted into walls. Folks butted into other folks. Boys fell across the snooker tables, scattering the colored balls under their running feet. Boys banged headfirst into bar stools and other ones turned pure flips in the air like shot cats.

One of the soldier boys, the lieutenant, turned his gun to shoot. Sack snarled at him and raised one claw, and the barrel of the gun melted. It just drooped down like a hot candle. That soldier threw it away, his eyes big as pies, and tore out.

Those yellow-bellies headed for the hills. Every one of them.

Harvey Lee Lipp got special treatment. At first, he came at Sack with a chair. But Sack turned and looked him full in the face, and that was all she wrote. Harvey Lee dropped that chair and ran like the back of his pants was on fire.

Sack caught him by the door. Swiped the seat out of him. Left five scratches across his pimply hams, deep enough so Harvey Lee wouldn't enjoy sitting down for a long time.

Sack finished by pushing him through the door and out on his ear. He scraped off some of his chin in the oyster-shell parking lot.

Crying like a baby, off he ran, a full moon shining on his back porch.

*

Sack! We showed this bad and stupid place!

We stood at the Bob-A-Lu's front door, knocked out of the frame, and saw the slowest, worst beat-up boys in the pack, still huffing and puffing toward the Bay filling station lights way up Highway 27.

Me and Sack gave a thought to chasing them, but decided Bob-A-Lu was pure enough now.

The job was done.

We stepped outside, and I slipped Sack's head off.

Steam came gushing out from my hair. I'd gotten so hot I had to swab the sweat out of my eyes. The little bit of breeze felt like rubbing alcohol dabbed on your forehead when you run a high fever.

The parking lot was about empty. And there was the story, same as always. A bug light. A shell drive full of dropped socks, key chains, billfolds. A full moon in a June puddle.

And something else.

Right there in the car nearest the front door was the biggest, life-changingest surprise I'd had in all my born days.

Behind the steering wheel of a green Galaxy, I saw a head. It stared at me with its mouth wide open, a blond head, two eyes like lit cherry bombs waiting to explode.

She sneaked down and tried her best to hide.

Oh, but I was found out!

*C*ISSY

I JERKED OPEN the door of the green Galaxy and jumped right in on top of her. Two white skinny legs kicked hard to get away.

"Drive!" I hollered. "You seen me now! You seen Sack! You spoilt it all!"

A high-heel shoe jabbed at my head, missed, and ripped a hole in the cloth top of the car.

"Can't you hear, girl?" I yelled in her face. "I said DRIVE!"

"Thang!" she begged. "Please, Thang! Don't do anything to me!"

It was a real girl, all right, gussied up for Bob-A-Lu. She had on this dress, red as devil skin. Her hairdo looked like a tore-open bale of cotton, and two eyes hid inside it like scared rats.

"If you don't drive this car, it's gonna be the worst night of your whole life, girl." My steely-clawed gloves clamped down on her baby arms. "I promise."

64

"I never drove a car before!"

"You better learn then," I went. "I ain't in no mood to just sit here waitin' on soldiers or the po-lice."

She grabbed the keys and held them out, trembling. "Here! You just *take* Harvey Lee's old car! I won't ever tell who did it."

"Drive! You *drive!* You the one that's got to! I'm The Wild Thang! The Wild Thang don't drive no car. DRIVE!!!"

It scared her so bad. Her little white hand twisted the key. She got that big green Galaxy to rumbling. I looked at the gearshifter. I knew the shifter had a lot to do with making a car go.

"I reckon that R right there means Race," I told her. "Move that stick. No, the *other* one. Put it on R."

She put it on R.

"Now," I growled, "GO! How many times do I have to tell you?"

I'll always remember something I learned that night. R on a gearshifter means Reverse. It don't mean Race.

We'd still be picking our teeth out of the front windshield except for a motorcycle we hit fifty feet back.

Awful noise comes out of a motorcycle and ten or twelve garbage cans crushed at one whop. The grinding kept on too, after she got us going frontwards. The heavy Harley hung on the bumper, and we dragged it right up the parking lot.

The car's rearview mirror got knocked out of whack by our tussle. I fixed it and saw that bike finally get shook aloose and leap up in the air in slow motion. A tornado of white sparks came out when it crashed in the oyster shells at the edge of Highway 27.

That girl gave a wild ride. Pine tree limbs whacked the car once when she got all four tires off the shoulder. A ditch wasn't a safe place either. She plowed through one place where wings of white water shot out on both sides of the car.

Halfway across this narrow bridge, she ran over an armadillo that first went one way and then went the other way and finally just gave up. She tried the horn, but it was one thing on this old speed barge that didn't work.

Down the road a good piece, I got her stopped under a fence of these mossy oaks. The whole car slid side-around in a big avalanche of red dust. The engine shivered and coughed and shook to death in the shadows, hid fairly good from stars and cars. Believe me, a good hiding place is one thing me and Sack always try to make sure of.

I put Sack's head back on, so maybe that girl wouldn't be able to pick me out of any jailhouse lineups later on.

Soon as the car stopped, her little tiny hands fluttered up to her face. It looked like she was maybe fourteen, but you couldn't tell. Lots of makeup. A ring on every finger, probably out of bubble-gum machines. She smelled to me like furniture polish, but I reckon it was some kind of perfume.

I couldn't see her after a minute. Sweat fell in my eyes and just burned too bad. I found a dry handkerchief in the glove compartment and stuffed it in one of Sack's eye sockets.

All of a sudden, her two burning-fever eyes popped out from behind red fingernails. Before I could budge, she plundered her hand down in her purse. *Something to kill me,* I thought. *This is it for me.* Only she didn't pull out a gun or a knife or even an eye jab.

It was this female napkin.

"Thang!" she said in her broke-to-bits voice. "Look here. I ain't no good right now."

I stared at her with that handkerchief hanging out of my eye. I didn't have any idea what that girl expected till right then and there.

"I know you can't be all mean!" she hollered. "You don't have mean ways about you!" Bony legs kicked up and down, and her little white hand poked that thing at me. "PLEASE!" she sirened. *"Say* something!"

I took Sack's head back off so I could breathe. She looked more scared than ever. It made me mad.

"I can't believe what I'm a'seein'," I said. "But you right, white-headed girl. I ain't all mean. I ain't hardly mean at *all."*

I reached over and stuffed Sack's handkerchief right in her mouth. The way she was worked up, the future of my ears depended on it.

"I got to figure something out," I told her. "I seen you watching me out'n this car. You'd tell the soldiers and the po-lice everything. Especially that part about The Wild Thang."

Her blond head shook no, no, no, that just ain't so.

"You ain't got to pretend," I said again, nice and polite. "I know what you'd do. I ain't no circus clown."

She shook her head no again, but her squirming eased off.

I could see her better now we weren't tussling. This dress she had on was a silky red thing with baby green polka dots. It looked like house insulation with stinkbugs crawling in it. The dress was torn in the arm and she had mud from someplace smeared on her elbow. She wore heavy makeup. Every time she blinked, it was like a neon sign. When she got my handkerchief out of her mouth to talk, it was pure red with the lipstick.

"Listen," she breathed up at me, those big hot eyes wide open. "I won't tell anything about The Wild Thang, not ever, if you just won't tell what you saw tonight!"

"What you mean?" I said.

She looked down at her high-heel shoes.

"I mean about seeing me and you-know-who down here at Bob-A-Lu."

"You and who?"

Her lip poked out so far you could walk halfway to China on it.

"Harvey Lee Lipp. He's not like you think. He's not really so good and squeaky-clean, I mean. He sweet-talked me into going out for a good time with him, then he drove down to Bob-A-Lu and—*I can't hardly believe this*—he locked me in the trunk. I had to kick the backseat out to crawl into the car."

I thought about it and felt a noodle of sweat fall off my nose. I nearly had to smile.

"Your Harvey Lee ain't really so brave, neither. He run when The Wild Thang showed. Took off like a scalded dog."

"You ought not be so proud of yourself," she said. "Anybody would want to get away from you. That awful suit you have on smells worse than a polecat."

That nearly brought an ugly temper up in me.

"You ought to just shut up that kind of talk, white-headed girl. It won't do you one bit of good to go and hurt my feelings. Especially when I'm tryin' to be nice and I ain't got to be."

"Well," she sniffled, "it's not easy to get all pretty and then get left out in the trunk of a car for two hours and then have yourself kidnapped by a boy in a roach suit and then made to drive ninety miles per hour when I never even sat behind a steering wheel before. It ought to happen to you some time."

"Harvey Lee locked you in the trunk? You could have roasted to death."

"He did it so I wouldn't go in there and sit by him in Bob-A-Lu," she said. "He said I might give him a bad reputation around Goshen. I tell you this, though. Cissy Barber is not the kind of girl to wait in the trunk of *anybody's* car.

I turned my head enough to see behind me. Sure enough, she'd kicked a hole all the way through the backseat of the car, strowing sheepy cotton balls and curly wire springs all over the floorboard.

"It works both ways," Cissy said. "This minute, I don't want anybody, ever, not ever in a million years, to know I ever got in the car with that creep."

Right then, out of the corner of my eye, I saw her sneak a look over at me. Her eyes seemed as deep as two well holes on a clear night.

I propped Sack's head in my lap, and turned his fangs and eyes toward her.

"This car," I said, real dramatic. "Is about to turn into one big problem."

"What do you mean?"

"I reckon we both know somebody's gone and stole it," I said. "I hear tell they hang folks nowadays for stealing cars."

That thought hadn't made a nest in her head yet. She looked at me funny, then she leaned back like all her air was leaking out.

"Shoot," she said. "Harvey Lee's gonna tell the police *I* did it. I can hear him now. That sorry so-and-so will claim he left me to watch his car, and that was the last time he saw his old green machine. The *creep.*"

She mashed something alive on the back of her neck. After a minute, sort of weak, she tacked on something that surprised me.

"It's a fun car, though. Driving it here, I mean."

There was a long crickety time before I got brave enough to answer.

"Listen," I told her. "The police might not ever have to hear a durned thing about this."

More crickets. Way off, I heard a screech owl.

"You got to promise first!" she spit like a wet cat. "Git your hands off of me!"

"Well, durn," I told her, drawing back my claw hand. Fur was bit out all over the back. "Girl, that hurt."

She glared over, kind of licking fur off her lips. Not one bit afraid anymore.

I couldn't believe this next. When I saw her face that time, just that way, fur and all, something inside of me stopped being the old lonesome Buddy. My heart sang a birdsong, that second.

"I'm sorry about what I just done," I said out of the clear blue, embarrassed. "I ain't really like that."

"That's good to know. For starters." But her eyes wouldn't stop scolding me.

I felt dumb. Dumb and tongue-tied and put on the spot. My cheeks burned all the way out to the tips of my ears.

All in the world I could think to do was pick up Sack's head and hold it in the air by its hair.

"I'm not really like this, either," I told her. "Not all the time."

"Oh, you're The Wild Thang all right," she said. "But you don't scare me. I've seen worse."

THE FIRST TIME

A POLICE CAR flew down good old Highway 27, wild as a hog.

I busted out the overhead light, then eased open the Galaxy door and hid behind it like a little baby back of a mama bird's wing. I was ready to run.

Cissy sat stubborn in the car with her arms folded, sort of matter-of-fact.

The black-and-white car came on. Its blue police light lit the woods, and all the trees and bushes looked like trees and bushes in a black-and-white scary movie. Spooky shadows stretched every which way.

All of a sudden, that girl was huddled beside me back of the car door. She seemed nervous as could be.

I reckon, sometimes, the devil in the car you know is better than the devil in the car you don't. Or something like that.

The cruiser flashed right on past. It rared up on two

wheels cutting the next curve, gunning down the road toward the Bob-A-Lu. Farther on, we heard the siren rip
loose again. It gave me the chills. A hungry wampus cat
sounds like that.

The oak trees and Spanish moss did their job. They hid
me and Sack and Cissy. Oh, we got a scare though. You
could see how a flash off a mirror or the chrome bumpers
might call like a lighthouse beacon to somebody with a
careful eye.

Evil eyes *would* be here before long. The potbellied pig
sheriff and all his police would roll up and down this highway, sniffing under every bush for The Wild Thing. Christian Soldiers too, thick as green ants, hunting under the full
moon for any little clue to what monkeyed up their precious Bob-A-Lu.

I looked at Cissy. Her hair glowed in the moonlight like
a golden girl's.

"You as worried of them government boys as I am, ain't
you?" I said. "I can look at you and tell."

She crouched and made a face. "My reasons are real
good ones," she said. "You can't trust anybody much that
claims to look out for you."

A screech owl hollered, way off. It came to me that she
just said something important. About her life.

I decided I'd say something important too.

"This little Indian is about to head for a hideout," I said.
"Got to git while the gittin's good. So, I reckon you got a
choice to make, white-haired girl."

"Cissy," she said. "Go on. You can say *Cissy.* That's my
name."

I nodded. "Yeah. *Sassy.*"

She waited, but I was finished.

"Well, don't get all puffed up, boy. Let me tell you, if
you feel like *your* whole night's been ruined, I'll just remind you. I've been kidnapped and made to drive . . ."

"Hey," I said, fussy. "There's the car, right there, white-haired girl. The keys are in it. You know how to drive already. I reckon this kidnap is over."

I waited.

Then I thought how that probably sounded.

"Sorry," I said, real quiet. "It's just been a nerve-wracking night. Kinda different."

"That's okay." She took a deep breath. "I know what you mean."

So. We listened to the engine cool down for a minute. She finally spoke up.

"Let's say I drive Harvey Lee's car back to the Bob-A-Lu," she said, "if I remember how to get there, and I can keep the car running, and I don't have a head-on collision with some guardrail on a bridge."

"Yeah?"

"I do that, they put me in jail, 'cause I've been a single girl and I'm unaccounted for. Or, worse, they send me to the crazy house. Especially if I tell the truth. If I tell how The Wild Thang sat right there in the front seat by me and showed me how to work the gears and took me off to the woods. And then that this big old fierce red-eyed monster everybody's so scared of turns out to be just sort of a weird country boy."

A weird country boy can feel himself turn red in the dark. But I never knew it till then.

"So that's a choice," she went on. "And I don't like that one a bit."

I wouldn't either, I told her.

"So then there's choice number two. Which is this. I plop down here in the front seat and wait alone in the middle of the night, all by myself, no telling how long, for somebody maybe crazier than you to find me. 'Cause I know you're going to be out of here in about two shakes."

"I got to go," I said. "Me 'n Sack get caught, it's worse'n

the crazy house for us. *IF* Sack and old Buddy ever get caught."

Cissy actually smiled, the first time.

"Well, *Buddy,*" she said. "Pleased to make your acquaintance. And who is this Sack?"

"I'm Buddy," I said. Then I patted my mossy chest. "This here, he's Sack."

"Okay, then, Mr. Buddy. I'll tell you the truth. I don't really believe I want to wait around for some bunch of bad policemen or peckerwood soldiers to find *me* out here by myself in these woods either."

I believed her.

"So I reckon I'm to choice number three."

My heart flipped like a pancake in a skillet when she said that. And these words then came pouring out all at once, like it was somebody else talking, not Buddy.

"White-haired girl. Cissy, I mean . . ." I looked at her, swallowed to keep on track. "If you'll come with me, you won't never ever again in your whole life lay lonely waiting for a boy to care about you."

She looked straight at me, surprised to death. Me too, if I'm honest. But I just looked right in her eyes and kept talking.

"My mama's gone too," I told her. "I never even had no daddy to remember. I ain't had nobody to look out for me except my brother Randy since I turned ten years old. Old Randy's gone too now. Shot by those Christian Soldiers."

It happened just when I said those words that two heavy trucks rumbled around the curve in the highway. Me and Cissy shut up and held our breaths again.

Through the twisty trees, I could just make out a place in the back of one of the Saracens where the tarp cover flapped opened. A row of soldiers with guns sat on a bench back there. Faces black with camouflage. On their way to the "disturbance."

"Please," I said, turned to her. "Me and Sack can't get no lonelier. We got us a secret place."

You don't ever know what makes a person say yes or no to things that change their whole lives. Sometimes, they just say it and then it's done.

"I reckon any old hole in the ground is better than where I been the last little while," she said.

My heart jump-started right then.

"My full name is Cissy Jean *Barber*," she told me. "You might as well know it."

"Cissy Jean?"

"Barber."

"I'm just Buddy. I ain't got no other name."

She nodded like she understood.

"You done met Sack," I told her.

"I met him twice, at least. He's sort of handsome, if you look close enough. Like my daddy was."

If I had a nickel for every thing she'd said like that, every thing that I didn't understand, I'd already be rich in this one night.

*

I gathered Sack up in the dark. A claw hand. The fur Cissy snatched loose. Every piece would be important, if folks with bloodhounds found this spot.

A dog like that could follow a trail through brimstone. Unless it ran into red pepper. Nothing fouled up a good dog's nose worse'n a dose of cayenne. So Sack always spilled a lot on the trail he came in on, and on the trail he booked out on too.

Still, he never left a piece of himself behind. You didn't take foolish chances when you got to be a legend.

Cissy was something else. Somebody to worry over. While I sprinkled around the pepper, I could already see how, in the daytime, that red dress of hers would stand out like a pillar of hot fire. We'd have to find something else to wear.

Or nothing at all, if she would put up with that. Pure and wild, that's how I lived out in the woods.

Oh, that was fun to imagine.

But it would only be imagination if we never got back to The Secret Place.

"Uh, Cissy," I said, tying a thong on Sack.

She sat in the passenger side of the Galaxy, rocking the heavy door to get it closed.

"I'm listening."

"Cissy, you done a good job. I mean, gettin' this car to here . . ."

She had the door closed now, and worked at rolling down the window. It took both hands for her. She stopped and put those eyes on me.

"Yes. And?"

I must have turned red again.

"You won't believe how easy it is," she said, patting the wheel with her little white hand. "The car does everything itself. All you do is aim it with the steering wheel."

My heart hopped up in my throat when I thought about it. Then I looked down the side of the Galaxy at the scraped-away paint—her driving. A half a bucket of dirt matted the grille. A pine limb hung out of the door handle on the back driver's side. The hood wore a deep dent, like somebody threw something out of the sky on top of it.

"Shoot," I said then. "I reckon if you drove it, I can too."

She smiled big and proud.

"You know, my mama got her head cut off in a car crash," she said, just as cheery. "So you be careful."

I looked at her, and she just grinned crazy.

*

Driving *was* easy. A breeze. It reminded me of playing pin-ball. You just pretended to be the ball instead of the flashing signs and barrels and flippers that hit the ball.

"Whee!" Cissy hollered, with her arm swatting at clumps of Johnsongrass. "Boy, we must be going thirty!"

It felt faster than the mad mouse at the fair to me. I was still trying to get it straight. Like a tractor, one pedal made it go and the other pedal made it stop. Fast, if you weren't careful.

On the blacktop again, I stomped on the brake so quick our wheels barked like dogs. Both of us had to laugh.

"You're not driving a covered wagon!" she went. "Go *on!*"

"I'll show *you.* Watch *this!*"

I flat out stomped on the gas pedal. And the car did what a good car ought to do, I reckon. It leaped onto its two hind legs and shot off like a scared rabbit. It threw Cissy slam over the backseat, into the springs and cotton stuffing.

Lucky for us, nothing moved along the highway right then. Nothing but that stripe down the middle, and dog if it didn't swoop all over the place. Me and Sack and Cissy, laughing as hard as she could in the backseat with her hair blowing, we did our best to keep straddle of that stripe. The needle on the speedometer shivered up to eighty, then ninety. The whole car rattled.

The needle hit 100. Telephone poles went by like fence posts. Cissy yelled and whooped in the backseat. All of a sudden, I lost my nerve and stood on the brakes.

"Yeeee-haaaaawwwwww!" went four smoking tires.

Cissy popped back up over the seat, like a surprised jack-in-the-box, and tumbled down into the front floorboard. I hugged the driver's wheel, in love with it. The tires squawled so loud. You could smell burning rubber and see tire sparks fly in a big swarm outside the window.

Oh, it was fun! Driving was fun! Hooray!

"Let me! It's my turn!" Cissy climbed halfway up in my lap. "C'mon, Buddy!"

"No way." I stood on the gas pedal again. "You already had a turn."

*

I rabbit-hopped that car on down the road for a lot of miles before I finally spotted my landmark in this rising summer fog. We never passed another car or army truck, and I took that to be very good luck.

The fog started to feel like good luck too. Cold smoke boiled up out of the creeks and swamps all over. Fog was easy to hide in.

I turned into the woods on a grown-up trail, and we bounced and bucked along an old train track until we came to a covered bridge. It was as gray as an old lady and shot full of bullet holes and held together by a million dirt dauber nests.

The bridge straddled this little lightning-fast branch off Old Mercy River. A rusted historical marker leaned away to one side. It always caught my eye: BATTLE OF PEE CREEK. The rest of the marker was shot to pieces, so you couldn't read a word about whatever happened at the Battle of Pee Creek. But I reckon it made sense for a marker like that to be full of bullet holes.

It was a battle marker for me and Sack too, our own personal battle of Pee Creek.

One summer night, right along this stretch of Highway 27, the moon had hound-dogged us through the woods. It was the first night we ever tried to make a difference in this world.

Scared to death, we stepped out of this other summer fog, a fog like this, thick as stewed oysters, into the headlights of a food truck, on its way, most likely, to feed the very soldiers that killed my brother. The driver panicked and ran slam off the road. His truck stampeded deer and rabbits on its way down to Pee Creek.

The onions and heads of lettuce and tomatoes jounced out of their crates and left a smashed white-and-red trail a hundred yards long back of that rig.

If you closed your eyes on the right kind of night, you could still smell the stinking ghosts of those onions.

Me and Sack hid out that first time while rescue folks showed up in droves.

First on the scene it was police and nervous Christian Soldiers with itchy fingers. Then directly a flashy ambulance rolled up with two big fat blond-haired sissy boys inside dressed like butchers at a grocery store.

Next, out of nowhere, curious diesel truck drivers rumbled in. They got news of the wreck on their CB radios.

Other soldier boys, lucky ones back from a hospital and alive but still in bandages, and a lots of tremble-legged little old ladies climbed down from a Greyhound bus that happened by.

Every one of the folks that night wore some kind of costume. Just like me. They found that driver out on his cab in the river, howling about "a wild thing," and they fetched him back through a drizzle.

The ambulance lights came on, and off moaned the meat wagon. Oh, the truck driver wasn't really hurt bad. A man hurt bad couldn't cuss like he cussed.

A policeman said they found whiskey in the truck cab. You could see the Christian Soldiers were all just disgusted by that. I reckon everybody just knew the DTs finally caught up with that poor trucker. Nobody believed the first word he babbled. Nobody even bothered to look for clues.

I got to feeling good, thinking back on that first night.

The world took away everything and everybody I ever had.

But on that night, me and Sack started giving back as good as we got.

*

Me and Sack and Cissy followed the rail bed and drove to the yawned-out entrance to that rattly old covered bridge. Before there was a railroad, there was a buggy road, and the bridge was built over the road in those long-ago days. It looked every century as old as it was.

"Cissy," I said, hoping for the best as I aimed the car at the dark opening. "You want to remember this covered bridge. It might be famous as a place in the Bible one day."

"Why's that?" She sounded a little tired now.

" 'Cause maybe someday people will say it's the bridge me and you went over on our way to The Secret Place for the first time."

Cissy didn't look at me for a second. She stared out a hole between planks in the covered bridge wall. The silver fog rose outside and the silver creek ran below.

"Buddy, you are one mighty interesting boy," she finally said.

Maybe it was my imagination, but I thought she turned to look at me then, and actually reached out her hand and touched my arm in the lightest way you could touch a person.

"You do smell just awful, though. Where did you get that roadkill you've got all over you?"

San Antonio

WE TURNED OFF that little pig trail about a mile past the covered bridge, and the bucking and bouncing commenced.

The Galaxy crawled up the steep, slick sides of purple-clay gullies. We bumped over dead pine trees the beetles had gnawed till they fell and scattered like pick-up-sticks. We rocked through the roughest little washboard streambeds ever carved out of Alabama's tough old hide.

It didn't help matters that the night turned out so foggy. You shouldn't pick one like that for driving a car through the wild woods. Even in the brightest moonlight, you couldn't see a stump ten feet ahead. You had to watch. Black leaves came up out of nowhere and swatted the windshield. I had to get out and pull a snake off the hood two times.

Let me tell you, though. Anybody that says a Galaxy won't make it a bunch of miles through the woods on a

81

dark and foggy night just never put Buddy and Sack and Miss Cissy Jean Barber behind the wheel. That old car grunted and clanked and spun its tires, but it still butted down saplings all night. Put a gun on top, you could have been in a tank.

Me and Sack learned to drive that trip. You can learn quick. Goose the gas, easy on the brake, aim the front of Mr. Car at the little things. That's about all there is to it.

I learned another thing too. Me and Cissy stopped twice to get out and pee.

A car made it rough on your insides, if you weren't used to that old-time rock 'n' roll.

*

We edged on. I bet we scraped bottom a dozen times getting through Bighead Gully, but that old car just kept rumbling. I knocked the outside rearview mirror slam off on one tight squeeze between two pines. The back bumper too, on a snag I didn't see. No slowing down, though. Sack knew where we were. Headed for the barn. Close enough to smell the feed.

In the easy places, we ran through thickets of ironweed and cane and mulberry and pokeberry. We scared out the possums and rabbits by the droves, but we never hit one.

Without headlights, we couldn't go fast enough to hit a turtle really. And we *had* to go without headlights. Once I saw a helicopter zip over us in the woods, then turn and hover in front of the moon like a hungry dragonfly.

Headlights in the woods would just call down the rockets and ruin. That would be the end of us.

After the helicopter flew off, Cissy tuckered out and dozed off in the seat. While she sawed logs, our trail connected back up to Pee Creek, miles deeper in the woods past the battlefield. That creek twisted and turned like a dying snake all through these parts.

I couldn't believe how pretty the moonlight made that creek water. It poured gold and copper over the black rocks. That sight made me start to feel back home again.

A big white rock split the creek halfway across. Randy said that rock was all that was left of the first white man in these parts. Him and his wagon got changed to stone by Indian magic.

At that landmark, we turned east. The moon wallowed out a hole on the horizon behind us now. I gunned the engine toward higher ground. You didn't want to drive on downstream. One of the biggest beaver-dam swamps ever pooled up there.

"Cissy! Cissy, look!"

"Look at what?" She sort of whimpered, stretching and waking up a little.

"Right down in yonder," I pointed. "That's Soggyboggy Swamp. That's where me and Randy ran into old Alligator."

"A live one?" She got half-interested.

"Uh-uh. I mean a person name of Alligator. This old woman that made her living killing gators and selling their awful hides. She kidnapped little boy dogs in towns all around here. Used a lady Chihuahua in heat to lure 'em. Then she came here at night and floated out in a johnboat and tied them dogs to plow traces and throwed 'em in the water."

Cissy scrooched up her face and put her hands over her ears. "She sounds real sweet."

I grinned.

"She went fishing . . . for alligators! And when them sons o' guns showed up for a dog snack, she gave 'em both barrels of a twelve gauge. Right in their chompin' mouths."

Cissy yawned. "So what happened to her dogs?"

I waited just long enough and said, "Let's just put it this way. Old Alligator had to bait her hooks all over again."

I drove on and we heard the sproinging and scraping of bushes under the car for a second.

"You know," Cissy said. "I hate a stupid dog."

She went back to sleep with her cheek against the door lock.

Sack got a kick out of that one. He squeaked and wiggled all over my legs.

See, Sack hates a dog too.

A coyote, a fox, even a red wolf you see sometimes out in these woods, they're okay. You won't ever see one of them lick somebody's boots the way a dumb dog does. Or roll over on their backs and show the whites of their eyes and make their nasty red lipstick tubes creep out just for a bite of moldy thrown-away honey bun.

Some animals are *wild*. Wild and pure. And that's the whole difference.

*

We bounced up to The Secret Place just at daybreak.

I declare that Mr. Car, who started out so strong, was just about gone by then. He shrieked and hollered, idling at the edge of the clearing. When I turned the engine off, it sounded glad. And me and Cissy could hear again, like it was the first time in our lives.

The red trees hummed like tree gods still lived in them. A mockingbird played this flute in the dark, way up a tree. Frogs squawled from their dewholes, and every blade of sparkling sweet green grass must have hid a purring cricket.

We were so tired, we went straight from the car, me and Sack, and flopped down in the vine hammock. Cissy stretched out on the front seat of the car, with the doors open for circulation.

I had spent five days making my hammock. I took and

soaked wild wisteria and other tanglers in river water. Then I boiled the vines in a vinegar I found in a sinkhole, made when wild crab apples fell out of a tree and soured in there with rainwater for a long time. Then, for a whole day, I cooked those vines, till they turned as soft as cotton. I weaved the hammock all together while I sat on top of the Indian mound and sang a song. I made the song up myself. It went like this:

> *Catfish, catfish swimmin' around*
> *Took a little trip down to catfish town*
> *Funny little whiskers, funny little grin*
> *You never do know where a catfish been*

That was the same song I sang that morning, lying in the hammock. Me and Sack drifted off to sleep with it. It was already hot, so I shucked Sack off, down to my cutoffs and T-shirt, and left him to be on his own there beside me.

I didn't care what she said. Sack didn't smell all that bad to me.

*

By the middle of the morning, the sun sizzled in the sky like butter in a hot blue skillet. We hadn't had all our sleep yet, but it was too warm to go on trying.

Cissy stirred first. She crawled out of the car with her hot-red dress stuck to her. In just a minute, she undressed down to her slip. I never saw a real slip before. It was fancy, white with little ruffles at the hem.

Me and Sack together looked like one giant spider, sprawled in a web. I waved one of Sack's arms when Cissy came up over the side of the Indian mound.

She groaned and straightened up, then her face came on like a happy light.

"Buddy! Look! Look at that!"

A hummingbird beat the air down by her feet. Her toes sported that red toenail polish, and that bird appeared to be mighty interested.

"Shoo! Git!" I waved my arms and kicked all around in the hammock. The bird flitted off a few feet, then stared back with this mean face.

"You'll be sorry, girl, if that hummingbird touches you with that stinger. You'll run a fever from now on."

She looked at me funny. "I touched a hummingbird before. They don't do any such thing."

"I saw one spit in a cat's eye," I told her. "That cat's whole head swelled up big as a cabbage. And its brain dripped out of its nose, and it *died* hollerin'."

"Well aren't you special," she said. "Then did you eat the cat?"

I saw right then she wouldn't be much for waking up all fresh and lively in the mornings.

The hummingbird zoomed off, loud as a robber bee. It zipped on up to the orange trumpet vine coiled around the hickory where I got my last blue jay eggs. That little green hummer wore a red reflector on his throat, and his wings beat so fast you just saw air.

"I do think they're mighty pretty critters," I said. "Dangerous as they are. But think how you'd feel if you was a beautiful flower and that thing showed up. . . ."

Cissy turned and looked at me funny and then just laughed.

"I declare," she said. "I never met anybody like you, Buddy."

Well, shoot. I didn't know exactly what that meant. But it sounded nice when she laughed.

Maybe she wouldn't be so bad before breakfast after all.

She pulled her gold hair—that's the color it was this

morning—up in a little cornshock off her sweaty neck and looked all around her at the green new world she lived in. A little breath of breeze came up, welcome in the hot.

"This is really a beautiful place," she said. "Shangri-la, Alabama."

That sounded nice. But I didn't know what that meant either.

"What did you think about all that mess last night?" I asked her.

She laughed again. Third time's a charm, I reckon. She took her white slip in her fingers on either side, like she might curtsy, then started to spin, around and around, with her face turned up to the sun.

"Wheeee!" she went. "I'm a wanted woman! I'm wanted all over Goshen! Hurray!"

She got dizzy and drunk on laughing and finally fell down. Me, I laid back in the hammock and puzzled and admired her. It was different from the way I ever saw a girl act before.

So we just laid there in the June of our lives, quiet like we were full from eating fresh peaches or a sweet watermelon. A red seed or two twirled down from those giant trees.

In a little, the wind pushed my swing back and forth, and I went off to dreamland.

She must have taken a nap too. 'Cause I saw her walking in my dream.

*

Later on, stirring, I noticed how high those red trees rose to the sky. You could have cut whole wagon wheels out of the trunks. They rose as tall as the columns on the front of the biggest church you ever saw.

No vine could crawl high enough to get to the crowns of those giants. Way up there, those short needles glowed like red fur in the sun. You didn't see a sick spot anywhere. No moss on the limbs, and no yellow fungus. Sometimes, cancers twist trees up like old Popeyes. But not these perfect red ones.

I couldn't even spot a bird in the high places. And remember, my eyes see pure.

Finally, though, I saw what was put there for me to see.

The Old Man of the Woods appeared if you looked long enough, like one of those hidden animals in a kids' book, the kind you have to find and color blue or red.

Oh, yessir, he was up there. Like all the other spirits that lived out here. Those people have forgot.

He hunkered down in the branches. He smiled with those big white teeth, smiled and smiled till all you could really make out were white chocks and blocks of sunlight where the grin used to be.

Cissy could have seen him too, but she dozed on.

*

After a long fun rest, Cissy finally woke me up. She did it by sneaking around behind me and trying to flip the hammock. It bucked like crazy. I held on like a man on a wild horse, but it finally threw me out onto the deep grass and red needles.

She dashed off down the side of the Indian mound. I reckon she thought I'd chase her. But I just laid still on the ground and rested and thought.

The grass on the mound felt so good. Cool and sweet. I wondered if King David in the Bible ever laid out like this, in those places where he lived when he took care of sheep and wrote those Bible poems. He wrote happy words about green hills. Maybe the grass back then wasn't full of redbugs.

When Cissy got back, I patted a place next to me and she sat down. She looked like she had something on her mind.

"Buddy," she said, kind of solemn.

"That's my name. Don't wear it out."

She rolled her eyes, green today as the light on the grass. "Listen, now. Be *serious.* I want to tell you a story."

"What kind of story?"

"You'll see."

I stared at her feet for a long second or two.

"Okay. I'll be listenin'. But I want you to listen to something first."

"What?"

"It's *serious,*" I said.

"*What?*"

"You're sittin' "—I waited till her head nodded yeah, go on—"right in the middle of a great big old fire ant bed."

She slapped at my arm. Then she realized I wasn't kidding. She looked down, and there they crawled, a little army of fire ants trying to sting whatever they held onto. Cissy scooted all around in a big fluster, brushing little dots off her legs, her slip. I don't think she got bit a single time.

"That wasn't very funny, Buddy."

"Go," I told her. "This time, I'll listen. I promise."

She started settling, checking this time before she plumped down on the other side of me. "I wish I had some chewing gum," she said. "I could tell this faster."

I sat up on one elbow and squinted. She shined so, with that hair like a dandelion puff and her skin gold. "There's something better than Juicy Fruit," I said. "You ever tapped fresh sweetgum from a tree?"

"Don't interrupt," she said. "I've already started talking."

So I forgot the sweetgum and settled back.

And this was Cissy Barber's story.

*

"The important part starts in San Antonio. San Antonio in Texas.

"That's a pretty good name for a town, if you think about it. It's not one of these worn-out town names you find just everywhere. I mean it's not a tired same-old, same-old name like Greenville or Columbus or Jackson."

I told her there was a town in Florida named Two Egg, and one in Alabama named Smuteye.

"I've noticed there's a Jackie's Lounge in a lot of towns here too," she said. "And nearly always some car place called Big-Hearted Eddie's."

There's a Goshen in the Bible, I told her.

"Right across the river from Hell," she said. "And I bet nobody swims across."

I told her Goshen wasn't so bad before The New Times.

"Anyway," she went on, "I guess Hell can be just about anywhere. Like in San Antonio, there was this hospital where they brought my daddy after his helicopter crash. He got shot down in the big battle out in California, back when everything first went all to pieces. He was a soldier before they called all of them Christian Soldiers, back at the very start of all the trouble."

I told her I didn't remember that one particular scrap, really. All that fighting out west and the bad parts up north just ran together for me. But she didn't pay much mind right then.

"There was a green Rose of Sharon tree blooming outside the hospital room Daddy laid in, and a mockingbird in that tree whistled like crazy. I always thought a mockingbird was good luck till then. But I was little.

"In that room, I remember a bunch of doctors that stood around in these white coats. Me and Mama walked in on 'em after the Air Force flew us in special all the way from Jackson."

I asked her Jackson, Mississippi, or Jackson, Alabama, or Jackson, Tennessee?

"See, now that's what I mean. Jackson's a name that's about like an old cow that's been milked to death. I mean the one in Mississippi."

"Ain't no Jacksons in the Bible," I said.

She stopped. "You sure talk about the Bible a lot, to be fighting so fierce against The New Times the way you are."

I liked the stories. I liked all those names, I told her. I liked Shadrach and Meshach and Abednego. And Nebuchadnezzar and Esau and Solomon. And Jethro and Nimrod. Besides, it wasn't the *Bible* I was fighting . . .

"Okay, Buddy, anyway. The hospital. Me and Mama walked in and it felt sort of fishy, right off. These doctors started fooling with their watches and cleaning the eyes of their glasses.

"Turns out they had a good reason to be nervous. Maybe they never saw a scary movie. But I'd watched plenty. I could tell what was up, in nothing flat."

What? I asked her.

"The Mummy! The Mummy himself was lying right there in the room. Right behind those guys.

"Did you ever see that movie, Buddy? The one called *The Mummy's Ghost?*"

You bet, I told her. That's the one where that four-thousand-year-old dead man climbs out of its grave in a moldy old sheet and drags one leg behind him all over town looking for a girl to be his queen down under the ground.

"That's the one. I never yet got over seeing *The Mummy*. I used to have bad dreams about that booger. He'd be dragging through a cornfield toward our house. Slobbering this brown stuff. Bugs crawling in and out of his face. He'd get up to my bedroom window and push his awful self right up to the panes in the middle of the night and peep in with one eye just throbbing. Shoot! Talk about a girl screaming bloody murder . . ."

You ain't got to worry about nothing like that around here, I told her. This is The Secret Place.

"I'm glad it's a secret, that's all I can say.

"Anyway, in San Antonio this Mummy thing was piled on the hospital bed, right up on the white sheets. It had some tubes and junk hooked up to his arms and running down its nose. Looked like Karo syrup they were pumping in."

I like Karo syrup, I told her.

"And this fly kept buzzing around and landing on the Mummy's head. He didn't have eyes or a nose or anything. Just those white bandages."

And a pet fly, I said.

"About then, Buddy, one of those fancy-dan doctors cleared his throat and piped up. I can still hear him, the way he said it."

She made her voice climb up high and schoolteachery.

" 'There's your hero, Mrs. Barber. We saved him. Go ahead and look Miss Cissy, that's your daddy!' After he said it, that feller worked his finger around his collar once real quick.

"Now, Buddy, that turned out to be one fine puffed-up proud bunch. I saw that when this other doctor climbed right up on top of the first one's back.

" 'Dr. Lee is right, ma'am.' That's what this next one said, something like that. 'What you see resting comfortably on that bed right there is a miracle man. When Paul Barber got pulled out of that helicopter, not a man-jack in this whole Air Force gave him a Chinaman's chance. But I tell you what—he raised up his cot and lived, that fellow did. Holy Science married the Holy Spirit. We really do have miracles in our time, ladies.'

"The next doctor down the row got the spirit about then. He whipped his glasses off his head, and I swear to you, Buddy, I saw his hair turn sideways.

"Oh, he laid a line of trash talk on Mama.

" 'Mrs. Barber, I can see by your face that you're keenly aware of the fact that we're not out of the woods yet. There are miles and miles to go. Cosmetically, I mean. But we're growing artificial skin by the yard right now out in our research laboratories and that, with plastic restoration, leads us to expect a full recovery.' He went like that, blah, blah, blah.

"Buddy, Mama boiled over the top of her pot right then."

Cissy's story was good, and I sat up.

"Mama shot out of that room. I could hear her high heels just a'going—*pop-pop-pop*—down the hall. And then, her courage ran out, I reckon. I heard this crying, just like some kind of awful song.

"Those doctors. It looked like the three stooges, except it was about six. They went runnin' into one another and boinking heads. I saw a nurse swoosh by the door like she was on skates. By the time I got to the hall, all you could see were men's big butts and flying sheets of paper and the fluttering tails of white coats.

"I tell you what. When everybody left, it got mighty still and quiet in that room. It got down to just me and the Mummy. Just me and him and that stupid fly.

"I remember every single sound. *Buzz, buzz, buzzzzzzz.* That mockingbird all out of tune. Those gurgling food tubes that sounded like a sweetheart straw at the bottom of a good milk shake."

"I like milk shakes," I said.

"Yeah, and there was this one other sound. Breathing. That Mummy, breathing. Into this heavy rubber bag by the bed. He just kept breathing, and that bag would fill up like he was blowing up a beach ball. Then down it shrunk. Then it filled up again. It just made you want to scream and throw up.

"They finally fetched Mama back. Her heel of her shoe was broken off. Sobs just bubbling up. Her stockings tore all to pieces."

"They caught her," I said.

"Yeah, those doctors caught her. But you should have seen that bunch. Mangled and tangled. One looked like he tried to put a thermometer up a wildcat's butt. Doctor Lee had his glasses broken. Another one pressed this white handkerchief up to his ear, trying to stop the blood."

Good going, I told her.

"I ran over to Mama, and put my face against her tummy and hugged her so hard. And Buddy . . ."

Cissy stopped and bit her lip.

"Way, way down inside of her, I heard something crying. The kind of crying that doesn't ever make it up to your eyes."

"I don't really remember how the time passed after that. They had some 'talks' with me and Mama. They gave us some books to read. But I do know that the very same afternoon, we climbed back on some rattletrap military airplane and flew home to Jackson.

"Mama sat in the back of the plane with some equipment, real quiet. She made me go up front, to watch the pilot move all the dials and arrows. I thought about Daddy flying his helicopter through the sky. Outside, the clouds looked so big and white and soft. They looked like nothing would ever hurt you again if you got up there among them."

"There's white-hot lightning even up there," I said, just to say something. But Cissy didn't stop.

"They gave us Cokes and two packs of cheese crackers on the way home. While we ate, the pilot dipped down out of the clouds to look at some of the fighting along one of the big highways. You could see it was bad, even from up where we were."

Bad how? I asked.

"This train loaded down with soldiers gored into a gasoline truck that got stalled—or left on purpose—across the tracks. The train and the cars were all just big fiery pieces now. The boxcars knocked down whole pecan trees, and the fields caught on fire. The flames went so high and burned so hot you could feel them right through the walls of the airplane.

"We flew right over it all, and I thought I could see boys' faces all in the black smoke, on their way to Heaven or somewhere.

"It was one awful mess down there. You could see people cut in two like worms. One soldier walked right down the middle of the highway dragging his cut-off arm behind him by the fingers.

"It got really hot inside the plane. I thought we might be roasted too, for a minute. Then I felt a cool hand on top of my head, and I looked up at Mama.

"She had a tear melting out of her eyes.

" 'Pray for your daddy, Cissy,' " she said. " 'He's close by right now.' "

*

"We lived kinda quiet in Jackson for a long time after that."

"Jackson," I said. "Mississippi."

"Uh-huh. Sometimes a man from the Army came to the house and sat in a starchy white uniform on one of our teensie little chairs. He had shiny black rat hair and a mustache. He always told me and Mama how Daddy was 'making good progress' and stuff. He would hand us an envelope with a check and salute Mama when he stood up to leave.

"A preacher from the government came too, after most of the worst fighting settled down. He was tall and kind of gloomy. He'd want to pray and hold our hands in the parlor, but I could tell Mama didn't like that. I believe he could tell too. After two trips, he didn't come back."

What did y'all do for fun? I wanted to know. You didn't just sit around the house all the time, even if your daddy was sick.

"We had fun when the check came. We'd go out shopping, if it wasn't Curfew Day. Mama always bought me books to read and blue jeans and sometimes a doll, even though I never really liked dolls too much. They have scary faces. All that plastic."

"What about your mama," I said.

"Oh, Mama wasn't too hard to please. She might buy hairdo stuff. Or some shoes. We'd top off some days at Nip's and eat hot dogs and cherry Cokes and french fries. Nip's was her favorite place in the whole world.

"But let me tell you about this one time. After the soldier brought the check, me and Mama went to the grand opening of this giant new store, one of those with a parking lot as big as some whole towns. It was the biggest store anybody ever saw in Jackson. Imagine if you took twenty big stores and threw a roof over the whole bunch. Shoes and fishing junk and car tires and toys and a whole section of nothing but pillows, piled way up high. Whole aisles with nothing but chocolate candy. A store like that."

The biggest store I ever went in was a Gibson's in Panama City, I told her.

"Let me finish. This is about what happened that day of the grand opening.

"See, to get a lot of people to come to the store that day, they borrowed a Christian Army helicopter to take off from the lot. For a stunt. When I saw that helicopter, though, I got real nervous. Mama cut me a glance and I knew she was thinking the same thing. It made both of us so sad.

"The job of the helicopter was to pour Ping-Ping balls, thousands and thousands of them, out of its doors and down on the cars and people. Some of the balls had numbers written on them in black Magic Marker, and if you caught one of those, you won a prize."

"I won a Wild Man from Borneo at the fair one time," I said.

"It's fun to win stuff, isn't it? And this is about something I won, maybe the only thing I ever will.

"We looked real pretty, me and Mama. She had on a green coat—this was in October—and was dolled up so her eyes looked twice as big as they were. Serious too. But when that helicopter opened its door and a soldier boy dumped the Ping-Pong balls and instead of falling they got sucked straight up in the air and sprayed all over kingdom come in this pure Ping-Pong blizzard, we both went to laughing. It looked like winter in a movie, with snow falling and people cheering.

"Folks chased little bouncing white balls all over creation. They crawled up under cars to round 'em up. They swatted with their hats to catch 'em. They stuck their arms down drainpipes and rambled through the weeds at the edge of the highway the way folks used to do when Easter egg hunts were still allowed. You never saw such carrying on.

"Well, sir, Cissy Jean Barber got one of those Ping-Pong balls herself, without anybody's help. I pulled it out of the hood of some teen-age boy's coat, a boy who was standing right in front of me. It landed in there without him even knowing. And I could hardly believe it. A black number 'two' was written right there on it!

"At first, I thought I ought to give the ball back to that boy. Except what happened was all too fast. And it turned out real, real bad."

What? I asked. You had a fight?

"The daddy of the boy saw me play pickpocket. He came over all bowed up like a fighting rooster and told his son, and both of them turned around. I swear, they just looked at me and Mama like two dogs eyeing a bowl of meat. You could see they were bad people.

"It scared me plenty. But Mama just stared a hot hole back, till finally they turned and stomped on off.

"So we forgot them. We took our little prizewinning ball and marched off to the store, through the first electric-eye door we ever saw. We went in and out twice, just to see that door work.

"And way in there past mountains of clothes and stuff, at a counter just working alive with people, I got my prize.

"They came in their own cardboard box. Two baby ducks, fuzzy yellow, peeping their heads off. A paper tag from this place called Hutchinson's Hatchery was looped around both their little legs, and on the tag was a Bible verse."

Ducks don't read the Bible, I told her.

"Here's what it said: 'For I heard them say, let us go to Goshen, Genesis 37:17.' Me and Mama hadn't ever even heard of Goshen, Alabama, before that. Oh, we laughed. I mean that was funny to us, for some reason.

"Buddy, I never had won anything before those ducks. Never. Not at a cakewalk. Not off a cereal box. I saved potato-chip bags for a year one time, but they stopped giving away girls' bicycles on TV before I could cash mine in. So that day with Mama, I was so happy I thought I might just pop.

"On the way out to the car, Mama just seemed so proud. She explained how even though those ducklings were little and gawky and just plain old yellow, someday they'd turn into real pretty white ducks with long necks and soft feathers. And, this was real sweet, Mama said that's just how it would be for me. She said I'd turn into something pretty. I won't ever forget that."

"She was right," I said. I felt brave.

But Cissy didn't look right. "Buddy," she said, "isn't it funny how the happiest feeling you ever felt can roll off the edge of a table all of a sudden and burst wide open like an egg?"

What do you mean? I asked.

"This. Those ducks never did make it to the car. And worse than that happened."

Cissy's eyes filled up, but I didn't say anything at all. It took her a minute to come on out with the rest.

"Buddy, I never quite saw how everything happened, out among all those cars in the lot. This was just at dark, so you couldn't make things out real plain.

"All I remember is just how *fast* it all went. Here we were walking, and then, poof, the duck box got snatched right out of my hands. I got knocked flat by somebody big, running by. I heard Mama holler, then this noise—*peep! peep! PEEP!*—and got up just in time to see who stole my box of ducks."

I bet I know, I told her.

"Sure. It was that man who looked so hateful earlier, him and his awful boy."

I figured.

"Well, that grown man took our baby ducks out of the box by the necks. He raised them way over his head . . . and threw them down as hard as he could. Right in front of us. Oh, he threw 'em hard. They bounced off the asphalt as high as my head."

My teeth clenched. Sack might just look those guys up one day.

"The man got all shaky like some crazy old country preacher and jabbed this long bony finger toward Mama and his eyes just burned.

"He said something like this: 'You the lady whose husband got in the news for killing them rebels out in California! Them was friends of mine he kilt, lady! My boys, fighting for worship rights! My boys, like I done raised 'em myself!'

"You could hear that man hiss like a snake, Buddy, every time he took a breath!

"Buddy, my mama always toted a pistol in her purse, loaded with ratshot. She went to dig it out, but it was scary and she dropped her purse, and then that old man was on top of her like a bad dog. He kicked the purse and everything in it up under the next five or six cars. Her stuff is probably still rolling across that parking lot."

Tears as big as marbles came out of Cissy's eyes now, so heavy they didn't stop on her chin but dropped right on to the deep grass.

"He hit my mama in the face, so hard. She fell and landed on the empty duck box. Blood just pouring out of her nose on that green coat. Her elbows scraped and bleeding. She couldn't get up.

"So you know what happened next."

I tried not to think about it, just looked up at the red trees.

"He took down his pants, and was holding them up with one hand. And that's when something almost unbelievable happened. Unbelievable as everything else."

I'd believe about anything after all this, I told Cissy.

"Out of nowhere, big as a monster in a monster movie, that black army helicopter come flying up.

"Oh, I was scared so bad. Mama was dead maybe. You couldn't hear anything, and the paper stuff from Mama's purse and all the other junk in the parking lot, a thousand squashed Ping-Ping balls and popcorn kernels and shopping bags and milk-shake cups and all kinds of everything, rose right up in the air like it was going to God. My clothes felt like they would just get sucked right off.

"I must have been screaming and screaming, because my mouth was open. But I couldn't hear a thing. It felt like the end of the world, when your screaming doesn't mean a blessed thing.

"I jumped up and down, yelling and crying so somebody might hear it. I waved my hands and pointed at my mama, just lying there bleeding with her dress hiked up, like a doll somebody broke.

"Then, like in this dream, two soldiers standing in the door of the helicopter spotted me waving my arms. They saw Mama too, then that man and his boy, running away now, weaving through all those cars.

"It took those soldiers about one-millionth of a second to figure out what was happening. There was a machine gun in the door. It swiveled around and made a noise like a sewing machine and red fire came out the nose.

"That running man and his boy tried to roll up under a truck, but it was too late for them."

What happened? I asked her.

"They just kind of disappeared. It was like watching the witch melt in *The Wizard of Oz*. Only instead of water, those two melted on the ground into this lumpy red soup. The truck they dove for wouldn't have done any good either. It blew up like a volcano when the bullets hit it. You could hear ricochets, everywhere, all in the air, whining like they do in a cartoon on Saturday morning."

P-chwang! I went. Like that.

"Like that. Only it wasn't a cartoon, but real as me and you right now. Black smoke and fire everywhere. Loud noise and stuff flying all over creation. Crowds of people, too, running all directions.

"I looked down on my dress and on my arms, Buddy. I had wet red freckles all of a sudden. Freckle drops of blood. Blood all over the car windshields and on people's glasses when they ran up to us, and on their white shirts too, like red sweat.

"I fell on top of Mama. I was afraid those men in the helicopter would shoot us too. Shoot us and fly on. See, I didn't understand it.

"They wouldn't shoot us though. They left us to see all the faces and hear all the voices. They left us to have all the bad, bad dreams two people could ever have."

*

"We spent a hard winter, me and Mama. We worried and cried a lot and hardly ever left the house. We played Hearts and ate too much soup, and we never went to school. Mama was a teacher, but she never darkened the door of that government schoolhouse.

"The soldiers came and built a big iron fence around the house and put a man on duty out there most days. We got a lot more money, too, even if neither one of us felt like spending any. Mama just asked the soldier who showed up on the porch to put the check in her account at the bank, and she came on back inside.

"Well, me and her figured this was about as bad as times could get. And then, just like they say about the darkest hour, came this bright ray of sun. A letter. From Daddy."

Boy. I bet it was one happy day, I told her.

"We didn't even know if he was still alive, really and truly. Oh, these government letters came and said so sometimes, but anybody could type up a lie on a sheet of fancy paper. We got to where we didn't believe hardly anything in the mail or on the TV or radio anymore."

That was smart, I told her. Because you *can't* nowadays.

"Anyway, Daddy's letter came in the spring. Me and Mama lived in a nice kind of Florida house with a carport, pink asbestos shingles on the sides, all that. We had a long sandy driveway and rambling roses grew wild in the front yard. Like I say, we didn't go out there. Just Mama, out to the end of the drive to visit the mailbox.

"Well, this one afternoon, she came in and the door slammed and it sounded like a different Mama in the house. *'Tweedle-dee!'* That's how she went, sort of like a bird. 'It's a letter for Cissy,' she said, all excited. 'And guess who sent it?'

" 'I can't guess, Mama.' That's what I said. 'Don't make me.'

"Mama said one of her corniest Mama-sayings then. 'That's not a fun girl, Cissy. Come on and be a fun girl.' That's what she said, or some saying like it.

"I told her I *wasn't* a fun girl. It wasn't fun to be me.

"Mama told me I ought to just listen to myself. She said I shouldn't be that way. She said I'd be sorry if I didn't take one guess at who sent this special letter.

" 'Okay,' I went. Then I guessed. 'It's a letter from Daddy.'

"She looked at me real hard. Like it hurt her feelings or something. 'I didn't know my own little daughter was a witchy girl,' she told me, and dropped it on my lap.

"I remember everything about that letter. The stamp, with the Christian Elvis on it. The way Daddy's name was typed in the corner. It looked so funny to see it spelled out, with all the numbers and ranks and stuff behind it like some kind of chicken from the other side of the world walked all across the envelope.

"But my name, Buddy, right in the middle, Daddy wrote

himself, in thick black ink. It looked like whoever wrote it was riding on a roller coaster when they did, but I could see plain it was my very own name. Cissy Jean Barber. I felt so proud, for some reason."

"You ain't got but one name in your life," I said, "if you're like most people."

"I opened the letter—it was fat—and took out another envelope. This one had Mama's name on it. She took it and started reaching for the Kleenex right then.

"I tore mine open and read it, first-grade letters and smeared spots and all.

"It said something about like this: 'Dear Cissy, I am your daddy. Mama says you ask about me a lot. I ask about you and Mama too. Mama says you help her a lot and you are a good girl. I will visit from the hospital soon. I will try not to get in your way while I am home, except when you want me to.'

"And Buddy, at the end he wrote, 'I am sending this with all the love in my heart.' I remember that part so clear.

"I read it out loud, Buddy. We squawled, me and Mama, till we got the letter good and wet and the ink ran through into the kitchen tablecloth.

"Mama said it would be a good idea to write Daddy a letter back. I used a real fountain pen, one with a blue cartridge inside it. I wrote it on paper that didn't have any lines. I remember how hard it was to keep the words from running downhill.

"Mine said something like, 'Dear Daddy, I am glad you are doing okay. Will you write me some more letters?'

"I put in how Mama told me he wrote some songs one time. One called 'Fuzzy Wuzzy Lovin' Man.' It was hard to read the grown-up writing he put in for the verses, so I didn't know all the words. I told him that.

"At the very end, I wrote how Mama told me not to

prank him when he got home. And I put on the bottom, 'We love you. We are doing good.'

"A lot of stuff happened real quick after that, Buddy. That letter, I reckon, was one of the biggest things that happened in our whole lives.

"Mama raised the shades inside the house and changed all the beds and sucked up all the spiderwebs with the vacuum cleaner. She dressed up and did her fingernails and wore lipstick and stopped sleeping all the time. She called a yardman, and he came and mowed down everything in the yard. A year's worth. That fellow killed a snake with fourteen rattles out there."

I saw a rattlesnake that had twenty-one, I told her. Not too far from where we're sitting right now.

"Well this one only had fourteen, but that was big enough. So, anyway, the day Daddy came, the house was getting painted. It was about dinnertime. That bunch of gray skinny old painters sat under a sweetgum tree in the backyard peeling boiled turkey eggs for their lunch. Mama fussed with some hair-curler thing, way back in the house.

"A big bunch of leftover paint buckets littered up the carport. White paint dribbled all down their sides and stuck the buckets to the cement. They smelled just awful. I couldn't even go out there.

"But I kept looking out the carport door. I felt all kinds of ways. I wondered if he would still look like the Mummy. Probably not, I reckoned. He'd be out of the bandages and all handsome again, like the man with that shiny black hair and those googly eyes in the picture on the back of Mama's bed.

"Well, I found out soon enough. Directly, up he rolled, in a big black Cadillac with a government tag.

"That car looked like a battleship plowing up the sandy driveway. Two little baby American flags whipped on either side of the hood. The driver wasn't about to let a puny bunch of paint buckets keep him off the carport either. The car crunched right through 'em, and they scattered and bounced around like bowling pins. Back of the screen door, I watched the big front tire paint a picture of itself all the way up the driveway."

That's funny, I told Cissy. A tire painting a picture of itself.

" '*Mama!*' I hollered, and stood on my tiptoes. 'Mama! Daddy's here!'

"I heard her hurry up the wooden hall. Already, she was laughing. She wore this beautiful dress, as white as a wedding gown.

"She flew out the door—boom! Right into this tall man in a blue uniform. He held onto his hat with three funny fingers. But she knocked the hat right into the spilled white paint.

" 'Paul!' Mama cried when she said Daddy's name. 'Paul!' she went. She crushed her face into that blue wool.

"I didn't look up yet. All I could do was stare at those three weird skinny fingers holding Mama's back. They were yellow, like old rubber bands. Too long and yellow for real fingers.

"Then . . ."

What, Cissy. You got to say.

"Those fingers . . . they . . . they reached. Right toward me.

"Everything in the whole wide world stopped. Right that second. Those fingers stretched out and got closer and closer to my face."

"Cissy," I said. "Come *on,* girl."

"Then he squatted down. Daddy. And put those fingers right up under my chin and picked up my face so I had to see his."

Boy!

"You couldn't even say Daddy *had* a face, though. It looked like a plastic baby-doll face that melted in a hot, hot stove. Only one big clear blue eye staring out.

"Buddy, I tell you what. I should have been scared from that day to right now. That's how horrible my own daddy looked."

I'm *tellin'* you.

"But here's what's weird. I *wasn't* scared. It was something in that one eye. Way down in there, I saw something that loved me. That eye burned the scare right off of me."

And what did he say? I asked her.

"He said, 'Cissy, I brought you a surprise.' He talked through this kind of voice box, so he sounded like a robot. And you could see right through his lips. Some kind of plastic. But that blue eye just twinkled like a little star.

"He brought something out from behind his back, in his other hand. And this hand didn't have *any* fingers.

"It was a beautiful little silver locket. Shaped like a heart.

"Daddy's big old nubby hand just trembled. I looked up at Mama, and she smiled, waiting so proud.

"She told me, 'Go on, sweetie. Open it. It's yours.'

"I opened it up. Inside was shiny silver, like some men's hair."

"It was a picture of him?" I said.

"No. A picture of *me*. A baby picture.

"I was about a minute old, I reckon. Lying in some crib with a hospital bracelet on my skinny little arm. Blind and dumb. No hair. Ugly as a little shaved bulldog.

"Anybody could see what Daddy meant."

Even me, I told her.

"Daddy told me, 'I carried that picture of you all this time, Cissy. I kept it three years now, and looked at it every day and wondered if I would ever see my beautiful little girl again.'

"That's exactly what he said. And then, 'I love you,

Cissy. No matter what else ever happens, you remember that.'

"Mama took us both by the hand then and said we better go in the house. She said Daddy couldn't stay long this trip, and he needed to sit down."

*

"That was his first trip home, Buddy. A good one."

I bet, I said. I believe it.

"He only came home one more time. And he never went back to the army after that."

She took a deep breath.

"Because the second time, he came in a box with a flag on top. Rode the train, all by himself, from San Antonio."

Oh no, I went. This story ought to have a happy ending.

"It's no real happy endings, Buddy. Everybody's got to die."

I dug at the ground with my toe and didn't answer.

"Anyway, me and Mama got that notification just like the other letters. At home, out of the blue. Mama brought it up from the mailbox, flapping it in her hand like a church fan. She already knew, I believe, without even opening it.

"She left it on the table while she baked two early apples pulled off a tree in the yard. We ate them with cinnamon and vanilla ice cream, then went out for a long walk. We didn't come inside till after the sun went down and it got cool. Mama made some hot tea then.

"She opened the letter with a butcher knife. She read it first to herself—I remember how her lips always moved when she read.

"Then she told me what it said, clear and loud. Oh, I remember it plain as yesterday.

" 'Cissy, your daddy passed away last week,' she said. 'We both knew that could happen, didn't we? He just had too many things wrong with him to ever get well again. He loved you very much.'

"She folded the letter back real neat and put it in the envelope. Then she gave the envelope to me, picked up her teacup with two fingertips on each hand, blew steam off the top with her lips pursed, closed her eyes, and took a sip.

" 'There's a picture of your father inside the envelope,' she told me. 'It's yours.'

"I won't ever forget what I felt, Buddy, when Mama opened her eyes after that sip of tea."

"What, Cissy?"

"She was gone. I don't know who was sitting in that chair, but it wasn't my mama. Ever again."

*

"The yardman came back. He went at the weeds again, and Mama and me went at the house too, scrubbing fit to kill. That poor fellow worked till you could almost eat supper off the lawn. The monkey grass looked healthy enough to get right out of the ground and come on in the house.

"Inside, we scrubbed bathroom corners till they gleamed like teeth. We turned up every chair and sofa and sucked the spiders and hair balls out from under them. We dragged down every curtain in the house and dyed them new colors and hung them back up in the sun.

"Mama said, 'It's got to be just perfect, Cissy honey. Perfect.' She'd say that and blow hair out of her face. 'He'll be back home in no time,' she said.

"Then Daddy was. Home for good.

"The day they rolled him through the front door, company filled up our little home. It was a tall forest of grown people to me. I never laid eyes on most of those folks before, but here they stood, and I tried my best to be a little lady. I helped the colored maids tote coffee cake around, and little triangles of pimento cheese sandwich and pitchers of iced tea.

"The room with Daddy's casket just overflowed with bouquets and flower arrangements. So many white lilies you couldn't count them all. I reckon that little house, if it's still there, smells like lilies to this day. One lady, I remember, got her dress snagged on a floral display and jerked it down.

"The Lay Governor came in the front door. A skinny black man with red eyes escorted him to the door, then waited on the porch. The governor wore a cowboy hat, like a rancher, that he took off right away inside. He brought a big Bible and went in and read a few words of it to Mama. She told him 'Thank you for coming.' He left in a white Cadillac with a gold cross on the side."

They got those same crosses on the federal cars in Alabama, I told her. But I reckon you know that by now.

"It started to rain in the afternoon. The whole day turned a little sadder. Lightning struck one time close to the house, and the air went funny. You could hear people talking, but you couldn't understand anything they said.

"Mama was strong as steel, Buddy. When two soldiers carried the coffin out into the dripping wet, one of the lady visitors started to cry. Mama hugged her and shushed her and patted her cheeks dry with a little lace handkerchief.

"Mama and me rode in the hearse with Daddy to the cemetery. Me and her stood right together by Daddy's coffin at the place Mama picked out for him, in a daffodil patch at the foot of a green hill. Oh, it rained. For some reason, there wasn't a funeral tent that day, and puddles stood in the grave.

"On up the hill, Buddy, you could see an American flag. It popped and fluttered when the wind got after it. Mama picked the oldest cemetery in Jackson. Over to one side, you could see rows and rows of white crosses where they buried dead Confederate soldiers a long, long time ago."

I've seen that kind of cemetery before, I told Cissy.

"Beautiful. Sad and beautiful.

"A preacher let the rain beat on his bare head and talked about the dead rising to heaven again, if they died fighting for The Holy Cause. Then a man with a golden bugle played taps. That's the saddest song. You could feel the notes of it washing down in the soft green ground, among all those gravestones.

"Mama was strong the next morning too. She took me by the swimming pool, dropped me off, then came back to get me at 10 o'clock. Two paper bags full of clothes were in the back seat of our Plymouth. Mama smelled like smoke, real strong.

"Here's what she told me, Buddy. 'Don't ask questions, Cissy. And don't look back. What's done is done.'

"I got in the car. Much as I wanted to, I didn't look back. I heard sirens one time, way up ahead. Then, in a minute, three fire trucks passed, and an ambulance, heading in the direction we'd come from. But I never turned my head.

"We drove for what seemed like the rest of our lives. Out of Mississippi and into Alabama. We finally outdrove the rain, and the sun blinded us and Mama put on some sunglasses. While she drove, the white road stripes reflected in them, squiggling like water snakes in a black river.

"It was just pure chance, I reckon. Or something. We passed a sign on the road—Goshen—and I remembered those two ducks. The funny Bible verse on their legs. I looked at Mama and she looked at me. This strange smile came on her face. We stopped and took a rental at a cinderblock hotel right on Highway 27. The Snow White."

I know the spot, I told her. Down from the mill.

"That's it. Fact is, that sawmill is part of this story too."

How's that?

"Mama ran up under a log truck on her way back from the beauty parlor. This was after we lived at The Snow White, oh, three months or so."

"And that makes you an orphan," I said. "Like me."

"Yep. In this old world, it's just me. Cissy Jean Barber. Fifteen years old. One hundred pounds. Tired of all that's gone wrong. Ready for things to go right."

Thank goodness for that, I told her.

Then she took my hand and squeezed it just hard enough.

*I*N THE PINES

WHEN YOU BRING somebody new to the woods, you show them the world at the very start. Up high, way up over your head, the green-and-gold leaves wag like tongues and tell every story that ever happened in this old world.

The men leaves talk about fighting chickens, and checker games, and fishing, and what kind of tobacco spits best, and how somebody found a gold coin from the Civil War times, the *first* Civil War, in a peanut field after a hard rain.

The women leaves talk about African violets and congealed salad made out of green lime Jell-O. They tell about birthing babies and how cold it gets when it rains in the winter and no children still live at home.

One of these days, I bet somebody will listen close enough to understand those stories. Right now, though, only other leaves on other trees can understand.

Maybe they'll always remember me and Cissy, and how we talked on the mound that day.

113

*

One or two things happened before I took Cissy on a stroll to see the wilderness, and I ought to mention them.

First, she told her long sad tale and both of us cried a little. Yeah, I cry sometimes too, if you didn't know it.

Next we hid Sack. I took him off the hammock, and we laid him down together in the burrowed-out side of that Indian mound. Sack would sleep in there till the next full moon.

While I rolled Sack up and made him into a bundle and slipped him into his croker sack, Cissy waited at the secret tunnel in the side of the mound. She studied the hole for the longest time. She pitched in a hickory nut, and it disappeared. Then she pitched in a rock the size of a coconut. It disappeared too, while she listened with all her might.

"You got a lot of nuts and rocks to go before you get that hole filled up," I told her.

She looked at me real serious. "I thought I heard something down there," she said. "It sounded like a baby squawling."

"Like a what?"

"You know. A baby squawling. Or a durned Siamese cat with a stomachache. Something like that."

It made my hair stand up.

"Cissy, that's spooky. Sometimes when I'm sleepin' up top here, I make out something too. This weird noise. Like a little baby pitchin' a fit."

Cissy leaned way over and poked her head into the tunnel now, like she was trying to lap water out of a well. I reached, ready to catch the back of her slip if she started to tumble in.

"It don't smell too bad down there, Buddy." She teetered back up and flung her hair in the sun and brushed the dirt off her hands. Her eyes sparkled. "You ought to go down and see what's at the bottom!"

Well, I was thunderstruck. Holes gave me the heebie-jeebies. Especially holes where you couldn't see any bottom.

"I reckon I ought not go down there," I said. "This being a grave and all."

We stood there, real uncomfortable, for a second.

"Oh, me," she said, finally.

"You can cry," I told her. "I done cried enough for today, but you go on."

"Buddy. Poor Mama and Daddy."

"You'll get over it," I told her. "One day."

"When?" she boohooed. "I wish somebody could tell me."

I felt like I ought to hug her so close, but I just kicked the ground. "When somebody else comes along and fills up the hole," I said.

I kissed Sack instead of her. I laid him in his place and covered the door to the mound with the square of sod.

It looked like it did the day God made it.

*

In the cool of the afternoon, me and Cissy took a long swim in the river, her just around the next bend and hid by a stand of black willows. While I played "otter in the water," I could see her white slip hanging in the willow branches a hundred feet downstream. The sun dried us off, then covered the riverbank with this gold dust that made us sleepy.

Later, we ate fresh blackberries and a panfried firetruck as big as my hand. A firetruck is a bluegill with a red swatch on the belly. Those are the best fish in the river.

We finally took a long nap, side by side under one of

those black willow trees that washed its long hair in the river water.

When we woke up, I got Cissy by the hand. And she didn't try and stop me.

She already told me all about her life. Now I wanted her to know mine.

When you leave a clearing with somebody who never saw the woods, you take it slow, like wading into a river you never went in before. At first you just go out to a place where the green waves pool up around your ankles. That's what me and Cissy did.

We eased out of the clearing into the trees and first looked over a sprig of green just hatching out of an acorn. I told her how that live oak tree might be growing here for five hundred more years and still be just a baby.

She poked at a clump of poison ivy coiled around a stump. I told her about one of the orphans at the home, a boy name of Terrell Tussey. He went out deer hunting one fall morning, and the first cup of coffee hit and sent him off to the bushes. He wiped his behind on poison-ivy leaves scratched up from the ground. His dookey hole swelled shut and he like to have died. After a week, the doctors opened him up. They had to use a five-gallon freezer bag to carry out all the stinky stuffing.

I showed Cissy some wild wisteria vines, how they could climb and choke down a tall tree like a nest of giant chicken snakes. She touched a Spanish bayonet plant that had stickers like a green porcupine.

I let her use my knife to cut a splinter off a fat lighter stump. Fat lighter is the very heart of a pine tree. Cissy smelled of it, while I told how the turpentine in the wood turns hard as a quarry rock. I showed her how a spark of flint, struck on another flint, will catch a fat lighter splinter right on fire. It's fire so hot and pure it burns blue, like the gas eye on a stove.

I gradually showed her, too, how the deep woods are more than just a bunch of plants. It's animals too. That brown thousand-legger, crawling like a railroad train over the leaves and pine needles. That banana snail, dripping down the trunk of a little red maple. Oh, and those two wrens, peeping out from a sourwood limb.

The woods are like water another way, too. They're never the same one minute to the next. Even in the shallow places.

I showed her a red cowkiller, prowling over the leaves on its way to some mischief. See them jaws, Cissy? It can tote a crumb of food big as a nickel. A cowkiller ain't like other ants. It's covered with bristly red hair. It sleeps alone and hunts alone and travels alone. It lives on its own for its whole life. The only time you ever see one with other ants is in a battle, when it shows up like Samson to kill all the puny little red Philistines.

Cissy said we ought to catch one and put it up in that fire ant bed on the Indian mound. I told her that was a good idea, except if that cowkiller stung *you*. . . . Well, just think about how it got its name.

Look yonder!

Boy, you're lucky, Cissy! That was a blue scorpion. Did you see it slip down the side of a tree and tear across that clear place? It's on its way to hide some of the stuff it collected, some of the stinkbugs and click beetles and those casts that horned owls throw up. That kind of lizard can raise up on its hind legs and run just like a man when it gets scared.

Cissy seemed amazed by everything. Really interested. But she asked me a hard question right about then. "Buddy? Do *you* ever get scared out here?"

I thought about the best way to answer that. I didn't want to tell a fib. That ain't the way to do.

"I reckon I do get scared, now and again," I told her. "I

might find a spot where a wampus cat has killed and eat up a grown man. Or I might scare a coachwhip snake out of the bushes. A coachwhip can flog a man like a mule skinner with a bullwhip if it takes a mind."

She edged a little closer and her eyes got a little bigger. "Where do *those* animals live, Buddy?"

"We're safe here," I said, real cool. "Animals like that are even farther on back in the woods. Besides, they ain't nearly as scary as people and what people do for no reason at all. See, people can hate you when they never even met you. There's nothing in these woods, nothing in any hole or holler or up under any log, that hates you like that."

With the sun passed over, some of the bugs started razzing us. I pulled a handful of onion grass and showed Cissy how to rub it on her legs and arm and back, to keep the mosquitoes off.

We went wading into the woods a little deeper. We saw a loblolly pine tree tumbled across a little branch. Wildcats and raccoons and every other kind of animal used it for a bridge. You could see their tracks in the mud at both ends.

We found another tree blown down, with five baby woodpeckers staring out of a hole at us. I didn't bother them. A woodpecker is my spirit bird, and when I saw one, it meant real good luck.

Those baby woodpeckers must have been extra-special. Cissy cooed, so sweet, down on her knees over the peephole in a place where the air smelled like a wild tea olive tree.

Something was on my mind. I took a deep breath and brought it up. It could have spoiled the kind of day it was turning into.

"Cissy," I said, looking away. "You might ought to hear something."

She turned. "Okay. What?"

"I been thinking, and I want you to know something. I don't care if your daddy fought agin my brother and what he believed. I know it weren't *your* fight."

She didn't blink or look away. "I don't even understand it, Buddy. Why everybody has to fight about God. It doesn't seem right to me."

I told her she was right. Fighting was wrong, and me and Sack wanted to stop it all forever. We wanted to scare it away from sleepy old Goshen like an old Bible story scared away sins.

Cissy forgave my brother Randy too.

*

After you get all used to the shallows and then the up-to-your-waist water, you can take a girl's hand and go out even deeper in the woods. Out to where most of the sun gets knocked off by bigger, older trees.

The shadows run darker here, but the magic gets better too.

In the spring, you tell her, all these white dogwoods bloom at one time. They look like brides waiting outside a church. And the ground sprouts lady's slippers, so many you'd think you were in a shoe store for fairies.

It's not all pretty stuff, either. Pitcher plants grow in the soggy spots. They eat meat—whole flies are a good lunch—and they'll suck your finger like a hungry baby if you let them. Ground mosses grow here too, cute as green little sheep. If you ever pick one up though, the stink it puts on your hands makes a skunk smell like honeysuckle.

This place is where you can sit and start to understand what the deep woods are really all about, I told Cissy.

If you keep quiet, the woodcocks come out and play. You can see them do a love dance, strutting like tom turkeys and thumping the ground to show off.

You can see deer come out of the trees and lick the stones up yonder. The rocks are salty, and the deer stand around them smiling, with their tongues hanging out.

And, Cissy, if you were to climb on up that hill over there, you'd come to a tree with some fruit on it that you won't ever find in a store. If you eat it, you'll see things. Things that aren't real.

You can have dreams and take off your skin and walk right through barbed wire or stout limbs. You might fly up in the trees and sit on a limb by an owl, and he'll turn his head all the way around to size you up.

Or you can sail off to some house in Goshen and go through the keyhole and hover over folks asleep with their mouths open in front of their TV set. Their faces will be weird and blue, like the TV just killed them.

"Oh, come on, Buddy," Cissy said. "There's not a tree in the world like that."

I shake my head, real serious. "There *is*. I ate the fruit a lot of times. The Indians used to eat it too, so they'd see signs from the Great Spirit. Maybe me and you will eat some one of these days. You'll see."

Right now, there's other stuff, I told her, and laid down. Like a nap.

She took the hint and stretched out on a soft bank of pine needles with me.

*

I told Cissy a story.

I laid here another afternoon, settled in the hollow of a tree, and waited out a bad storm.

You get bad storms around Goshen in the summertime. The thunderclouds throw white pitchforks of lightning and the wind rips through like jet planes. It rains a gray forever and the whole day smells like something you dug out of the ground.

This particular rainy afternoon, it came to me how I might be like a turtle on the bottom of the river. Over my head, the limbs of the big trees beat one another in the fast current till the bark broke off. Little trees bent over and put their faces to the ground. You couldn't hear a thing. I felt like if I said three words, they'd turn into bubbles and rise up through the rain and pop at the top of the sky.

Finally, when the rain stopped, the fattest sun you ever saw came out, and drops of water hung as sticky as honey just everywhere. I popped out of my hiding place, along with about a million other birds and bugs and things. You could see steam rising off the tree trunks and smell new flowers opening.

Then, I told Cissy, I saw the most beautiful thing ever.

A slender little green snake slid through black cherry leaves, right over my head, and all the drops on the leaves fell at one time, like somebody spilled a jewel box.

That's what the deep woods are like, I told her. Every single thing you took for granted is newer and more important some way. It feels like whatever happens just never happened before. Ever.

Cissy sat up. "So, is there always stuff to eat out here too?"

"Shoot, girl. What are you talking about? Without getting up from here, I can show you a whole grocery store full."

I pointed right off at a skinny little birchy-looking tree.

"See? That's a persimmon, right there. They're so sweet and good they'll break your heart. But whatever you do, don't never *ever* eat a persimmon that's green. It'll turn your mouth inside out, girl. Get those pretty orange ones. In fact, we'll pick a bunch before we go today. We won't have this tree many days."

"Why? Do persimmons go bad?"

"No, that ain't the problem. The problem with persimmons starts with a *P.*"

She looked shocked. "You mean 'poison'?"

"No. Uh-uh," I went. "I mean *possum.* Once a possum smells big sweet persimmons like these, he'll climb up the trunk and not come down for a week. He'll eat persimmons till he's drunk and falls out and busts wide open on the ground."

"Ugh," she said, wrinkling up her nose. "What if a possum fell on you while you were asleep . . . "

"If a possum doesn't get them persimmons, crows will," I went on. "Or a hog bear. Oh, yeah, those live in these woods. Didn't you know? And if all those other critters don't beat him to it, Brer Fox will figure out a way to climb a tree and get that fruit. The point is, everything in these woods loves a sweet ripe persimmon. Including *me.*"

Cissy pointed to a stand of light green trees on farther.

"I see red things in those trees, Buddy. Persimmons?"

I nearly popped, I felt so excited. "Just as good. Those are wild plums. Sweet as candy. And over yonder, just past the plums, that's a bullis vine. It's covered with wild purple grapes so fat you can't hardly put two in your mouth at one time."

I stopped and pointed then, so she could follow my finger to the next sight.

"Now look. Up a little higher than the vines."

She squinted her eyes, straight into the setting sun now, big and hot orange.

"See that hole in the trunk of that tulip tree?"

"I can't—oh, wait, I see it now."

"See the bees working alive up there? All around that hole? Fact is, that whole tree, from that knothole clear to the ground, is one giant comb of honey. I took and drove a railroad spike I found in the side of that tree, at the bottom.

It's a poplar tree, and they're naturally full of sweet sap. But *this* tree. Honey runs out of it. You can just about live on that stuff when the fruit goes out of season."

Cissy smiled so big. "Honey! I could eat honey by the jarful!"

"Cissy, we got fish in the river. We can find wild apples and huckleberries and so many different kinds of nuts the squirrels have to go to nut school to learn 'em all. Old Randy showed me which plants are good. Cattail root and dandelion and poke sprout and dock and fennel. We can go on the other side of the river any day of the week and pick up a bushel basket of salty black mushrooms and sweet white ones too. You won't believe this, but there's wild corn out here some places. It's better'n corn back home. Especially if home ain't but a prison for boys."

"Or a hotel room at the Snow White full of roaches and rats," she said real quick.

"Roaches and rats sit on the devil's lap, down in the bad place," I said. "Those are his favorite pets."

She made a face and shivered.

"Devil walked over your grave." I took her hand again— it was a thrill every time—and we sat up. "We better go back and feed the fire, Cissy. It gets cool by the river at night, even in the summertime."

She looked on ahead, up to where the woods turned thick black and the trails disappeared. "What about up there?" she asked.

"We can save that till another day," I told her. "We've seen a lot."

"Good stuff," she said. "And—whoa, Buddy, what's *that?*"

Her bare foot nudged a white thing the size of a hard hat, buried under straw and leaves. I pulled it clear. A turtle shell.

"Oh-ho!" I said. "Cissy, you're pure good luck. This here is something *special!*"

I quick scooted around and found a dozen hickory nuts under a shagbark a few feet off. I filled up the turtle shell with them and shook it. *Hey-na-ha-ha. Hey-na-ha-ha.* My rattle made good Indian music.

"Let me!" She shook and did a little dance. It was fun. Some of the hickory nuts spilled out under our feet, but we just stomped them down and laughed and "hey-na-ha-ha-d" even louder. We whirled and kicked and shimmied. Finally, we ran out of gas and giggled together lying back on the ground.

Oh, me. I was surely in love.

"Count—count them pieces of the shell," I told her, all winded. "On the—that turtle."

She counted, then swallowed. "It's thirteen."

"That was one—for each month of the year—woo!—if you had an Indian calendar," I said. "Thirteen."

She laid there with her face close up, those Cupid's-bow lips by my face.

"We must have lost a whole month, in modern times," she said. "I reckon that's why time goes so fast."

"I reckon," I told her. She was real close. So close it was dangerous.

In my mind, a wild, wild imagining took hold.

Cissy reached out and took part of me and made it feel good in her hands. I closed my eyes. She tugged at me and the warm milky feeling came.

God walked in the woods right then.

God was inventing the whole world. The world was coming out of God, right out of inside.

Look out. Oh.

There it is. The world and sky and stars and all.

"You messy thang," she said, wiping her hand on a fern. "Look what you done."

I made my mind stop. I made it come back to the here and now. But the wild thrill still ran all inside. At first, I couldn't decide if the air sparked with lightning bugs or if I was woozy. Then I could make out the little eggs of cool green fire on the tails of the insects.

"Cissy," I said, real husky.

She leaned so close that she was the sky now, and the world and all the woods.

"Cissy, it's good here. I promise."

She just sat there like a bump on a log. I reckon if she had something to say, she didn't feel like saying it right then.

We sat a minute longer. Down the path we'd come, the woods seemed deep and dark already. Woods get black, black, black out here at night in the hidden places.

Then I had an idea.

I scratched together a little pile of dry leaves and poked around in the gummy ground under that till I found two chips of flint. It's the commonest rock in Alabama.

You can build a little fire when it's an east wind, like tonight, and when it's just past a full moon. You can feel the fresh air over Old Mercy River.

And on nights like this, you hang a white vine or string over a fire. The lightning bugs will come land on the white vine by the millions. I can't say why, but they do.

And when all the lightning bugs cling on by the thousands and light the way, you've got a torch. You can follow it through the darkest woods back to home.

So we followed that homemade torch, happy me and Cissy, back to our Secret Place.

BOTH OF US dragged in from the woods. Our tongues hassled down to the ground.

I hadn't realized how far we'd gone. Or how tired all that scary business in Goshen still had us. Anyway, right when we limped back in, it was time to curl Cissy in the hammock and cover her up with her red dress.

We were tired, like I said. But I wasn't too tired to notice a miracle. All of a sudden, it struck me. Life felt good. *My* life. Too good to be true. Cissy so pretty. That little smile of a new moon up in that sky. Those whippoorwills singing all out of tune.

I took our lightning bugs and dropped them real careful, still holding to the vine, into the bottom of a white paper sack I kept for my clothes and stuff. That bag of bugs shined happy, bright as a Saturday-night revival at a country church house.

I tied the bag to a long stick, then poked the butt of the

stick in the grass so it stood over the hammock, bobbing its head. That little light of mine glowed for my sleepy girl.

Cissy lay there, dreaming a dream.

All the rest of my life, I'll remember how sweet she looked that minute.

*

I walked down to Old Mercy and laid down myself, on my back in the deep sweet grass, and let the cool river air flow over me.

The sky frowned a little now. The moon played hide-and-seek with froggy clouds, and trees shook in the wind now and then like big shaggy animals just coming out of the river.

I laid there looking up for a long time, talking to God.

God talked to me, too. And God did me this big, big favor. God let me remember something about my brother Randy as clear as if it happened yesterday.

I reckon I thought about Randy because of all Cissy told me about her family. Her recollections sparked mine, the same way one lightning bug goes off and causes ten more to flash.

In this one remembering, I jostled along with lots of other people, a whole moving flood of folks, across this parking lot on the way toward the big front gate of a football stadium. It was the Goshen Bowl, one chilly fall night.

Music played somewhere, and boys sold Cokes in the parking lot, and I could smell hot bread in the ovens of a big bakery across the road. Everywhere, people wore red-and-black clothes and shook red-and-black shakers. All together, they looked like red wasps swarming on a giant nest.

The closer I came, the louder the stadium buzzed, till finally I could make out individual people hollering their fool heads off. It really got to me. I couldn't *wait* to go inside and see what was happening. *Two bits, four bits,* they hollered. *Six bits! A dollar!*

Hurry! somebody said, pushing past. *Almost time for the kickoff!*

I hurried and hurried, but that parking lot seemed like it would never end. See, I was little, walking to still another place in the world from the stupid orphans' home. The home never seemed to be close to anything good.

I hurried through dropped pieces of light bread and strings off bologna wheels and red-and-black seat cushions and old rusted bottlecaps and lost plastic combs. Every step, I kicked something out of the way, or dodged some big fast-moving man and his little boys, or went by some car with a pretty girl inside and a boy too. The boy would look at me hard, with his hand up under the girl's fuzzy red sweater.

Finally, I paid the face inside the ticket booth and gave my ticket to a police lady and elbowed through the gate with all the others and swam through that bunch of people under the stands and out the tunnel and into the stadium seats.

I came to open air. Like heaven must be, a big and green place, with a brightness all over it, even when it's dark outside.

Here boomed some other kind of world. Pretty cheerleader girls in red-and black skirts jumped like circus monkeys. Big drums made my liver turn a flip when I walked by, and the clarinets made me taste sour milk in my mouth, and girls with glasses and teen-age bumps played flutes, and trombones knocked hats off when people got too close. Everywhere people, more people than the Lord ever meant to put in one place, unless it was for a battle.

A perfect green grass field sparkled down there, white-

striped and marked with numbers, the most peaceful-look-
ing place you ever saw on this earth.

And that peaceful Shiloh was where the battle raged.

Boys in red-and-black jerseys walked up to other boys in
yellow-and-white jerseys and everybody growled and
hunkered down on their all fours like animals. When they
did, grown-ups on both sides of the field screamed like
Jesus had jumped down off the cross naked and run right
across the fifty-yard line.

Like it all meant life or death.

Randy, my brother, was one of the boys on the field. He
wore a red jersey, number 13. I could pick him out just by
the peculiar way he leaned into the huddle.

I watched him on the first play. A whistle blew and
Randy's red-and-black team trotted up to the line and the
quarterback got behind this other boy in an embarrassing
way. Nobody moved. Things turned strange and still, the
way the air gets before a bad storm.

Pow! The two armies clanged together and people
screamed and a helmet rolled off like it had a head still in it
and somebody's shoe went flying. Maybe the collisions had
some plan, but nothing really made sense. It knocked the
breath out of me how hard those big boys hit together, how
hard they crashed on the ground.

Only one player didn't fall like all the others.

Randy was the greatest football star ever for the Goshen
Red Tops. I got to see him that magic night when he made
football history in the state of Alabama, and God let me
remember every detail, like it played on a movie screen.

Randy took a weak pitchout from a falling quarterback
and dashed past a mound of people who wiggled like they
were dying. He skittered through two tacklers like a skink
in a woodpile, then jagged for the sideline. Three skinny
blockers went ahead, but they all fell down on their faces in

the dirt when they saw huge snot-blowing, screaming line-backers ahead with their eyes out on stems. A whole other mad-dog pack of players in yellow jerseys streaked toward Randy too, licking their fangs.

Something else lived in Randy, though, in those days. He was just not a man that boys in yellow uniforms could stop.

He juked, spun, stutter-stepped. He dodged and shim-mied and squirmed for daylight. He broke free of grabbing hands and turned straight up the field like a compass nee-dle.

A man beside me in the stands jumped to his feet! His mouth made an *O,* and a holler came up from his chest like out of a bellowing rodeo bull.

"Go boy! Goooooooooooo!"

Our whole side of the stadium went red-and-black with jumping, hollering souls like that man, all with their mouths open and their tongues stuck out screaming, with popcorn flying and people you never knew beating on your back for pure joy.

"Randy! Randy the Red Top!"

He dodged one tackler with the same quick move a little silver minnow gives the very second your shadow falls on it. Randy butted another enemy player flat on his fanny, like a young red billy goat. Then—look! impossible!—he broke through five yellow soldiers like a cheap wooden gate and cut back into the open field again.

A packed stadium and five hundred extra spectators in folding chairs, and twenty-five college scouts and a half-dozen cheerleaders in Goshen red-and-black yelled like one single person.

"Randy! Go boy!"

"Red tornado!"

"A boy gets to be a man like this!"

"Fast as a durned crazy bottle rocket!"

"Go Red Top!"

What Goshen people saw that night dropped their jaws. They watched young David sling his way through an army of Goliaths, and leave them all falling down. They marveled at a teenage Samson, slaughtering hated enemies in sissy yellow helmets.

"Go! Go Randy! Hurrah!"

Fans whooped and somersaulted with joy. The trombones and horns in the end zone pooted away, playing the Goshen fight song!

"Touchdown! Touchdown Randy!"

God gave me that night to remember. I hadn't thought about it in six years. But tonight, by the rushing waters of Old Mercy River, it flickered to life, wonderful to see.

Randy ruled the roost. A red spinning top. A blood-red bowling ball. A fiery hot summer breeze burning yellow leaves.

He knifed through the line where linemen gruffed and grunted like stupid buffalos. Or he didn't even bother, and just rumbled over boys like an eighteen-wheeler loaded with anvils on a coast-to-coast run.

Eleven times that night he danced in the end zone, then floated high as his teammates mobbed him and glided him to the sidelines on their shoulders. Ten times, he tossed the ball to a beaming coach. But the very last time, he passed the coach by—the surprise of a lifetime!—and made his way to somebody special, somebody watching starstruck from the bleachers.

He lobbed the ball . . . to me!

To Buddy! His little brother! Little Mr. Nobody, picked out to be Randy's brother in this world.

He flipped his last touchdown ball to me. He spread his arms wide, as wide as his smile, and threw one fist in the air. He jigged a little victory dance, held up by the whoops of his teammates. Then he stopped dancing and did a miracle thing. A dream thing.

Randy reached north, and his arm stretched out, stretched and stretched. It telescoped up over the north rim of the stadium, through the million cars in the parking lot. It passed the bakery, out to the dirt road already clogged with red taillights, the retreating army of disappointed Enterprise Wampus Cats fans.

His arm went up the Chattahoochee River, out beyond the Wiregrass, through the rolling Red Hills at Onion Springs, past the big white capitol house at Montgomery, and on even farther, north and northwest now, past the boggy cotton fields up in the Black Belt and on into the Black Warrior country, the rock ribs of the mountains, and directly on to the big, waiting, weathered paw of God Almighty—to the Coach at the University, Tuscaloosa, Alabama, Football Heaven, U.S.A.

The Coach wore this earnest smile on that old wore-out mule saddle he called a face. He took Randy's young hand almost tenderly. The flashbulbs caught them both, the Coach and Randy, unbeatable, undefeatable, forever legends.

This strange night, God showed me that memory while I laid there by his river. It happened just the way I said.

Still, you can't live on memories.

The Coach has been dead so many years his bones are loose on the ground somewhere.

And old Randy, he's dead too.

*

I made my way back up the little slope to the top of the mound where Cissy slept. Most of the lightning bugs in the paper sack slept too now, so the dark crept closer. I turned over a piece of wood in the fire place, blew on the coals, and teased up a little hot flame.

Squatting with my palms out, I got lost in thought just a second and drifted off. Then I heard Cissy move in her sleep, and I glanced over.

I about had the shock of my life.

Straight above her head, staring down from the branches of one of the red trees, glared the most terrible, terrible thing there is.

A wampus cat.

Just the snow-white tip end of his tail moved, twitching mad. You could see his killing teeth, sharp as steel knives. His eyes blazed red, and you could hear his bowels groaning like they were full of live men.

I broke out in a sweat you could almost hear.

Real slow, I eased my own eyes over to Cissy in the hammock. She lay in the vine net like a big caught mermaid, sound asleep, her mouth opening and closing a little when she breathed. I tried not to move when I whispered her name.

"Cissy!"

A hiss answered me from the tree.

Sweat fell in my eyes. My lips dried to my gums. *This is it,* I told myself. *This is the end of me and her.*

"Wampus cat!" I said out loud. "Please go away!"

I closed my eyes and got ready to feel the steel claws sink in my back like blazing fishhooks.

"Wampus cat, you ain't got no reason to harm Cissy. She don't even know there's a thing as bad as you in the whole world."

The wampus gave this low, ugly growl that almost made me mess in the fire and put it out.

I swallowed something as big as a baseball. "You go on and do whatever you want to me," I told him, with the most awful sights flashing through my mind. "But just please carry me on off and eat me under a tree so that poor girl ain't got to see it and know."

The tears pure filled up my eyes again, and I added, "She's seen enough stuff like that to last her whole life."

A minute went by, slow as cold syrup dripping off a spoon. Then another minute oozed past.

I was surprised I was still alive.

I dared myself. I counted to three, then made my eyes look back up at the tree.

The empty limb still bounced.

The wampus cat was gone. You'd have thought that wild creature just disappeared in the thin air.

I fell back flat, so relieved. I breathed big swallows of sweet, cool, delicious air.

Oh, Lordy, it felt great to be alive!

*

Sprinkling.

I woke up with drops misting my face. They felt good on my teen-age bumps. The bumps get bad in the summer when it's so hot. Sweating that way inside of old heavy Sack doesn't help.

Far off, it thundered, and right away I remembered. My head jerked toward the limb where I last saw Mr. Wampus Cat.

Empty. Empty as a Monday church pew. It seemed like a bad dream. Thank goodness.

But when I looked to check on Cissy, that old worry bird flew right back into my head again.

Her hammock swung ghost-empty too, back and forth in mid-air. I stood up and walked over and touched the vines where she should have been, just to make sure.

Cissy was gone. This flash of bad black lightning struck in my mind.

I jumped up. The empty hammock, just that second, re-minded me of the swinging bridge me and some boys from the orphans' home saw up at Rock City one time. A man said a hundred Indian girls jumped off that swinging bridge in the olden days to keep from getting humped by Davy Crockett.

Cissy, I reckon, didn't know about that. But where was she?

I checked out the limb in the red tree one more time. If that wampus cat caught Cissy, he could be out there in the woods this minute, cracking her pearly little bones in his teeth and sucking the golden juice out.

"Cissy!" I hollered. "Hey!"

The rain started in. Big fat drops fell, and red needles too, spinning in from all over the place. Even in this dark, I could see the sweet gums and other trees show their white leaves. One bad storm was on the way.

"Ciiiissssssyyyyy!"

The rain swooshed in, and the wind bulled at the red trees and at me and everything else around the mound. Down tumbled our lightning-bug lantern, and all the bugs woke up in a blue-green surprise. The lantern leaped across the top of the mound and blew off into the trees like a haint. Limbs popped in the dark, and the hammock bucked like crazy.

The strangest thing happened, though. Over the howling wind, blowing in from faraway someplace, I could make out music. An old song, like somebody singing along to a scratchy old Victrola at their grandma's house:

"Don't you remember Sweet Cissy, Ben Bolt?
Sweet Cissy, Sweet Cissy, Ben Bolt?"

I heard that same song one time on a Mighty Mouse cartoon. Oil Can Harry was tying a helpless girl mouse to the railroad tracks, laughing and twisting the ends of his greasy mustache. This train came up fast, on its way to squash her perfect little hairdo, to mash her brains right out through her big pretty eyes.

But Mighty Mouse zoomed through the sky straight for the train, his fist in front of him and his cape popping. You just knew he'd make it to her in time. He'd stop the train and save her at the last possible second, like he was sent from heaven.

You couldn't forget a cartoon like that. The faraway song in the woods brought it all back. I saw again that mouse girl on the railroad track, who kept her mouse eyes closed and sang through those pretty red mouse lips at the last second of her whole life.

Empty hammock. A lost girl's song. A dream about my own dead brother. River a'thundering, full of white rain.

I got real scared.

"Cissy!" I slid down the Indian mound. "Stay where you are! Don't go no closer to the water!"

I tore out, chasing in the direction I thought I heard the song. The riverbank slipped me, stumbled me.

"Cissy! Stay right there! It's a wampus cat out!"

The rain came harder out in the open, away from the red trees, and it stung like a bucket of ice-cold sewing needles flung out of a passing jet plane.

I wouldn't stop, durn it.

"Cissy! Don't go no farther! Cissy!"

The rain beat on the world. I stopped to catch my breath. *Boom* went thunder. I couldn't even hear my own teeth chattering. Then, so faint, I picked up her singing again.

"Don't you remember Sweet Cissy, Ben Bolt?
Sweet Cissy, Sweet Cissy, Ben Bolt?"

Thataway!

"Cissy!"

I scrambled up onto a blown-down tree trunk, dead so long the trunk oozed water between my toes like a brown sponge. Ferns licked my bare muddy ankles. I held my hand level across my forehead and squinted.

There!

Oh, thank goodness!

Cissy leaned over the fast water, right at the riverside. She held a long green willow wand in her hand and skimmed it around and around on the raging fast part of the river. Her mouth opened and closed, and singing came out. She was dressed in just her white slip.

"Hey! Hey, Cissy!" I flew down from the dead tree and lit in ten inches of gooey mud. "Hey, girl!"

Cissy didn't turn around or stop singing. Around and around went that willow cane, like a needle playing the record of the old song she sang. That soggy slip clung to all her pointy places. Shoulder blades poked out of the back of it, and her hair fell down her neck like cold spaghetti.

I felt happy. I felt like screaming bloody murder at the top of my lungs too, both feelings at the same time. I wanted to pick her up by her ears all the way off the ground and jerk a knot in her. And I wanted to hug her and love her and tell how much better a live pretty Cissy walking by the river was than a dead ghost Cissy in the black guts of a wampus cat.

Why didn't she stop? What on earth was she wandering off to do?

"Cissy," I yelled now, close enough now to make out her soaked face. "What's the *matter?*"

And that's when I just stopped. You could have knocked me over with a little titmouse feather, when I understood.

Why, Cissy *couldn't* hear me!

She wasn't even awake!

Cissy was sleepwalking!

I stumbled through river weeds all the way around her and marveled at this thing.

Cissy, sleepwalking!

I never saw it before in my whole life. That seemed like a thing you only saw in cartoons too. How on earth could a person walk around in their sleep? I can't put on a sock or a shoe with my eyes closed. But here the girl stood, happy and free, with that willow reed in her hand like it was any sunshiny Saturday afternoon with the fish jumping and the bluebirds flying by.

I watched, just dumb, and her pretty red mouth opened:

"Don't you remember Sweet Cissy, Ben Bolt?
Sweet Cissy, Sweet Cissy, Ben Bolt?"

I crept up so close I could see her voice box purr in her throat. I never saw a person hypnotized, but I imagine they must look like that. I waved my hand in front of her nose, but she never noticed. Just kept right on singing.

I honestly didn't have any idea what to do with a soaked girl walking in her sleep. Maybe if I'd had a sister instead of Randy I'd have known.

I thought the best thing was to wake her up. So I reached out my hand and put it on her bare white shoulder. Little beads of rain ran down my fingers. I shook her real easy.

"Cissy? You okay?"

The song stopped. She turned to me and opened her eyes. I won't ever forget it. She blinked at me like a roosting chicken hit with a bright light.

Oh, I learned something then and there.

Don't never, *ever,* wake up somebody in the middle of a sleepwalk. And if you've just got to, make sure you got your doctor bag ready.

I'm not a sissy, but I couldn't stop her.

Cissy clobbered me right in the face with her fist, so hard my nose shot dark goop all down my chest. She raked my cheeks, and her sharp girl-claws left a row of pink streaks like I'd been asleep for a week on a chenille bedspread. She screamed so loud my ears tried to jump clean off my head.

But even a bigger shock would come.

I stood there beat half-silly and started begging her to settle down. But when she heard my first sentence, she screamed something terrible and leaped like a crazy woman off the riverbank, way, way out into the fast current.

Strong black monsters in the water grabbed her and pulled her right under.

I panicked and screamed at her now.

"Cissy! You'll drown! Oh, please!"

She bobbed up, and then I saw a different look in her eyes and face. Someway, she'd come back, from some lost place. It was *her* again now. Cissy. In bad trouble.

She hollered, raised one arm, fought off the whitewater hands that clawed her face and pulled it down. She screamed my name now—Buddy! Buddy!—and sank again.

Lucky for her, I swim middling fair. Still, it took every bit of iron in my body to fetch her out of that torrent. I caught her by the hair. Lucky for us both, she was too sopped to fight me out there in the flood. It would have been the end of us both.

I kicked and flailed and swam with her slip strap in my teeth, dog-paddling and side-kicking and doing anything I could to get us back to the bank alive. Limbs in the water tore at us and we rolled over sharp rocks, but we held on to each other.

We landed nearly a quarter of a mile downstream and crawled out in one wet pile together.

Sputtering and spitting, I left her and alligatored way on up into the grass and weeds. My nose bled everywhere. I stuffed some Spanish moss up my nostrils to stop it. I threw up too, from the pure scary shock of it all. I tell you, I was a mess.

Cissy came back to her right mind, little by little. At first, she just lay there all freaked, way too still. After that, she sat up and looked at her hands, the palms and the backs, then the palms and the backs again.

Oh, she cried then, tears harder than the rain. She bit her lips and hugged her knees and moaned and laid down and rolled in the wet leaves.

It was a sight.

NEXT MORNING, ME and Cissy sat by the campfire and steamed river mussels we found washed up on the bank.

A whole big wad of those goodies tore loose from some safe place on the bottom when the rain came and the water stampeded. I took a half-dozen mussel shells at a time and put them on a piece of pine bark over the hottest part of the campfire. They looked like devil fingers, long and black, grabbing at the smoke.

When the mussels steamed enough to make the shell yawn, we gobbled them up. I sprinkled mine with little jibbles of vinegar weed, and Cissy squeezed wild blackberry juice on hers. Between helpings, we talked about the weirdest night yet.

"It happens when there's some kind of trouble about to come," Cissy said. She sat on the ground in the shade of the big red trees now, out of the blazing sun. While I cooked, she dabbed at my nose and black eye with a sponge of wet Spanish moss. "I can't help it, Buddy. It's not really me."

"Ouch!"

"Sorry. It hurts there too?"

"Just when you touch it."

Every time she dabbed at a hurt, I made a noise through one side of my mouth like water dropped in a hot skillet. Oh, I milked those bruises for all I was worth.

Cissy wised up, finally. She dabbed a place she knew wasn't hurt—my ear—and when I said "yikes" she got disgusted and threw her whole soggy slip at me. She folded her arms around her knees and rocked back and forth with her hair swinging. I felt sorry for her. All of a sudden, she looked like a tiny little lost girl.

"I don't guess you'd know, if you never had it happen," she said. "Something just takes you over."

I thought about Sack. "Well, I might know how that feels," I said.

I handed her a serving of mussels so hot the tongues panted out of the shells.

"It's like this," she said. "When I was a little girl still wearing diapers, a mouse or something gnawed through a wire in a wall of the house in Jackson. The wire started smoking and smelling awful and burning a hole through the sheetrock wall."

She caught my eye. "Just by pure chance, Daddy got out of bed to get Mama a glass of orange juice. She had a cold or something. Anyway, he found the smoldering place and dashed that glass of juice on it and saved the house from burning down. It was lucky for all of us."

I rolled the next bunch of shellfish out on the fire. "What's that got to do with walking in your durned sleep?"

"A lot. You'll see. 'Cause, first thing, Mama got up and went in to see about me in the other bedroom. And guess what?"

"You broke her nose and gave her a busted lip."

"Smarty-pants." She threw a cooked mussel. It hit up on my forehead and stuck like a leech. Both of us got a big laugh.

"Buddy, you're not hurt so bad," she said. "You laugh too easy."

I leaned up and kissed the side of her face. It was real soft.

"Cissy, I love you," I said.

She was quiet for a second. Then she reached and took my hand.

"I'm sorry I hit you, Buddy," she said. "I wouldn't hurt anybody on purpose. Much less you."

It sounded like every bird in the world sang when she said those words.

"If you'd get that nasty oyster thing off your face," she said, "you might get kissed, too."

I did. And she did.

All during that first wonderful kiss, I heard the river run faster, smelled her hair in the morning. The sun sent out the brightest flash you ever saw, and golden light fell as hard as rain fell the night before.

A crackling noise stopped us. I looked down and saw the fire burning up the pine-bark slab in my hand. I blew it out, it took me two puffs, and then put some fresh mussels on to replace the ones I turned to charcoal.

"Oh, me," she said. "Where were we?"

"Right on top of this old Indian mound," I said. "Thank goodness for that."

She picked up the conversation again. "Now listen, Buddy. When Mama went to check on me that night the house nearly burned down, my little bed had all the covers kicked off. And you won't believe what else."

"Probably not," I told her.

"The window was raised and the screen poked out."

"You sleepwalked right on out of that joint," I said. "And you a little girl. How did you know the house was on fire?"

She made this face, but Cissy couldn't make an ugly one. "That's what I'm telling you. I *didn't*. I can't to this day tell you why it happened. Or why it happened last night. It just did. Something dangerous was around, and off I walked."

"Sounds like Sack," I said. "He can tell. You can just feel it in the air when something ain't right . . ."

She rolled on. She didn't want to be compared to Sack, I reckon. "Mama came in and saw the empty bed and screamed so loud it woke up the neighbors. Lights came on all up and down the street. They found me out in the front yard, dragging my blanket and old Raggedy Andy.

"And now listen to this part, Buddy." Her voice swooped down low. "I pitched a fit when they woke me up that time too. I don't remember it, because I was little. But I heard the story enough times. And look."

She twisted a leg up under her self then, so I could see the ball of her foot. A white scar shaped like a *C* hid in the dirt under there.

"When they woke me up that time, I hit and screamed and kicked the sharp edge of a lawn chair," she explained. "I had to get eighteen stitches."

I thought about little girl Cissy, lost in her own front yard, walking in her sleep. That poor little child and a beat-up redhaired ragamuffin. Ain't the world funny?

"You got a inside eye, Cissy. You can see stuff other people ain't allowed to. You might of been born with a cawl over your face. That's what I think."

She nodded her head and pulled her foot back. "I guess, Buddy. I went sleepwalking two other times. Two that I know about, anyway. Once, somebody broke in the house and stole the TV. Nobody even knew it until the next morning. But I sleepwalked that night. I climbed the stairs and went all the way up in the attic. I was *scared* to go up there most times. Oh, it caused trouble. They couldn't find me the next morning and thought I got kidnapped.

"Really kidnapped, I mean. Not like this."

"I bet they coulda put out a bowl of chocolate or something and lured you out," I said.

"And there was one other time."

She got quiet and looked down at her hands like she all of a sudden didn't know who they belonged to.

"I walked in my sleep the night before all that stuff happened with Mama and me at that store. With the Ping-Pong balls and helicopter and the awful men. I never told a soul, Buddy. But the night before that happened, I went sleepwalking and got halfway to downtown Jackson before a car nearly ran over me.

"That woke me up. I panicked and fell over a guardrail in my nightgown and rolled down a ditch and landed on some broken chunks of concrete at the bottom. Didn't get hurt bad, but it scared me to death. I got home without Mama ever knowing. It took me about half a bottle of Merthiolate to paint all the scraped places."

"I put that Merthiolate stuff on a redbug one time," I told her. "Right on the tip of this, uh, this place I got that you ain't. On top of old salty dog. Man! I thought that medicine would burn me *up!*"

She giggled. "I bet. You're not supposed to put Merthiolate on things like a salty dog. It says so right on the bottle."

She was going to say more, but this yellow fly got after her, up in her face. She batted at it. It gave me a chance to change the subject.

"Cissy, you never feel any different ahead of time? You

never know it's going to come over you?" I swatted at the yellow fly too. Two against one, it gave up and left.

She shook her head. "Never. I go to sleep feeling just like I do every other night. Nothing itches or feels peculiar or out of whack. Then it happens, like you saw."

"I know whoever wakes you up better be careful," I finished up. " 'Cause you'll just sure clean their clock."

"I'm grateful, if you want to know the truth, Buddy. Walking in my sleep might save my life one day. Maybe it already did."

A picture flashed in my mind again. I remembered the awful slobbering mouth and burning eyes of a wampus cat in a red tree.

"I declare you had a good reason last night," I told her. "Cause that wampus cat was set to eat yore pretty little face for his supper." I leaned in close and made my eyes big. "The second I came up, his old black lips peeled back and out flared those bloody tushes and—"

We stopped. A sound interrupted us, a strange one, so far away you couldn't really be sure you really heard it. A little boom in the sky. Like when a jet breaks the sound barrier. But different.

Right then, Cissy's finger shot up toward the blue forevers.

"Buddy, look!"

I sat up. But, honestly, with just one good eye I had trouble making out where she pointed. I squinted and tried to follow the red tip of her fingernail.

Then it came clear. You had to refocus and look high, high up, higher than you'd ever look to see most planes. Way out there, this teensie silver piece of nothing flashed along. But something was wrong. This long thin stripe of white smoke went across the sky until it got to right . . . there. Then the white trail changed color. To black. Black as burning oil poured on a pond to kill the mosquitoes. Black as a tire skid.

"What's happening, Buddy?"

"Maybe it got shot."

Her eyes went to little green squints. "Shot how? I don't see another plane."

I leaned up close to her. "I heard about fights with rockets down in Florida. They kill each other from about fifty miles away and don't ever even know the people they're killin'. Maybe those rockets can hit a plane too."

It worried me, this ugly business in the sky. Then it got worse.

Right before our eyes, the ghost jet broke apart without a sound and fell in pieces, shimmering like so many dimes and nickels, falling toward the ground.

We forgot all about the mussels and the fire and the kiss and the pine bark and just watched for a long time.

"Cissy, look," I said. "That's a man dying up there. If you never seen one."

It was the wrong thing to say. I don't even know why I said it. Cissy turned her head and didn't look again.

*

It was her idea.

She'd be the one who went out this time, up to the edge of the woods where we walked yesterday. She'd gather up a lunch for us, picking out the best things in all the places we found on our walk. Wild figs. Persimmons. Pecans out of season off a crazy volunteer sprouting out of a dry red gully. Honey from the poplar trunk.

Her blues didn't seem to last long. Fifteen minutes. But I got the feeling she could use some time alone, after that. We all do, I reckon. I knew the plane on fire reminded her of a daddy she used to have.

She made a fuss over me, before she went. She bathed my black-and-blue places for real and kissed my hurt eyelid again.

All while she fussed over me, my mind was in this other place, a place where things with her got really good.

In that imagining, Cissy swallowed my old salty dog with her salty cat and rode on me and rode on me till I saw sheets of white silk blowing all up in there where the sky should have been. She put her little red lips to my chest, so soft, and kissed the freckles and made all the hurt in the whole world go so far, far away.

I came back just in time. Like slow motion in a movie, off she went, toting a little stick basket I made a long time ago for fruit and nuts. She stepped slender and shiny and proud down off the Indian mound. I think maybe she was somebody new just that second, on her first trip into the wild woods. Somebody I never met before.

She disappeared into the summer green, and I closed my eyes for a few minutes.

Soon, a sleep drip started in my head. I love to feel that drip, falling out of a silver cloud in my dreams.

Drip. Drip.

First, one eyelid trembled, then the other. Oh, I felt beat up and tired from the long nights. My breath came in and went out, clean and slow.

My fingers relaxed, tuned to the drip, slow and steady.

Last to drift away, my ears. From deep, deep down in the start of a sweet sleep, I heard the tapping of a woodpecker in the leaves of the red trees.

I hadn't dreamed about a woodpecker in a long time. It's my spirit bird, because of the red hair.

I went to sleep and had a dream. I was the woodpecker, and the woodpecker was me.

This was the dream.

Go way back, even before the olden days. The whole world just created.

Old God got together a bunch of angels to paint the birds and fish and rocks and trees and all the rest of the brand-new things in the world. Before this, things were plain black and white, like old *Gunsmoke* shows.

God got bored with black and white, and no wonder. A black-and-white rainbow rared across the sky after every black-and-white rain fell. A black-and-white sun sat in the black-and-white sky every afternoon. The leaves on the trees in autumn and the flowers in spring, they were black and white too.

So God blew a horn in heaven and called all the perfect gold-and-silver angels, men ones and women ones, and let each one choose a can of paint with a beautiful color in it to paint the world. Then God put them to work.

The big hairy men angels took their cans of brown and gray and dark green paint and went to work, painting the big stuff. Angels never have to sleep, so they painted up a storm, all night and all day. They painted mountains and rocks and the trunks of trees. They painted deserts and the green rivers and whole volcanoes and all the stuff like that.

The women angels gathered up their cans and took their brushes made out of angel feathers and got right to work too. They painted all the details—clouds in the sky and meadows on the mountains and waves on the ocean. They colored the sunrise and lemons in trees and all the bright pretty wings of things, like butterflies and June bugs.

The little angels, the children of the men and women angels, didn't get left out either. God let each one pick out a little bitty bucket of paint. Some took light green and dabbed it on leaves and hedges and the backs of turtles and the tails of parrots. Some took baby blue and touched the cornflowers and speckled the guinea eggs and sparkled light on the lakes.

That's how everything in the world got to be its color. That is, *almost* everything.

See, there was one problem.

Try as they might, none of the angels could get the lid off one of the best cans of paint. The red one. Bright bold red. So just that minute, every plum in the world was white, and every strawberry black.

God said that wouldn't do. God wanted red plums and strawberries and a lot of other red stuff besides.

The angels took turns tugging and tugging on the lid of the red paint can. They turned blue in the face and broke their fingernails and lost some of their feathers. Nobody had any luck.

So God tried. God got a screwdriver and turned red in the face trying to prise off the lid. (Oh, faces could turn red as roasted apples in Heaven, just not down on Earth.) God struggled with the can till he broke off the handle of the screwdriver. Still, red stayed put.

Naturally, God got all bent out of shape. Maybe God even cussed, but it was nice cussing, you understand.

Finally, God went over to one of the windows in his big house in Heaven and looked down at the world with this wrinkle over one big eye. God studied the situation.

What kind of world would it be if every apple stayed green forever? If those cardinals flew snow-white from tree to tree? How would yellow coalfires look? What would Alabama, God's favorite state, look like if the clay dirt was turquoise?

No, that wouldn't do, God decided. Red was part of the big plan, and only red would do.

Still, the lid wouldn't budge.

The angels tried even harder. They heated the can of

paint. They froze it. They heated one end and froze the other.

They asked the biggest elephant on Earth, strong as it was, to try and suck the lid off with its trunk, but it couldn't.

They got God's own bird-dog to bark at the can, to scare the lid off. They rolled the paint can down a steep hill into a golden wall. The can hit the wall, and it rang like a bell and woke up a bunch of lazy saints asleep under some blueberry bushes.

But no matter what anyone did, the lid stayed on tight.

God got flustered. "What will I do?" God asked one angel. "Leaves turning white in the fall. Lime-green baby cheeks on a cold day. Bright yellow fire engines, when people get around to inventing those. IT JUST WON'T DO!"

Now it just so happened that a bird was flying past at the very second God finally got all overwrought and started hollering and throwing stuff.

This was a black-and-white bird. It had *stayed* black and white, because it got scared when it saw all those big angels swooping down in gold-and-silver dresses, with long fingernails and voices way up high and splashing buckets of paint. That bird never saw angels before. To a little bird, they looked scary as those monkey things in *The Wizard of Oz*.

To hide, this little bird drilled a hole in a tree with its long sharp bill and jumped in. It laid low till the angels finished with their painting binge. Then this Woodpecker, because that's what this black-and-white bird was, came out and flew around for a long time, taking in all the new sights.

It really admired all the fancy new colors and stuff to see. As long as the colors were on trees and hills and other birds and not on Woodpecker.

But when Woodpecker heard God yelling, it thought

maybe it could help. It didn't really know what to do. But it would try. After all, the Woodpecker thought, God made all this stuff down here. When the Woodpecker played and hung out with the other birds or ate or just sang a song, it had God to thank.

So the Woodpecker flew over and perched in the window sill where God stared out. The bird could see God was in a really bad mood. God had torn out big pieces of beard and thrown them on the floor.

"Can I help?" the little bird said. "I'm Woodpecker."

One of the angels saw Woodpecker and got madder than ever. "Aw, beat it!" the angel yelled. "Can't you see God's not in the mood for jokes right now?"

But God, who was nearly over his snit fit and feeling a tad guilty, raised an eyebrow and saw the little bird. God sighed and picked the bird up on one finger.

"What can you do that all of us in Heaven couldn't do?" God asked Woodpecker. "Everyone in the place has tried to open this STUPID CAN OF RED PAINT and nobody can do it!"

God pointed at the can of paint, dented and dinged, but still sealed tight as a drum.

The little bird flitted over to the lid.

"Hmmm," Woodpecker said. "I'm not for sure about this. But maybe none of you used the best tool."

With that, the bird drew back its head and *RATATA-TATTAT!* before you could blink, it drilled a hole through the lid of the red paint can with its sharp beak.

"LOOK!" God cried out. "MY BEAUTIFUL RED!"

Out gushed the prettiest color of paint Heaven had ever seen. Bright red. Red as the Red Sea. Red as red silk and alligator eyes.

God was so excited. God took out a brush and went personally down to the world to paint red things. God wanted them to be as red as they were supposed to be.

And here's what happened to Woodpecker.

When the bird hammered that hole in the lid, paint splashed all over its head.

God decided Woodpecker looked perfect that way, black and white with its crown of bright beautiful red. And when you see the red on any woodpecker's head, you know God left it just that way for a badge of honor.

And that, in this dream, was how Woodpecker got a red head.

*

I stirred, but didn't quite wake up.

I felt the sleep drip.

Mmmm. Warm.

Drip.

Drip. Drip.

I came out of the pleasant dream, swimming up fast, the way it feels when you swing way, way out over a river on a rope and let go with all your courage and drop toward the water and splash so big and sink like you might sink forever.

At last, you start back up toward the eye of white sky way over your head.

One kick, two kicks, three.

You see the white get bigger, bigger, bigger. Your lungs might pop, but you kick and chase bubbles toward the light.

Close! Nearly there!

Out of the dream you bust, with sleep dripping off, breathing sweet air, your teeth white and laughing, happy to be back in the world again!

Happy.

Until you see.

Hung on the same limb where the wampus cat watched.

A man.

Burned bad.

Dangling by a parachute.

Blood dripping from one boot.

Drip. Drip. Drip.

Was I awake?

I felt the top of my head.

Wet. My hand came down wet. Warm blood.

Oh, no.

Not in The Secret Place!

"Help me . . ."

His voice was weak, faraway. A gold cross shined on his flight suit, bright as a flaming sword.

"Help me. Oh. Please."

I jumped to do it. Before Cissy came.

I trembled, but I climbed the tree to help him down.

SKY KING

I HUNG MY toenails and fingernails in the bark of the giant red tree and started up. I clenched my big buck knife in my teeth like a pirate. I could have used a patch over one eye too, it was swelled up so bad.

About twenty feet high, I twisted around to check my fall. The Indian mound looked from up here like a baby comfortable asleep under a green blanket of grass, snug in a lump, all warm and peaceful.

Sack *is* asleep in there, I reckoned. Resting up till the next full moon. Like there wasn't no danger to him in the whole wide world.

But I knew better. Me and Sack, we both knew. It all came down to something like this parachute man in the end. We got found out. Now we'd have to go on to the next place or find the next skin to live in. We knew all along it might happen.

I surveyed out over the rest of The Secret Place, while this worried so-and-so inside of me spoke up all by itself.

Cissy, you need to go on now. Keep going and don't look back, girl. Everything about this world just changed.

The sorry sight just above and off to my right said it all.

There swung a mess of a man in the broad daylight. I reckon it was a man. The thing was scorched so bad you really couldn't tell.

The helmet was all smoked up inside and stained with something awful. The orange flight suit smoldered in two or three places, and the smell of burned skin and melted plastic got worse the higher you climbed. I figured in about another hour, once the blowflies got used to the altitude, the reek would knock a buzzard out of the sky.

I climbed on, concentrating, getting my good finger-holds and toeholds, spitting out pieces of bark and grit, squinting through my one good eye.

I tried not to think what it must have been like in that Christian fool's airplane when the rocket hit and fire foomped out of the dashboard and burned him as bad as a weenie dropped in the coals at a cookout. I didn't want to imagine what he thought on the long float down either, watching Old Mercy River get bigger and bigger and never knowing if he might land smack in the middle, tangled in all those parachute strings.

The pilot made a sad coughing noise, then gave a deep hurt sigh and swung in his straps a little.

I got to considering.

Here I was, scratching my way up the trunk of a tree about like that woodpecker in my dream. The afternoon was hot enough to melt the brains right out of your head. I poured sweat, and it fell in my hurt eye and stung like fire. I was all beat up myself. But here I went anyway, dead-set on saving whoever that slap-out-of-luck, burned-black-and-hung-in-that-nylon-spiderweb fellow was.

Why should I care? This was a Christian Soldier. Maybe

he was the very fellow who killed old Randy. It might be wrong against my own brother if I saved this fellow's life.

I latched onto the side of the tree, thinking about this situation for a second. Me and Sky King both hung side by side for that long minute in our lives.

The devil on my shoulder whispered then. It would be easy. I could cut his parachute cords and let him fall. Fifty more feet and that would be the end of his sad life.

He deserved it.

I swung out over empty space to reach the red tree's next limb. I rested on it, a little shaky, to catch my breath.

I tried to piece together all the things I felt right then. I looked out far enough to see the edge of those wild places where Cissy went in the woods that burned so green. The Secret Place. Sack laying yonder. A river galloping past.

This was the whole world for me.

It was the world I chose, wasn't it? And Randy showed me how the world you choose is worth fighting and dying for. I remembered that lesson clear as a bell.

I stood up on the limb and catted out to where the nylon parachute cords held that pilot off the ground. I almost lost my balance and grabbed at the cords, and I plucked one by accident. It made a noise—*brrrruuummmmbbb!*—like the thump of a fat bull-fiddle string.

My knife flashed. I could cut the strings and not think twice about it. Sky King would fall, and be as dead as old Randy after he hit the ground. He'd go to a place where the only wars are over who gets to sit closest to the big white throne and who gets the first helping of honey and locusts.

I thought of this too. What if Sky King still wasn't dead after he hit the ground?

I knew what to do. I'd crush his head with a river rock. I would make myself do that.

I thought about my own poor brother with bullets coming in the front side of him and going out the back, and the pity just flew right out of me and up through the sunlight in the trees.

I never killed a man, or wanted to. I only scared them and let the legend of me and Sack gather up over these parts like a summer thundercloud. I reckon that legend made me special to folks some way, the way Randy was special to folks while he lived. But now a new day was here.

This thing with Sky King—I had to do right by Randy.

I made my heart hard as flint.

I squinted up at the white flower the silk parachute made over us. The sun burned clean through the other side of the cloth, brighter than the brightest thing that ever was. I raised my knife and the sunlight flashed again.

I touched the first parachute cord. The blade melted it, and the cord twanged in two pieces, one piece up, one down.

The blade whispered through another cord. Two more. The load below me bobbed and twisted, and a groan got loose from the horrible thing.

I didn't listen, no sir. That burned so-and-so wasn't a man I cared about now. Bad folks like him killed Randy.

I swiped at two more cords. Sweat dripped off my elbows. Off my nose and ears. I rained like a rain god all over the ground down there, and all over Sky King too.

I looked down at him. The cut parachute cords trailed over his back and on beyond, dangling with his arms and legs. He hung spread-eagled now, facedown, turning in a slow circle. His burned back showed through a rip in the flight suit. Horrible bubbles the color of beer suds boiled out of his pink skin.

The sight of that made me want to jump clean out of the tree. It made me want to leap out into space with my knife and land on him like Tarzan springing on a bad lion he *had to kill* to stay king of the jungle forever.

I wanted to get the rest over with quick.

Quick, quick. But little carbonated spots popped up all in front of my good eye, and then a sour mash of stuff choked its way up my throat. Hot, awful chunks filled up my mouth. I tasted vinegar. I tasted something else that I hated.

My balance got away for a second, and I teetered on the limb.

Old Buddy didn't fall. My heart beat wild and I wind-milled my arms, but then I caught on and closed my eyes and swallowed and bit my lip. After a minute, the sick wave passed.

Quick.

I gathered all the rest of the parachute cords in a bundle. I saw spots again, but thought, *Durn it, I'll cut them all at once, I'll get this over with all at one time.*

Sky King would fall the rest of the way out of the sky. That's the way he started. That's the way he was meant to finish.

I could throw his sorry bones down a gully or pile some sticks together and burn him till his ashes floated right back up to the sky. Me and Cissy and Sack could go back to living free and easy then, like nothing ever happened. . . .

I heard Cissy just that second. *Bud-d-d-d-y!* Like a voice calling you to come home, supper's ready.

"Hey!" she went. "You listening?"

Far below, calm as a minute, she stood there. Wildflow-ers stood in the circle of sunlight with her.

"There's a way to do it," Cissy said. "You got to climb higher up and bring down the other end of those ropes. Those cut ones still tied up on the parachute. You'll have to tie them to the others to ease him on down."

No panic. Steady in the voice. Nothing like you'd think a girl would be with a bloody burned man floating over her like a monster in a space movie.

I could see again now. Right under Sky King, with her arms spread wide, that's where Cissy waited. I saw that she'd stand there and try to catch him when the ropes broke, if she had to.

"Cissy," I went. "I wanted to kill him."

And, right that second, I felt all the hateful cords stretched so tight and angry inside me just pop, and my soul floated loose again and it fell out of that tree and landed safe, safe and sound, in my little girl's skinny arms.

I closed my eyes and fought the tears, but they came anyway and stung my bruised eye like a swarm of bees.

It hurt so bad to be me right then. Something had almost happened inside of me that wasn't right and wouldn't ever be right in the history of the world. But Cissy saved me.

She saved me from killing a man.

"Buddy? You okay, sugar?"

I leaned out over the limb and nodded so she could see my face, and see I meant it.

"We got to get him down pretty quick, Cissy. He's bad."

I cooned the limb clear back to the tree trunk. With the knife in my teeth again, I started climbing higher. My face opened straight up toward the sky, and I hugged the trunk of that tree. The sun glowed like God's good heart up here.

I wiped my eyes on the parachute silk when I got up higher, and I asked God to please forgive me for what I almost turned into. I thought of my brother, poor old lost Randy, and I broke down and cried again. This time, I dropped my knife.

It was a heavy thing, and it fell fast. The knife bounced off a limb. It ricocheted, ringing, twirling end over end, spinning and shimmering. It flew right past a falling red leaf on the way down.

I saw the knife clear the lowest limbs, but then my heart slammed into a wall. It dropped straight toward Cissy!

And she didn't even see it, staring up with her arms wide like somebody praying for rain.

She didn't have time to even move.

Deadly as lightning, the knife flashed toward her innocent face.

It missed.

Oh, it was lucky. Mr. Buck Knife sank clear to the handle in the soft ground not two feet away from her.

She jumped to one side, way too late, like a coiled snake just popped out of a hole.

"Yipes!" she hollered, so faraway down there. "Hey, crazy boy! You trying to kill somebody?"

No, not no more, I told myself.

Not ever again, dear God.

*

We got the burned man down and made him as comfortable as you can get a man who is cooked to the bone just about every place on his whole body.

We laid old clothes in the deep sweet grass on top of the Indian mound. On the pocket of the flight suit, scorched so I could barely read it, was a name, JELLICO. Almost the same as that city in the Bible where the walls came tumbling down.

Me and Cissy carried Sky King in our arms and settled him. He hurt so bad he just passed in and out of wakefulness—*ping! ping!*—like when you pull a string to turn on a lightbulb.

I fetched up some river water in a hollow gourd. Cissy put a hand behind his head, and I cradled the dipper up to this hole I took to be his mouth. Sure enough, I saw teeth and a tongue inside. I thought he might eat the gourd, he wanted the water so bad.

Cissy cut off his clothes, most of them. Oh, it would just

about make you puke up a meal from a week ago to see what was underneath. Skin the color of scorched Spam, oozing yellow bubbles. Just so awful. Only his stomach and the thighs of his legs weren't cooked that way.

We tried all afternoon to keep him warm. Hot as it was, he shivered and shivered. I finally went and hauled Sack out of his hole. Blankets stayed stashed and dry in there, and we took those and built a little canopy over him. It was careful work. Anything that touched him, even blankets, hurt so bad he hollered and thrashed. Still, unless you kept the heat close, he chattered so hard I thought his durned teeth would break.

I did know enough to help one way. The reason blood came through his boot and dripped on my head was plain when Cissy trimmed the flight suit. His legbone, bad broke, jabbed clear through the meat of his leg above the knee.

I took some stout green sticks and undid his shoelaces and used all that to make a splint. Cissy pulled the leg out straight to make the bone go back in. She did a pure brave thing, because he screamed and went into the blind shakes from all the pain. But she didn't let go till the bone disappeared back under his skin and I could tie the leg up stiff.

Sky King seemed to feel a little better after that. The moaning eased off, and the sleep looked more like real sleep, not like somebody who died every few minutes.

"Buddy," Cissy said, after he dozed off once. She blew a string of wet hair out of her face. "It ain't but one way to save his life."

"I know it," I said.

She came all the way over to me, where I sat sweating by the fire trying to boil some water to wash him, and she put her arms around my neck.

"You just got to," she said. "He's a human being."

I looked down and fiddled in the fire. "You'll be by yourself."

"I won't let the fire go down," she said. "I'll be too busy taking care of him to be scared."

I thought another second. I didn't like it, leaving her in the deep woods at night to go get medicine or kidnap a doctor or something. Not with a wampus cat out, able to smell cooked meat as good as any creature that ever lived.

Finally, I told her, "Hey, I know. I've got a great idea!"

I kissed her, all excited. I picked a stick out of the fire with a little burning ember tip and waved it in front of me on a quick trot down to the old Galaxy.

In twilight, the fire made a pretty design reflected on the side of that car, orange in the shadows. I thought about how strange it was that something so beautiful as fire could hurt a man so bad.

Mr. Galaxy was covered with limbs and leaves. Me and Cissy had camouflaged it. Hard to believe it was just hours ago when we grumbled to a stop out here after our wild getaway from Bob-A-Lu. That seemed like years and years ago.

I dragged that branchy mess off the car hood, screeching it over the metal, and tossed the leafy limbs out in the woods.

I climbed into the driver's seat. Man, I was an expert on cars now. The key waited in the ignition. I turned it. Nothing happened at first, just the cranking noise. It caught, smoked, and sputtered. Then it died out.

Twice more it caught for a second, then coughed to death. I squinted down at the lights on the dashboard. A long red needle on a dial pointed at that ugly word.

EMPTY.

I might not know how to drive a car, but I sure knew what that word meant.

I got out and slammed the door behind me and walked back up to the Indian mound, real slow.

"I'll have to get to Goshen the old-fashioned way," I told her. "The way me and Sack always do . . ."

She looked up with big eyes, full of tears.

"He started to talk," she said. "Buddy, he's still real alive."

I squatted by her and gave her a hug.

Let those tears come on, darling.

I knew what this felt like for Cissy. Worse than the burns, worse than the suffering nerves.

Her daddy might have been lying there.

I saw it plainer than ever, how close I came to doing wrong.

*

"Mama! Mama, make it stop!"

One long hour of suffering and hollering later, the soldier's voice sounded as parched as the rest of him. I gave him more water from Old Mercy River and he laid back with his eyes shining. The lids were burned off and I didn't really know if he could even see. He just stared faraway, like he was seeing past the moon and the stars and way on out there to the places yet to come.

"You just hush now," I told him, after the cool splash from the gourd. "You'll be all right. Just save your strength."

It was full dark now, and the tree frogs and whippoor-wills raised a racket like dogs fighting in a shed. Cissy got real quiet, concentrating on the bite of food she cooked over the fire. Some for me, before I struck out for Goshen, and some for her and the hurter.

It smelled delicious. Pecans, toasted in the skillet, and wild pears and black cherries boiled down soft. Cissy took pride in her first supper, I could tell. She stirred the food real serious, and jibbled up little spice leaves in them.

I wolfed mine down. And hers, since she couldn't find her appetite. Good food. It did like fireworks in your mouth. I thanked her too many times.

Before I left, I wanted to help Sky King one last time.

Cissy had found some quail eggs. We broke them in a clay bowl and poured them right down the soldier's throat.

It must have made things better for him. He didn't thrash so much. He seemed to talk in his right mind. Called his mama and daddy and somebody named Jenny.

"He's got a family," Cissy said. "I reckon they're worried about him."

I comforted her too. "It's all right to worry. Bad stuff happens to all of us, I reckon."

He took more water and a taste of the fruit a little later. You wouldn't believe how he relished that bite, chewing it and making sounds.

I got a creepy feeling just after that. The campfire reflected in Sky King's eyes, and you could see it was just a little boy down in there, under all that hurting. Just a little boy about to die, no matter what.

Cissy appreciated me staying a little longer. She didn't really realize why though. And I didn't have the heart to tell.

I've seen a lot of stuff in my life. I've seen the janitor at a school get struck by lightning and his clothes blown right off and the soles of his shoes melted, and he still lived to tell kids about it for years, pushing a big broom down a hall.

I've seen a black dog on its hind legs crash through a plateglass window and walk right up to a piano in a funeral home full of people and play it, looking around and laughing with his wet red tongue hung out.

I've seen an old widow lady get blinded by her own

chickens. I've seen an army of ants get under a baby stroller and haul it toward their nest with the baby sound asleep in it.

I've seen a little plaster bust of Abraham Lincoln on a mantelpiece start talking and cussing and spitting so vile it had to be buried, and even while the shovelfuls of earth got poured in its red mouth, it kept on shrieking and hollering the dirtiest words you ever heard.

Anyway, I've seen enough to know, after a good hard look, when the life light is running out of a man's eyes like the water down the hole in a tub.

Oh, there was a minute when I thought he just might make it. You get full of hope sometimes and it clouds your judgment.

But after I went down to crank the car then came back and got that second look, I knew. Sky King wore the death's-head, and I saw it plain.

No need to leave Cissy alone this night. I loved her too much for that.

Sky King hollered again. "Mama!"

He moved the crispy little nubs on one hand, raised the arm a little like he waved good-bye to somebody, dropped it again.

I settled in closer to Cissy, just to wait.

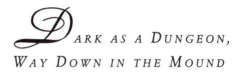

DARK AS A DUNGEON, WAY DOWN IN THE MOUND

S O .

I never had to bust Sky King's head open with a chunk of river rock. Or hold him under water till the bubbles stopped coming.

He died all by himself the next morning, just before the sun floated out of the treetops.

Cissy had tuckered out. She sat there and made hoot-owl eyes, her head nodding. Believe it or not, I wasn't sleepy by then. My worry wart was itching fierce.

I took a break from Sky King and watched the river run by in the soft light. A kingfisher flew from one pine limb to the next one, hunting breakfast. A school of shiners leaped out of the waves and hung in the air like something ready to hang on a Christmas tree.

That's when it happened. Sky King gave his last scream to this old world. He reared up from where he was lying on top of the Indian mound. He grabbed his burned chest and whooped, and his fingernails raked out fresh blood.

167

Me and Cissy jumped up and held to him while he
bucked and hollered and dug in the dirt with his heels.
Cissy was so scared.

I was too, if you got to know. I've seen a lots, but I never
saw a man die right in front of my eyes.

I don't know why he couldn't just go on off to sleep, the
way people pass away in the movies. Or why he didn't have
the good sense to go down with his plane in fire and glory,
if he was going to die anyway. He could even have broken
his neck on a limb of that tree, or landed in the river and
just disappeared quick down into the two-hundred-pound
snapping turtles and the water rattlers.

But Sky King stiff-armed the death angel for one hot day
and a night. He made *us* suffer too. Oh, we worked hard to
save him. I even waved little mimosa leaves back and forth
over his face to keep the gnats off in the day, then the mosquitoes at night. Cissy looked up at the moon and said
prayers like she meant every word.

The way things went there at the end, you could almost
believe Sky King might make it. He talked plainer and
plainer, even if the words didn't make much sense. He
stopped trembling like a twenty-year-old dog and got real
peaceful.

But at the end, just when we all felt a little comfort, he
bawled like a castrated hog and shook loose from the
world.

He laid still after that, and the river gnats clouded down
on him.

*

Oh, Cissy squawled and squawled.

I squawled a little too.

"I was gonna kill him," I confessed. "For what he
done."

Cissy stopped crying then and turned toward me. Her eyes looked like two red rubber stoppers in a tub.

"You never should have thought that. All he ever did to you was just float down out of the sky."

I didn't have an answer. Some part of me knew she was right. But maybe Sky King did more than that to old Randy. It made me confused and hurt. Then Sky King died.

"Cissy." I just shook my head. "Don't get upset at me. I got to feel what I feel." My eyes burned all over again.

After a minute, she slid over and put her arm around my neck and dabbed so soft at my hurt face.

"You're a good boy, Buddy," she said. "You're not bad any way."

But Cissy didn't understand. She couldn't see a feeling that grew like a thunderstorm in my head. Until it went off, that is, and shot out lightning.

"I ain't crying just for him, stupid. It's *me and you* too. Can't you see nothing? It would be nice if somebody would live, Cissy. Just one stupid time."

Oh, it shocked her. "Buddy," she said, and that was all.

I kicked the ground, miserable. "Ain't you ever heard of a miracle, Cissy? Couldn't it happen just one time?"

She didn't answer. After a second, I realized that was an answer too.

I still sat. For just a minute I could see the reflection of the moon, sawed off on one side. It rolled lopsided out of a cloud. Then it got blurry and sad, and I lost it.

"Cissy," I told her. "You'll be gone one day too. I just know."

It was a long time before we talked again. The moon went away and it got to be good light. The bluejays pinched each other up in those red trees. A leftover lightning bug or two popped in the grass, and mourning doves made that sound somewhere.

What happened next with me and Cissy might not sound right. But it doesn't really matter what anybody else thinks.

She turned to me. She kissed me too. And we just melted together.

We didn't care about anything. We didn't even care if a dead burned man laid just ten feet away, staring at the big black circling buzzards up in the pink sky.

Nothing could stop that kiss.

Nothing but her, just when things could have gone on to the end, forever and ever, amen.

*

After a little, Cissy sat up and brushed the sweetgrass off the back of her arm. Her hair swung down her seashell back.

"We got to bury him," I said, still floating a little above the world. "Right away."

She made a sharp little noise for an answer. "Oh, Buddy. Look. The fire ants."

I didn't look. Not yet.

"Those durned buzzards up there worry me more than those ants," I told her, squinting up. "But I got a plan."

"What's that?"

I took her little white hand. "I'll tell you. But you got to promise something. Promise that you'll kiss me like that again sometime, Cissy."

She flipped her hair and eyed me. "You're back to yourself now, Buddy."

"You did it, Cissy."

She smiled. "It made me feel good too."

Oh, it was love. My ears rang with it now, and it clanged in my chest and roared through my head like a log train.

At least the two of us had one thing in the world.

Love.

And we also had this dead chunk, lying stiff on his back in the dewy grass.

"Might as well get it done, Cissy," I sighed, at last. "Gonna be a hot one."

"This is where he came to die," she said. "I wonder why."

*

It was only about seven in the morning, but you could already feel the heat off a mad white sun. On days like this, the tall trees just stood there sweating. The air turned into thick, hot, clear, melted, sticky glass.

That Christian Soldier would smell horrible and swell up like a boiled weenie in an hour. That's what a shot deer did in weather like this. So I got motivated.

We asked a prayer over the dead man, a long one. Cissy said the words, and I clenched my eyes tight and tried to call up God with my brain.

Forgive his sins and us too, I prayed. *We're sorry we don't understand nothing that's going on down here.*

After the ceremony on top of the Indian mound, Cissy grabbed hold of one of Sky King's big burned feet. I took the other foot, and we dragged him over the slick grass to the side of the Indian mound nearest the river.

We sent him over the edge. Whee! Sky King was stiff now, hunkered sort of into a sitting position, and he went down the grass side looking so durned much like a boy on a sliding board it would have scared you. At the bottom of the mound he stopped—*bump*—then pitched over to one side. You couldn't see it, even that close, but the secret door where Sack hid out in the mound was right there.

I sidewinded down the slope behind Sky King, then went to work. I lifted the grass tussocks off Sack's hiding place and tore out the river rocks and made the entrance hole as big as I could. I brought Sack out real careful into the broad daylight. Cissy stared hard at him.

"He's gross," she said. "I don't know how you stand him."

"He's good luck," I said. "Here. Touch the croker sack. You'll be able to feel what I mean."

She reached out her hand, real careful.

"RrrrRRRR!" I went.

She snatched those fingers back quicker than a man touching a hot horseshoe.

"Don't *do* that, Buddy. That's not funny."

"Sack, don't you growl at that pretty girl," I scolded him out loud, shaking the croker sack. "That there's *my* girl-friend."

I thought it would be polite to introduce Sack to every-body, so he met poor old Sky King too.

"And that one there, he's gone on to be with all the an-gels," I said. "Or maybe the devils. There ain't no way to tell by looking."

Cissy held her hand over the secret entrance to the mound. A cool wind from the hole blew her hair.

"That hole must be deep," she said. "Feel that breeze. Like air-conditioning."

"The cool breath comes out of a water well that same way," I said. "Hey, did you see this?"

I brushed some crickets and spiders out of the way of an old hard clay door frame. "It's the Indian door. It goes on down in the mound."

"It must be old!"

"I reckon." Now I threw dirt out between my legs like a dog. "The Creek Indians lived here before white people and stuff. They built this whole mound with just the pore dead people from one tribe. They buried people year on top of year till this mound got taller than a two-story house."

I tore loose some more rocks and dirt from the entrance.

"That's a lot of people," I said, finished up. "So there."

She peeked down the entrance hole now, and her eyes got bigger.

"It smells funny. Old."

She tickled me. "Sugar, the sun ain't hit down in there for about a million years. It's dark and it's full of old moldy bones and junk. Besides, it ought to smell funny. It's a *grave.*"

"You know what?" She pinched my arm.

"What?"

"I'm not going down there."

I looked behind me at the poor burned soldier. Maybe he was already swelled a little in the sun.

"It'll be cool down there. It won't be dark, Cissy," I said. "We'll have us a torch. I can make one real quick."

"I don't know."

"Look," I said, finally. "I can't hardly get him down there all by myself. He's big as a skinned mule. You got to help me bury him, Cissy.

"Mostly," I added on. "I'm scared of holes too."

She bit her lip. I could see the clock parts working behind those big eyes.

When she nodded, I felt lots better.

*

We got busy.

We gathered up some broom sedge and some fat lighter knots and some wet poke and green sticks. Mixed together and tied to a fat lighter knot, you had a torch that would burn for thirty minutes.

I know how to build a fire with flints or rubbing two sticks. I knew how to hold a broken whiskey bottle over dry leaves too and focus the sun to kindle a fire.

Believe me, though, it's a lot quicker to use plain old Red Top matches. I always kept some in the bag with Sack.

I struck four at once and held them till fire fluttered up at the end of the torch. Cissy brushed stringy white hair back out of her eyes.

"I don't guess it would be right to just sink him in the river," she said.

I grinned like a goat eating briars. "I promise, you ain't the first one to think of that."

She looked right on at me, sort of hopeful.

"Trouble is, he'd get all gassy and float up one of these days. Somebody would find him for sure and want to know how he got there and how his leg got set and all kinds of questions like that."

"Oh."

"And besides, it ain't right. Like you said. When a person dies, you bury 'em."

She hesitated, a sign of second thoughts creeping in.

"It's hot, Cissy. Let's don't stand around."

She gave in.

"Well, I'm not going down that hole *first.*"

"You ain't got to," I promised. "But I need your help."

*

The graveside service commenced.

I bent low in the cave door. "Ready?"

"Uh. Not really."

"But you're comin'?"

She did her shoulders funny.

I smiled big. "You gotta see down there," I told her, pretending like I knew. "It's wild."

I poked the torch in front, down the hole, real slow. "Help me watch out for snakes. They get washed down in places like this by the rain sometimes."

The tunnel lit up ahead of the torch, and I followed the shining streaks of moisture down the walls of the mound.

So did Cissy, after she took one more deep breath.

We scrabbled along on our butts, kicking dirt clods along, the torch out ahead of us. Cissy never turned loose of my shoulders.

"Are we almost there?" she wanted to know. The second time she asked, her whisper sounded bigger, all echoes, like she said it into a microphone.

"Hear that? I reckon we're close," I told her. "Watch that spark there."

We slid down a little farther, the close walls fluming orange and throwing shadows. The air smelled peculiar. Chilly.

Then, up ahead, this big black space yawned like a lake of coal tar. The room lit up as we slid into it, one behind the other.

Cissy held tight to my shoulders and bit my back with her teeth.

"I don't want to look," she said. "I changed my mind."

I lifted the torch high over our heads. Some mean little cinders popped off and danced all down my arm. But I steadied the torch, and orange light changed the room. Me and Cissy made flickery big shadows on the wall.

"Yewww!" Cissy went. "Skeletons!"

A dozen, all sizes, laid on little hardened mud platforms. The bones weren't white, like you'd think. More like a honey color, with some dried pieces of leather tied to the bones here and there, and shed hair under the heads. The air smelled older than the oldest book you ever opened. Beads and little bone needles and arrowheads and junk covered the floor.

I took a look at Cissy and saw a girl with eyes that couldn't get enough in them at one time.

"There's a little baby one, Buddy. See?"

It was pitiful. The little thing curled around something brown, that might have been a toy about a million years ago. The baby looked like it was still crying from a stomachache after all these years.

The cool air crackled. The fire in the torch ate some dry sedge and flared up. We had some time left.

"Here, Cissy." I gave her the light. "Now this is going to be hard, but I've got to fetch Sky King down. You won't be alone but a minute. While I'm gone, you need to try to find a clear place on the floor where we can lay him out."

She ought to have complained. Nobody would want to be left alone down here.

But Cissy seemed to forget anything she ever felt about being scared when she saw that little baby skeleton.

Maybe people never think about babies even having skeletons, much less little white ones with bones like a tiny bird. But here one lay. And how could a baby be scary?

"Cissy?" My voice zoomed around and around in the cave. "Did you hear?"

"I think Sky King might like it here after all," she said, sort of faraway. "You go on."

"Hold the torch like this," I said. "So the fire don't burn out too fast. And I wouldn't touch too much. Maybe it's like knocking over gravestones or something."

I scratched back up the hole, bound for the bright circle

of sunlight at the end of the tunnel. Coming down was sure a lot easier. I never used my fingernails once. Going up was different. But I grunted and heaved and played worm till I reached the top and oozed out.

The sun blasted down so bright that it hurt my eyes. For a minute, I felt like a bat flopping around. You could purely hear the heat, banging on the world like a hammer on an anvil. It took me three eyefuls of tears before I could see the buzzards.

Ten of them waddled around old Sky King. Their stinky old wings spread out like evil enemies of Jesus mocking how he hung on a cross. More buzzards than that swooped low, wheeling round and round in a funnel cloud over the mound. Turkey buzzards, with horrible scabby heads and eyes that don't blink.

It only took me a second to send those puke-pigeons back up toward the clouds. I'm a deadly aim with a rock. Black feathers got left all over the grass.

"Durned rotten butthole eaters! Stay gone!" I hollered and threw rocks even after I knew I couldn't hit them anymore.

Oh, they had pecked old Sky King some. But after all he'd been through, you couldn't really tell and it didn't really matter. I just grabbed his ankles and tried not to look.

By the time I got him to the hole, I heard Cissy's voice float up.

"Buddy! Hurry, please! This torch is burning low!"

I broke a new kind of sweat then. I jumped in the hole like I lived there all year, then tugged Sky King by the charcoal-hard ankles and yanked him down behind me.

Nothing to it now, with gravity to help. I blinked away the green gloomy dark after the bright sun. By the time I could see, Sky King was on his way home, halfway down the shaft.

Cissy met me at the bottom, her face shining like a jack-o'-lantern. The torch burned about half as bright as it first did.

"Got him!" she said. "Way to go."

"Uh. He's heavier than he looks."

"Hurry," she said. "I made a place right over here."

We laid Sky King down among all those Indian bones. He didn't look like a Christian Soldier right then, and all those other bones didn't look like Indians. They looked the same down here. Dead and gone.

Cissy fixed his head on a scrap of Indian blanket, then we stood back and took our last look.

Maybe it's not reverent, but it's true. Sky King looked so funny after a minute that we started to giggle.

"He's ready for anything, Cissy," I said. "Look."

Sky King's arms sort of hovered at his sides, like a cowboy about to draw his pistols. I reckon all those Indians just had that effect on a soldier boy.

"Don't laugh any more now," Cissy said. "I'm gonna say the last prayer he'll ever get to hear."

Her voice sounded a lot bigger than she was.

"Close your eyes, Buddy."

"I ain't needin' to, Cissy."

Sure enough, just that second the torch snuffed out and the room got black as what it was. A grave.

Cissy grabbed my hand extra tight, but went right on with her prayer.

She stayed brave. Maybe things scared her at first, but she could find courage mighty quick, then keep it burning. Quicker than most people I ever met.

"Dear Lord," she whispered, "this man needs to go get in some cool water up in Heaven. Amen. And take care of all the other ones in this Indian mound too. Double amen."

"Double amen," I said.

Double amen, said our echo.

At least, we *thought* it was our echo. Truth is, maybe something spoke out loud. Something that was left to stay inside that mound in peaceful cool dark forever and ever.

Amen again.

TRY SCARING HALF the people in Goshen one night.

Then escape from soldiers through the woods with a girl and a car. Keep somebody from drowning in a fast river. Two shakes later, try to save some burned-up dude that floats down from the clouds out of nowhere. Stay up all night to keep him alive, then watch him give up the ghost and die after all you do. To top it off, go drag him down a dark hole halfway to the center of the earth and lay his bones to rest.

It'll wear you out.

Do all this in the blast-furnace heat of Alabama summer, and you can see why we hugged the shade of those big red trees the rest of that day. I hid the parachute in a hollow tree. Twice we nibbled some wild grapes and took a dip in the slow part of Old Mercy River, just to keep cool. But mostly we just snoozed.

I kept guard duty when I could manage, worried over something. I couldn't quite put my finger on what.

For some reason, way down, I expected trouble. But I just saw the most common scenes in the world. A porcupine with a green apple in its mouth humped it toward the woods on the other side of the Indian mound. A blue heron stabbed between its feet in the river. Yellow butterflies staggered through every now and then. Everything seemed perfectly normal.

Cissy slept so hard I worried about the buzzards coming back to get her. Three or four of those things could just about tote her off, being light as rabbit fur and all.

I made a decision in my own mind to treat her to something special this night. Something wonderful, that would get her mind off all the trouble we'd seen.

I thought hard about what to do. And, finally, I came up with just the thing.

Yeah. The foxholes. That would be perfect.

After that, I felt starved for food. I thought about getting up and limping over and pulling up one of the fish traps. I just knew a big yellow Appaloosa catfish winked and blew bubbles in the bottom.

But instead, I curled back onto the flattened grass where I'd just been lying. I put my hand over on Cissy's shoulder and watched her smile in her dreams.

Sleep cranked its motor, and pretty soon I thought about a dark room and a tunnel going into it, with a circle of bright light at one end.

*

I was born in Florida, Randy told me one time. Came into this world in a dazzling bright citrus town. The tallest thing around wasn't a tree, but a silver water tower with spray-paint writing about high-school seniors all over it.

I remember the place in little pieces. I reckon the memory fit all together one time, but someway, growing up, it fell and busted. Now I always had to puzzle the parts back together to figure out what happened.

The man that lived with Mama at my house always smelled like Three-in-One oil. He had shiny black hair, combed straight back. He bought me a red tricycle with tassels on the hand grips. In the house, we had a picture on a wall, me and this Daddy in the yard. I was perched on the trike, my white toes just barely reaching down to the pedals.

Randy told me later how it wasn't our real daddy. But I never understood any of that. We just called him Daddy and went on with things. It's only nowadays that I wonder what happened to the blood-kin daddy. My father. Randy said he just went away one day, but you never know.

Anyway, the daddy I knew worked in a factory where men scalded the skin off oranges in huge boilers. His job, he told us, was to keep the machines boiling.

"Keep boiling, boiling, boiling . . . keep them oranges boiling . . . Rawhide!" He'd sing that for a joke at the top of his lungs in the shower at night.

He said the boiler-room job went on no matter how many folks fainted from the orange juice fumes or fell into the pasteurizers. Just keep them oranges boiling, hee-ya!

Daddy's skin felt scratchy on the cheeks when he kissed me to sleep, and you could smell gin under the Three-in-One oil. Mama made sounds in their room at night like a mourning dove. Then she breezed around the house every morning opening windows and chasing out the moths that got in no matter what screens you closed or lights you turned off. She let me drink coffee, mixed with condensed milk so it was gold and sweet.

Mama worked at the factory with Daddy, adding up numbers and stacking papers with her long red fingernails. Her face was so pretty. She held me in her lap and read me

The Jungle Book and Brer Rabbit stories, but she was so pretty I could hardly pay attention.

Maybe I was three when they both went away, Mama and Daddy, on the big boom day.

*

The boom that afternoon was so loud it shook loose the rattly jalousie windows on the back door of the Florida house and crashed them down the brick steps like a glass waterfall.

The noise woke me up from a good afternoon nap. Bagheera too, my best friend those days. Baggy jumped up in the playpen like a cartoon cat, turning two or three different directions at the same time, scared half to death. He jumped the playpen rail and raced up under the chifforobe and meowed out loud.

Randy told me later how all over town the sirens went off and people ran up and down the street, hollering and swatting the hot red sparks that fell down the necks of their shirts and stung them like wasps. Randy said some folks stood on their lawns with garden hoses, squirting the shingles on top of their houses to keep them from catching on fire.

But I never saw that. I only heard a world go boom. Like a hundred jets flying through the sound barrier over the house at one time.

Weird things happened all the time out there, in Florida World. I didn't really give the big boom a second thought until Maria Grazie, our babysitter, flew out the back door without even closing it.

With the coast clear, I climbed out the hole my brother Randy smashed through the slats of the playpen before I came along.

Randy was a tough baby. Maybe he couldn't hold a tractor up in the air over his head like Superboy. But he could make a playpen sorry for the day it was born.

And that's how me and Baggy got away.

We toddled past the refrigerator, by the lumpy brown food and the piece of cheese on Baggy's food plate. Baggy turned his nose up at a piece of cheese, but every morning Maria Grazie peeled the plastic off a slice of yellow American and left it on his menu anyway.

The fact is, *I* ate that slice of cheese. Every day. I stole it while Maria lay on the couch with one foot in the air and talked forever on the phone to some girlfriend. I sneaked through the hole in the playpen, gobbled the snack, and made it back in. She always thought my nap lasted longer than it did.

Every evening, I heard Maria brag to Mama and Daddy, when they got home, about Baggy's big appetite for cheese. All three of them would laugh, and I felt like the cat that swallowed the canary.

Me and Baggy padded through the empty house. It had giant old rooms. Ghosts cracked their knuckles in the corners. Shadows of banana leaves tossed and nodded on the walls. Most houses in Forest City were pink shoeboxes with green lawns and white carports and pink-and-black Buicks. But we owned an older place, the kind Mama said she loved for the "atmosphere."

Me and Baggy passed quick by Randy's room. A poison tarantula lived under the bed in there. Randy told me. He said he saw it all the time. It licked its slimy lips and blinked its red eyes in the back of the closet. It waited behind the white curtain on his window like a big devil hand. Because of that, I didn't *ever* try to go in Randy's room.

We slipped on back to Mama and Daddy's instead, and it was one big mess. Rolled-up dirty socks and a sweaty baseball cap and a hairbrush so full of Mama's soft yellow hair you couldn't see the bristles. A pair of torn stockings trashed the bed. An old black banana got one day blacker on the floor.

This afternoon, a dirty pile of cigarette ashes and butts covered Daddy's white pillow. The big boom knocked it right off the back of the bed, I guess.

Water was sloshed on the wood floor out of Mama's pet fishbowl too. A goldfish flipped around on the throw rug, but Baggy turned up his nose at it. Like some kind of cheese.

Not me.

I still remember how peculiar that thing tasted. It wiggled all the way down to my stomach.

Believe me, a catfish wrapped in wet poplar leaves and steamed over a low fire is a better way to go.

Maria Grazie never cleaned Mama and Daddy's room, but nobody seemed to care. I bet nobody ever cleaned at Maria Grazie's house, two streets over, either. Why would you even bother? A whole baseball team of a family lived there, in a pink shoebox squeezed between Mr. Bewley— the dope fiend—and that deaf couple whose scary little girl could read your lips a block away and know everything about you.

Maria Grazie really only watched TV in the afternoons till the folks got home and Randy came in all sweaty from beating up other kids on the playground. Maria Grazie primped, she ate Spam sandwiches out of the refrigerator, she read a movie-star magazine.

I loved her a lot.

The day she went outside and stayed for three blue forevers, though, I got a little nervous. Even more after she came tearing back into the house to catch the phone.

I would have answered it myself, but I didn't know how yet. I reckon, though, I could have done as good as Maria.

She picked up the receiver, then put her hand over her mouth and shot this weak-eyed look at me and Baggy. We got caught peeping around the door frame. Maria saw us and dropped the receiver without even hanging up.

We ran like crazy. We scrambled back through the house, scared to be spanked. The sound of her hard shoes on the floor chased Baggy under the chifforobe again. I even tried to climb back in the playpen, but it was a tricky business to handle in a red-hot hurry.

We needn't have worried.

Maria Grazie snatched her pocketbook, not us. Her keys hit the linoleum-tile kitchen floor. She banged her head on the cabinet, hurrying to pick them up. She knocked the carport door wide open, and the wheels of the car barked like four dogs when she raced off.

I couldn't reach the telephone to hang it back up. It swung like a clock pendulum. Baggy thought it was purring, and got all interested.

How did I feel right then? To tell the truth, I got real, real mad. It griped me to be left behind on a trip. If Maria Grazie wouldn't take me along to the store, or wherever she went, then me and Baggy would fix her little wagon.

We knew some stuff to get into.

We meddled in the sewing-machine drawers and pulled big red and black and yellow and green thread hair balls off the spools. Baggy rolled in the thread like a giant orange monster caught in a net. He batted spools all over the room, and chased them down again, and his eyes blazed like green fires.

I yanked the cord, and the cat clock with the moving eyes jumped down off the kitchen wall. Baggy sniffed the clock, and his tail puffed up, like a real cat was dead on the floor.

In the den, I fiddled with the radio knobs. I made the

radio man talk REAL loud, then not talk, then talk REAL loud. A radio was something me and Baggy knew how to work.

Mama and Daddy could make music come out. But I couldn't. Everywhere I put the needle, there was just radio talk. *Serious* talk. On one of the stations, you could hear police sirens and ambulances howling in the background.

Me and Baggy went and found my bottle in the refrigerator and I let Baggy lick the orange rubber nipple till he got enough. I took my turn, then. When the milk ran out, I threw the bottle in the sink with about a million other dirty dishes. Instead of water, two roaches splashed out.

Well. Now what?

The kitchen door, the one Maria Grazie left by, still stood wide open.

So we eased ourselves out, me and good old Baggy the cat. The sun lit up everything out there, and everything was green.

Baggy darted out into the yard, but I saw broken jalousie glass spilled like diamonds all down the stair. One step at a time, I scooted down. Me just three years old and still in training pants that had a little wet dirty place in back.

Oh, how fine to be free as the breeze in that backyard!

We watched lizards do circus tricks on the elephant ears in the flower bed. Those things did magic! A lizard would be green one minute and then—*snap!*—like that, the color of a pink house shingle.

I wanted to learn that trick one day.

Baggy was bad. He pounced on a lizard in the monkey grass. That little dinosaur opened its scary mouth, though, and hissed and blew up a big red ugly bubble on his neck. Baggy went *yikes!* and shot straight up in the air as high as my head, and that lizard slingshotted six feet off in to the elephant ears with one jump. Baggy acted like he meant to let that lizard get away all along. Like lizards taste sour to a cat.

Something funny happened too. Ashes started to fall out of the sky, even though the sun was shining with all of its might. Gray ashes, like the first snow ever in Florida World, Florida.

You didn't see ashes fall out of the sky too many times in your life. When you're just three, you don't get concerned. Not with lizards to see up close.

Me and Baggy next struck off to check on the trash pit. It was an adventure place too. All week, we'd haul the garbage down there. Then, early Saturday morning, Daddy would let Randy squirt the whole pile with Three-in-One oil and then lean way down to touch it with a cigarette lighter. The fire came all at once and made a noise—*whump!*—like somebody whopping a rug on cleaning day.

One time, Randy pitched a whole ten-pound bag of Mama's potatoes in the fire, one at a time, pretending he was a big-league baseball player. Daddy spanked him for that with some of the neighbors looking.

On this day, the big boom day, me and Baggy strolled right up to the edge of the fire pit and peeked in.

Down in there, big leftover chunks of log as gray-headed as old ladies in church huddled together. They smelled awful. At the bottom of the trash pit, you could see the other things that wouldn't burn. Ham bones and tinfoil and metal springs and rubber gizmoids. A piece of old Buttermilk too.

Last week, Daddy pitched my broken-down old wonder horse in the pit. I loved Buttermilk, even if he hurt me on the mouth when his head snapped off. I bounced mighty on him. I reckon the head should have been glued on better.

I wouldn't have burned Buttermilk myself. Daddy was as

mad as fire when I got hurt, though, and he made the pit flames jump and snap, then pitched my wonder horse right into the hot fevers. Old Buttermilk burned and melted, all but one side of its plastic face, that part with its big brown eye. It stared at me, sad as a horse's eye could look, while all the rest melted down to a glob.

Later on, when I was seven or eight years old, Randy cut a picture out of a *People* magazine he found in the library at the orphans' school. He gave it to me so I could take it to the second grade and show it.

It was a black-and-white two-page picture of the Florida World orange juice factory, how it looked after the boilers blew up and the fire burned and the ashes fell and the whole thing and everybody in it went to kingdom come.

The Big Boom Day.

That picture showed a big black-and-white hole in the ground. It looked like that fire pit in our backyard, full of gray heads and bones and gizmoids too, with ugly black stuff piled around. One of the heads had a wet eye open, staring out of that magazine picture forever and ever.

There was a lot to study in that picture, but the saddest part was that drove of firemen that stood around the crater edge, spraying their hoses. You could just barely see their faces. But what you *could* see told the story.

They looked like men that would quit their jobs as soon as they got back to the fire station.

All of a sudden on this day when I was three, for no reason I could tell, Baggy turned and ran like cans were tied to his tail, right back up the steps and toward the house.

Maybe a spark of fire fell on his nose. Or maybe he just didn't like what he saw in that pit. Whatever happened, he left me all by myself out there.

Way off, the moans of Civil Defense sirens started in. You never heard such a horrible sound.

Well, I still can't tell you why. But when Baggy took off that way, then that siren kicked up, something made me shiver like a whole herd of rabbits ran over my grave.

I got spooked and tore out for the house too.

The ashes fell thicker now over the backyard. I ran as fast as I could go, and I climbed up the back steps, one huge step at a time, right through the broken glass. I jerked open the door, and me and Baggy scurried in, and I climbed a stool and made it onto Daddy's big chair in the living room.

I started thinking all kinds of scary things.

Maria Grazie would never come back. My brother Randy either. Nobody would. It would just be me after today.

I huddled in Daddy's big chair, quiet as a stuffed mouse, waiting.

Out the window, the bushes got darker and taller and the sun shrank, till finally it was just a little dried orange on a tree.

Now the house got really spooky. I could see inside Randy's room a little ways, and I watched every minute for his deadly tarantula to come out from under the bed.

My heart beat so loud I could hear it.

What was the matter with this place? Where was Mama? Where were Daddy and Randy?

It was okay now if Maria Grazie never paid attention to me again. Everything would be okay, if she'd just come back this minute.

After forever, I saw two headlights sweep the carport.

I scrambled down from the chair. I was so scared my stomach hurt. But I didn't know what scared was until the door opened.

A woman I never saw before came in.

She never knocked. She was dressed like Mama, in the

same factory jumpsuit. Her hair was the same yellow color as Mama's and pulled back tight in a ponytail. She chewed gum and wore Mama's red fingernails.

This was a trick. An evil trick. I knew it was.

This wasn't my mama!

"Oh nooooo!" I squawled. "I'm scared!"

"It's okay, Buddy." The woman gritted her teeth and showed them, sharp and fierce. Smut dirtied her wet apron. A shiny hurt place showed on her cheek. "Everything's going to be okay. You just come with me."

"Waa! I want Mama!"

"Your mother, uh, she asked me to come take care of you, Buddy."

She grabbed my hand, this imposter mother. She held it too hard.

"No!" I told her. "Mama!"

She knew. She knew something was the matter.

The woman broke down and cried like a baby. She curled up in the middle of the floor and beat the tiles with her fist.

"Oh, Lord. Oh, Lord. Oh, Lord," she told the floor. "I'm not strong enough for this. Oh, Lord."

BEFORE ME AND Cissy stirred again, the moon burned blue over the treeline. That lopsided old piece of rock felt almost as hot as the sun.

We were parched, sleeping through such a day. One hundred degrees, if it was one. Long after dark, we got up and walked stiff in the joints, the way zombies walk, down to Old Mercy River.

We got on our hands and knees to guzzle the water, just like wild animals. We splashed it all over our dry faces and down our dusty backs. The goose bumps came up in a flock. Brrr, that river ran cold. Cissy dunked her head under, and her white hair streamed when she came up with her mouth wide open.

Something popped its tail out on the river, then dove under. A beaver, probably. Pink and big up on the bank and scrubbing at ourselves so serious, we must have looked pretty peculiar to that critter.

"Cissy," I finally said, lying back with my hands behind my sun-burned neck, "I slept so hard I'm still groggy."

She just shook her head. The girl couldn't even grunt yet.

The moon eased on up out of the trees, brighter than usual, an odd blue. Sometimes there's magic in a moon like that, and it must have been that way tonight.

Right off, I saw something I never saw before.

A family of bobwhites tiptoed by, just a few feet from me and Cissy. The mama and daddy led the way and the whole bunch of babies followed like they were tied on a string.

I knew by this sign it would be an unusual night. You just don't see bobwhites out after dark. They roost out in the field, cozied down in a circle in the broom sedge till just their eyes show and the little gray feathers blow on top of their heads.

This blue moon brought them out like it was high noon.

*

A patch of blackberry vines grew by the water. I got to thinking and had an idea.

Too burned-up lazy to crawl, I just rolled over in the grass three or four times. Then, as careful of the stickers as a starving man can be, I pulled off fat blackberries and crammed them in. They tasted like fruit might taste one day up in heaven.

"Cissy," I said, with my mouth full.

She lay still, one white hand waving in the water. "What, Buddy?"

"These are the best blackberries you ever tasted."

"Uh-huh."

I glanced over. She stretched out by the water in the soft blue light, pure as the day she was born, staring out into the wildest parts of space. You'd have thought maybe the heat hurt her brain some way.

"Blackberries are mighty good for you."

"Uh-huh."

I pulled a big handful and rolled back, over and over, up the grassy bank. For a joke, I made a noise like a car crashing into her, real slow, when I snuggled close.

She didn't even snicker. Just lay there like a jellyfish, or something with all its bones cooked soft. Like a sweet apple baked in an oven all day.

I slipped a ripe blackberry in her mouth. She didn't help or hinder me. Her white teeth turned purple and the little black seeds got on her lips. She chewed one time, two times, without a sound. I pushed another berry past her stained lips. She ate this one a little faster.

After four or five fat juicy berries, you could see a light coming back on in her eyes.

"Buddy," she finally said, through a mouthful of purple teeth, with a deep sigh. "You know what?"

I told her I didn't.

"I believe there's a prickly pear cactus or a board with a nail in it under my back. Something sharp. It's about to kill me."

"Roll on your side."

She did. Sure enough, she was lying on a green pinecone with sharp hard edges. Her back, just above the straps of her slip, wore a big pinecone tattoo. I kissed the place to get it well, then chunked the pinecone in the river.

"Whew," she said, settled back. "That feels better."

"I reckon so," I said. "That old bad pinecone hurt you."

"Thought I might die," she said.

"It was just a pinecone."

"The heat, I mean. It got so hot today. I woke up one time. Buddy, it was scary. Big black things coming out of the woods and sniffing all around the Indian mound. Bad things. Bigger than circus elephants, but blurry, like shadows. You couldn't see if they had eyes or mouths."

I leaned back to stare at the stars.

"Maybe you didn't imagine," I told her. "These woods are a real strange place."

"Thought I was gonna die," she said again.

"No ma'am. Sky King did that."

*

If the biggest, fanciest chandelier in the whole world fell off the back of a pickup truck doing ninety miles an hour, the blacktop road would look like the sky that night over The Secret Place.

A million little crumbs of glass shined up there, some with little comet tails, some welding-torch blue, other ones yellow and red and green and pink.

There's nothing else in the world as pretty as heaven on a night like this. No wonder everybody wants to go there. Trouble is, you have to die.

I love to pick out all the star shapes. A crab and a bear and a man with a club and a lion skin. Two twins and a flock of seven angels. A scorpion too, if you think that's what a scorpion looks like.

I never figured out how people named the stars. It takes some powerful imagination to conjure up a goat out of those five or six bright ones right there. Or a lion out of those yonder. Oh, the big dipper is an easy one, because that's just what it looks like, a dipper gourd. But most of those other collections don't look like much of anything.

Since the old ones are so bad, me and Cissy decided to name a bunch of new constellations.

Tonight, we spotted The Hogdog. Yonder flew The Skinny Cat and The Fat Cat. Sometimes, you could find a shape in the black places between the stars. We said hello to The Cowboy Hat. Cissy herself named that one.

Fresher now, and cooler from the river and the night, she seemed to be getting happy.

"It *is* a cowboy hat, Buddy. And that over there, that's Mama's Wedding Ring."

I told her I'd take her word.

We saw a star fall. We both closed our eyes and wished a wish.

The river went by sweet and smooth.

"Don't tell your wish," I teased her.

She did her mouth. "I'm not about to," she said. "It won't come true."

"Mine already came true, Cissy."

"Shhhh!"

"Oh, but I made another one. And it'll come true tonight if you'll walk up in the woods a little piece with me."

She rolled her eyes, oh boy. But I could see the stars twinkling in there too.

"After me and you cooked in this heat all day like potatoes in tinfoil, you want to go tromping off on a walk? You're crazy as you look."

"You won't be sorry," I told her. "You'll remember it all the rest of your life, Cissy. I'll show you the best thing you've seen in the woods yet."

"Buddy, I've seen stuff to remember all my life. Just today, enough stuff to last me a pure lifetime. Why don't we do *nothing* tonight. Or something I'll forget in about five minutes?"

"Please?" I stood up and tugged at her arm now. "Please Cissy? It's the best surprise of all."

"Bud-dy!" She said it all flustery, but she stood up anyway.

Just then, we both stopped stone-cold still.

Away off, out in the darkest places in the deep woods, the wampus cat let go a blood yell.

Some poor thing just met its maker.

We hesitated, but then I felt sure again.

Old wampus already had his supper this night. He wouldn't hunt *us.*

I took one more glance at the sky, then led Cissy on up under the trees.

Maybe those stars didn't look like a Hogdog after all.

Maybe they looked more like a starry-toothed Wampus Cat, watching the world, waiting, never blinking.

*

The trail toward the foxholes threaded through one pitcher-plant bog and over two woody hills. We got all sweaty again. Her slip soaked through, and I took my shirt off to travel in just my pair of cutoff shorts.

On the way, we stopped under a grove of magic trees the Indians called "See-Me-Know-Me" trees. I jumped up and pulled down a low branch, holding it while Cissy picked off four bright red fruits. They looked like dates, except for the scarlet juice.

"You just have to trust me on this," I told Cissy. "You never saw stars till you see 'em after eating these."

She was cautious, like always. "This business won't make me sick, will it, Buddy? I don't think I could take one more thing today."

I ate one to show her, putting the whole thing in my mouth and spitting out the black seed. It wasn't bitter, but it tasted something like medicine anyway. I tried my best not to make a face.

"No. They never made me sick. But this fruit is real strong stuff. You won't want to eat them again for a while. Something about it."

"I'm not sure I want to eat it *now*," Cissy said. "Not if it makes you see things. This girl's seen about enough for one day. I don't need any help."

I chewed another fruit, thinking of what to tell her.

"Have you ever had a dream," I asked her, "that felt so real and good you wanted to go right back and have it again after you woke up?"

She said yes, she had.

"Well, this feels just that way," I told her. "It's the most relaxed, comfortable kind of feeling. Like everything's going to be okay from now on. Then you start to see things. And they just surprise you. You can't help but feel even better."

I let go of the limb, and it swooped back up into the tree. But Cissy still didn't look convinced.

"Look," I said. "I'm eating three. You just eat one. This little one. You'll learn what to expect that way."

"Will you take care of me? Promise you won't let anything bad happen?"

"I promise, Cissy. And not just tonight. Every night, as long as you want."

She reached out and took the fruit.

*

"Whew!" I told Cissy. "Now. Those pits right there are the foxholes. We're here."

She flopped down on the ground and put her noggin on her knees. The fruit had given her a headache right off.

"I haven't been this miserable in my whole life, Buddy. I'm not taking another step."

"That's fine. You just sit there, Cissy. You'll still see why we come all this way."

The foxholes weren't really made by foxes, not unless foxes grew as big as cows in the olden times and could dig like badgers. I just called them "foxholes" when I found them out here in the woods.

A grown man could stand on his tiptoes in the bottom of most of the holes and not reach the top. Maybe forty or fifty in all spread back through the woods in this area. God only knows what they really were, or how they got here. Maybe falling stars hit in a bunch one night.

One hole went down so deep you couldn't see the bottom, even in broad daylight. Once, I threw in an Indian cane spear and never heard it land. That spear might still be falling.

Anyway, as soon as I hopped into a shallow hole, the real reason we came was plain to Cissy. It smelled funny down in there, and the air went electric with mosquitoes, but I didn't care. I kicked into the old moldy leaves on the bottom.

"Ta-dah!" I went, my arms spread.

She sat by the hole and looked down with her eyes as big as plates. Blue plates, glowing.

"What *is* that stuff, Buddy?"

"Fox fire! It's what you call fox fire!"

A wet cool blue kind of fire coated my feet and stained my ankles. Cissy looked down at me with the most amazed face you ever saw, like a girl at a surprise party, her face shining over the birthday candles.

"Fox fire! Fox fire!" I hollered. "Cissy sees a fox fire!"

I picked up a forked stick. I turned back the top three or four inches of leaf in the hole. The plow rut blazed. The minute those buried leaves hit the air, they flamed to life. The end of the stick flared. You could see giant wolf spiders running through the leaves. Their legs dripped blue phosphorous.

"Help me up!" I asked Cissy. "Let's check another hole!"

She gave me her hand, and up I bounced. I put my cool blue hands on her cheeks. It left these glowing hand-shaped tattoos.

"It makes me—dizzy to look at you," Cissy said.

"Wooo! I'm blue! I'm The Blue Thang!"

She laughed a real laugh. The first one since Sky King came down. It did my soul much good.

"Look in that hole, that shallow one!" I said. "I'll check these over here."

We hopped to it. Cissy squealed when she turned back the leaf mold in the hole she chose.

Green fox fire! Green as her eyes! Fox fire that crackled and glowed!

"And look! Look at this!" I held my arm up, smeared to the elbow, crimson-red like a stoplight.

"Mine looks so beautiful, Buddy. It smells like a lime. It's so cool!"

Oh, Cissy was excited. She didn't waste a second. Her hand smeared the green fox fire up and down her long legs. While she talked, I dabbed red fox fire designs on my own legs. Blue and red. I glowed two colors! My arms too, all the way to the shoulders.

I hopped out of my gloryhole. I was just in time to see Cissy start to show off like I never saw before. And, I swan, her slip was off. She'd thrown it over a huckleberry bush ten feet away.

"Watch me, Buddy! I'll do you a trick!"

Quick as a flash, she climbed three limbs high up a handy wild beech tree. Cissy's blue cheekbones lit up when she smiled, perched now on the low branch with her green legs dangling.

First, she kicked like a swimmer on the edge of a pool. Her legs went like this—green, GREEN, green, GREEN, green.

Next she made those long legs go *V* and back together, *V* and back together. A green blur. All the way up to *her* secret place, where the color changed. That place yelled out red, bright red. She'd reached up with her hand and dabbed on some color.

Oh, she put on a show. Her legs made green scissors. Green diamonds. Green alligator jaws. Green bug antennas.

Finally, she flipped upside-down on the limb, like a monkey-bar trick on the playground. Her red and green and blue hair waterfalled to the ground and her green, green hands hung down.

She made hand signals in the air. Two green dinosaurs talking. A giant green bird flapping past. A green church, green steeple, open green doors, see green people.

Now, she swung on the limb, upside down, forward and backward, forward and backward. Higher and higher and even higher Cissy swung, like a flying electric girl on a circus trapeze.

When she let go, I couldn't believe it!

She turned one green flip in mid-air, then feathered down right in front of me, light as a fairy. A green fairy that smelled like lime.

She smiled and kissed me so sweet.

Maybe it was the most wonderful night of my life so far.

I wanted to show off for her too.

"You ain't the only one that knows tricks, Tarzan girl," I bragged, smearing red wavy designs on my chest and stomach. "I went to elementary school too. I been on a monkey bar."

"Woo!" she said. "Touch you." She looked at her hands funny. "Hey, Buddy."

"What?"

"I feel real good."

I grinned and winked my bright blue eyelid. "This stuff goes through your skin and gets your blood drunk," I told her. "It's something I didn't tell you."

Oh, I felt it myself. My blood whistled through my brain, and white sparks flashed on and off all around the edges of my eyes like lightning bugs.

"Quick!" I said. "Look at us! We're on a merry-go-round!"

I began to spin, fast, around and around, and so did she. The pools of color in the foxholes smeared and blurred. Cissy flew by me again and again, dancing a maypole dance, green and red, green and blue.

"Hey!" I heard her say, farther off and excited all over again. "This hole over here has *yellow* fox fire. Lemon yellow!"

I hummed while I turned, the world loop-de-looping, this googly music playing, like that big midway a long time ago. I heard a carnie squawl. I heard Danny Dynamite say something. Voices sounded the way they do under a boat dock, near and far away at the same time.

"Whooooo!" I sweated colors down my chest. "Whooo! Cissy, I'm The Wild Thang!"

She stood close again now. Her hands and arms and face glowed like yellow Jell-O with a light under it.

"Gotcha!" she said, and pat-a-caked my back with a lemony hand as I wheeled by. "Gotcha good! You're it!"

She dashed off through the black dark, fast as a bolt of yellow spring lightning. Her whole body glowed as she ran.

"Yeeeeee-haaawwww!"

I pulled up and stripped off my shorts, quick as a flash. If Cissy could, Buddy could too. Then I tore out after her. My knees flashed. My fists pumped like red-hot pistons.

My little man stood straight out, red as a stick of dynamite. My balls swung down, blue as the fuzzy blue lights on a Christmas tree.

Oh, she flew. Fast for a girl. Fast as me, but not faster.

"I'm—gaining!" I went. "You run—like a girl!"

If you listen to that kind of jive in a race, you slow down. Trouble was, Cissy didn't. She streaked on, faster than ever now, nimble as a yellow deer.

She flew ahead of me, tree to tree. I thought of a yellow curtain burning in a house. Or what old Moses saw burning holy on the side of that mountain.

"Cissy Barber, Cissy Barber, Cissy Barber," I chanted. I leaped over roots and thumped faster. A trail of flashing red footprints followed her fresh yellow ones. "I'm gonna catch you, Cissy Barber."

Old Randy used to win every race on the playground. But that was Randy. I ran as fast as I could, but I couldn't catch up to Cissy.

The faster she fled, the brighter she burned. Yellow and green and blue, and one juicy spot of red.

I could feel the sweat pour off me now, and see it fall in blazing colors all over the ground.

Run! Run boy, or you'll lose her!

The sound of a raging forest fire crackled in my ears. Fire everywhere. A world made of fire, leaping and burning up. Cissy's hair blazing. My body lit by pure flames.

What?

She disappeared! Where was she?

Aha! My lucky break!

"Oh! Oh, shoot! Buddy!"

Up I thundered and raised my arms over her like God after a fistfight with the Devil!

Cissy fell in a hole. One of the foxholes. Lucky for her a shallow one, silver in the bottom like a pool of moonlight.

"Girl, you hurt?" I asked, out of breath.

She giggled.

"Well, if you ain't hurt," I said, "then watch this!"

Her giggling flat stopped.

Here's why.

Buddy danced a love dance.

Around and around the hole I strutted, slow, so slow. I dipped my head low and threw it back high, with my arms in the air. I stomped the ground like a fine tom turkey. My glow-in-the-dark self wrote a long love note, one letter at a time. I bowed and lorded and showed her all a boy could show. Fine and fearless and slow.

"Buddy, you look great!" Cissy said. The girl I loved.

I saw her bright red invitation, floating like a valentine on a silver lake.

Not yet!

I turned and turned, fast as a top now, giddy and dizzy, slinging and sweating out all the bad of the last two days. I yelled to stars big as marbles, to a blue-eyed moon. I babbled like one of those folks struck by lightning in church, those that lay on the floor and twitch like they're coming to death.

I flew and flew around the silver pool with my fairy girl in it, her golden arms and green legs and red door wide open for me. I went in circles, faster, faster, like those crazy tigers under Sambo's tree, turning to butter they ran so fast.

Then, the accident. I fell. The bank gave way and I tumbled down into the foxhole. I landed on a dry silver ocean, splashed silver fire over my face and hair, drowning, out of breath.

"Lordy. I'm so drunk."

Way off somewhere, a little happy bird, Cissy welcomed me. "Whee! Wheeeee!" She threw blazing silver leaves high in the air.

No doubt about the happy now. No other night of my life came close.

Warm sweet breath lit my cheek.

I opened my eyes.

Burning blue lips.

I kissed them. A sweet hot fire ant taste. I could smell old leaves and pieces of wild gingerroot and white threads of mushroom and thick-odored leaves. Yes, and fresh lime.

What was better than this?

Nothing. Ever.

We couldn't wait anymore.

The red part of me and the red part of her joined. At last. Just that easy. Colors flew off in all directions. I tried to put myself inside her all the way up to her heart.

I was Cissy now, and she was me.

We loved. We shook and shivered and delighted. We went at it like we wanted to die that way together.

And, finally it all came to one pure note of music, clear as a bell, echoing, going away to nothing in the woods, lost in a million trees.

Her soft green eyelashes flickered against my cheek.

I lay still and closed my own eyes and thanked the stars in the sky for this second.

Beautiful stars. A blue moon.

"I don't ever want to be apart from you, Cissy," I said so fierce. "Never."

"Never, Buddy," she said. "We won't."

Sleep came to us soon after that. Dreams in color.

Happily-ever-after dreams.

Part Two

THE TWO GIANTS

THEY SHOT ME when I was still asleep.

The explosion and pain out the end of that shotgun scared me a foot high. I landed sitting straight up in the bottom of that foxhole. Frightened to death, kicking like a baby rabbit in a nest with a bushhog coming.

Oh, I thrashed and scratched, bound to jump up, scramble, run off. Only something was wrong.

My hand.

They hurt my hand. Real bad.

I looked down through blue gunsmoke and howling scary shotgun echoes.

What was that?

Two fingers off in the leaves, curled up like white snails.

I made myself look at my right hand. Little nubs stuck up where fingers used to be. White gristle on the ends, clear as the end of chicken bones.

I grabbed my poor stubs. After a second, up rose the

blood. The sticky red stuff bubbled out and ran down my arm and off my elbow. I felt pain, pain so bad I could hear it in my ears like chain saws ripping corrugated tin.

Not another sound in the world. No birds. No running river. Not the hot morning swelter of the woods or even the *pat-pat-pat* of blood dripping on dry rotted leaves.

Over the foxhole, glaring down, stood the two men that shot me.

"See there, Derl?" one growled. "I told you he weren't dead." The one that talked wore a thick black beard and pointed with his shotgun. A little pearly glob of smoke flowed out the end of the gun and rose toward the sky.

The other man stared. His whole left eye was pure white, like part of a boiled egg. He noisily spat a rope of tobacco juice off to one side. "Reckon you right. He's still wigglin'. Looks like he might try to get up and run off."

The big man with the black beard talked again, a mean dog's voice.

"Somewhere you got to go, nekkid boy?"

I just sat there bleeding in the hole, so shocked and hurt I couldn't answer.

"Heh!" the one named Derl said. "Cat got his tongue, Jeeter. Maybe he don't like our company."

"Reckon not."

"I believe he'd like to skedaddle," said Derl.

Jeeter, with the beard, winked his eye. "Well, Derl, why don't you take care of that?"

Derl moved quick for a fat man. He hopped down in the hole and without any expression at all kicked at my head. He wore the heaviest iron-toed army boot you ever saw. The kick missed my temple, but he rared back again and caught me in the small of the back. I reckon the boot had a cement block in it.

Things went black—*boom,* like that—black as the inside

of a black cat up under a black house on a long black night.

But I stayed part of this world long enough for worry to grab me hard one more time.

Cissy.

Where was Cissy?

*

The sun popped crazy back into my brain after a spell. I don't know how long.

I could see the tall walls of the foxhole now, rising like the sides of a grave. It scared me. I tried to get up. Something stayed bad wrong. I couldn't make my legs work. Just my arms. All I could do was crawl around in the leaves on one hand and one elbow, like a broke grasshopper.

The two giant men showed up again, at the rim of the hole. They towered over me. Their heads went way on up to the sky, tall as the tops of the trees.

I tried to make out all the details I could, while they studied me right back. They wore gray uniforms, the same uniforms worn by rebel soldiers, but their fatigues looked like they hadn't been washed in years. The man with the beard—Jeeter—cradled Mr. Shotgun under his arm. The gray sleeve hung down, the insignias ripped off.

The details told it all. Call these men runaways. Deserters. Outlaws.

Randy wore the same gray uniform one time. But if I had to bet, these two men were in an army all their own now.

I almost wished they'd been Christian Soldiers instead of two renegades. At least I'd have known to expect the worst.

"He ain't even knocked out," Jeeter said, words I made out over a sawmill whistle screaming in my head. "Derl, you kick like a girl."

Derl blew up and yelled back, tomato-red in the face.

"You the one missed him with a shotgun, Jeeter. If you'd let *me* shoot that thing one time—"

Jeeter cut him a look. The angle of the barrel shifted just the littlest bit. Derl shut right up.

I got a better look at Jeeter when the gun moved. His face went in and out of focus, right in the middle of a bull's-eye of white fire. Thick black beard. Mean black eyes. A mouth like a fresh cut.

I tasted blood in my own mouth and spit it out. I noticed how something slicked the toe of Derl's boot. My back felt wet, down to my waist. I still couldn't feel much of myself below that, but a warm, far-off tingle was coming back to my toes. I couldn't stop looking at my hand. It was killing me, throbbing, bleeding like a fountain. That made up for a whole lot of missed feelings in my feet, I reckon.

I might be okay, if I could just lie still a little longer. I closed my eyes, tried not to crawl, not to hurt.

My thoughts flew like birds anyway. Straight to Cissy.

Thank goodness, she was gone. Somewhere. Thank all the lucky stars and all the good angels that kept them lit. She was better off anywhere else than in this foxhole.

Maybe she was watching from the trees right now, scared stiff and wondering what to do.

For one panicky second, and this shows you how crazy the pain made me, I thought she might be burrowed down under all the leaves in this foxhole, hiding.

Then good sense came back. She really was gone, all gone. Like there never was such a person.

Maybe she walked in her sleep. Or if she got up to go pee, she ought to say a prayer every time she peed, from now on till the end of her life.

Whatever happened, I hoped it saved her.

I wished I'd walked in my sleep too. Or gone to pee. Or just done anything except what I did.

Just lay here while bad men walked right up.
I got caught sound asleep. On my home turf.
Maybe a boy ought to be shot for that.

*

I heard a *thump-stumble-thump* directly and opened my eyes.

Jeeter and the shotgun stood over me. He'd hopped down in the hole with Derl, and now both of them stood right there.

My eyes crawled up Jeeter like a spider. They went all the way up legs and belly and neck to his mean face. Past his head, blue sky showed and a flock of birds tore by, getting the hell out of Dodge.

"What's your name, soldier boy?" Jeeter grunted. "We found your parachute back up by that hill. We know whose side you're on."

He jabbed the shotgun barrel in my ribs, so hard something crunched in there. I couldn't really feel that either.

I didn't say boo. He was lying about the parachute, testing me.

Under the beard, that rebel's face looked like it knew everything a shotgun could teach a man. The skin was full of pimple holes and blackhead pits. He looked like a wanted poster on a tree at the edge of a dove-hunter's field after a rotten hunting season.

"What kind of goddamned nekkid sombitch are you?" that Jeeter wanted to know. He spit tobacco juice all over me.

I hated him so bad for that. I thought of revenge, and I remembered Sack. Tears stung my eyes. Old Sack would get even with these boys for this. One day. Just wait. He would.

"You done blowed his fingers off and filled his navel up

with that backy juice, Jeeter," Derl said. "Now see can I blind him in the eyes."

Derl leaned down. He smiled, and it was ugly, a crooked crack that split his face like if you dropped a pumpkin on a hard road.

He shot a stream of tobacco juice—*splat!*—right at my forehead. It made a noise, it smacked me so hard. My eyes burned and watered, and the sky turned red as ham gravy.

I knew they'd finish me then. I just tried to empty my mind. I conjured up a picture of Cissy in all her rainbows the night before and waited for that shotgun to sneeze and that big white light to come on forever.

A funny feeling. I wasn't afraid.

I could smell those soldiers, the stink of their clothes rotting. I heard church music. I remembered one of my teachers at the orphans' home, who used to walk funny due to polio. I saw a colored boy carrying a hurt dog up onto the porch of a shack, laying it down on a beat-up couch with a yellow-jacket nest in the arm.

Cissy flashed into my mind, deep in the woods, running away through the green ferns on long fast legs like a deer.

Jeeter put his face down close for a look at me now. His ugly beard opened up in the middle again, and this old yellow smile slowly poured out of it like egg.

"Derl, gimme your lighter, boy. I can stop that hand bleedin.' "

He cricked the lighter with his thumb. Fire gushed up, orange and blue. Jeeter leaned close.

I shut my eyes again and wished so hard to be in another place. Out in the thick dark cool woods. Down under the fast white river. Up in the air, with the flying blackbirds.

The burning smell came real strong. I tried not to feel. I listened for the sound of a wampus cat, screaming in the woods. But something else did all the screaming.

I remember twisting around and how their black boots struck at me like snakes, over and over.

This was what the wicked world gave boys like me.

*

After the torture, there came and went a long minute when those bad men just stood there over me, all out of breath. They sucked air like big horses after a race.

Jeeter looked happy. I guess they just got a kick out me, wiggling like a caught fish in the bottom of a hot boat.

Derl had an idea of his own then. "Jeeter, I know. Let's jab a sharp stick up his peehole." When he said it, his whole face brightened up.

Jeeter rolled his eyes.

"Derl, I swear. All you think about is cramming' a sharp stick up something's peehole." He sounded disgusted. "Same as that rabbit yesterday. And it dead."

Derl answered quick. "You *owe* me, Jeeter. I got us the hell out of the unit, didn't I? You'd be dead like the rest of 'em. Ain't that right?"

The quiet weighed down. Finally, Jeeter shrugged, put one leg back up on top of the hole and bounced out.

"You go right ahead, Derl. Take one of those sticks there and sharpen up the end. You got a right."

Derl's face lit up. He pawed around in the leaves and found a green limb. He was as fat as a bear. I watched him take his knife and peel the limb and trim it up. Directly, he turned back to me, a sharp white whittled point aimed out of his fist.

"Go to town, bad boy," Jeeter said from up top. "He's all yours."

That hateful thing hunkered down to torture me some more, squatted between my skinny freckled legs with that walleyed grin all over his face. He leaned in, the pencil-sharp stick ready to jab clean up inside me a foot or more.

Something in that awful second brought my mind back.

What happened didn't happen by plan or even by luck. It just happened.

I swung at his fist. Hard, with my good hand. The fist with the stick in it. Hit it straight up. And the stick, oh, it was sharp for sure. It jabbed right through the soft place under Derl's jaw. It went in like a nail through bread dough.

"Guggghh!" Derl went. It must have spiked his tongue clean to the roof of his mouth.

He fell back, clucking, grabbing at his lips with both fat hands. Under his chin, the stub end of the stick dripped clear spit with the blood.

I got ready again, to hear the angel song you hear at the end of your life. I closed my eyes and listened and waited.

But that never happened. I heard a squeal instead of a song. I looked again at Derl, on his hands and knees, his one good eye fixed right on me, with the life draining out of it like the picture on a TV screen after you turn off the set at night.

"God damb!" he managed to say. "Thom a bidge hurd me . . ."

Then his good eye flickered up in his head, and Derl pitched pig-forward onto his nose, right between my legs.

I could see why now. The sharp end of the stick poked clean out the top of his head, just out the crown, like a little red arrowhead.

He had a long rackety fit, ugly and bloody. Then Derl was gone.

I killed a man.

He wanted to hurt me bad, but I fought back. And I killed him.

The shock went through me like lightning.

He was alive just then. Now he was dead.

Oh, me.

I heard a dry click, like popping knuckles. My head swung up to see the long nose of the shotgun, two feet from my face. Point-blank.

I saw it coming for the third time. He'd blow my brains out all over the brown leaves and the green fairy moss on the foxhole walls. Nothing could stop it.

"Close your eyes and pray to that fuckin' Father of yours, you sorry Christian bastard," Jeeter growled. "This is the end of the line."

My hand hurt so bad. I looked at that old friend, burned black on the tips of two dead fingers. Poor hand. It never did anything to this man in all its born days. It was never lifted against anybody except to scare some humility into folks that needed it. For that, Jeeter and Derl hurt me so bad.

I thought about the boy named Lester in the Bob-A-Lu. Maybe he was doomed, but he never backed down. Maybe Randy stood up for what was right that same way.

"Go on. You go on and shoot," I told him. "I ain't afraid to die."

Jeeter heard it. I watched his face screw up back of the beard. He looked like pure blind rage came over him. He shook so bad the gun wobbled.

"You little fucker." He growled and slobbered. "You beg, boy, and I might go ahead and kill you with the first shot."

"Go on. Shoot," I said again. "This world ain't no good place with folks like you in it."

I didn't care. I closed my eyes and saw Randy, waving "come on, brother, come on."

Something changed Jeeter's mind.

Down came the gun. He glared at me for a long minute, then he hopped in the hole and turned his dead friend over with his boot. Derl's eyes stared wide-open at the blue sky. A bubble of blood clung to his lips.

"Nekkid boy, I'll teach you to be afraid of me," Jeeter snarled, like a black-lipped dog. "You'll be afraid of me and *beg* me to shoot you before this is all done."

He didn't make this next too personal.

He just took another step straight over to me and raised the butt of the shotgun in the air over the top of my head like it was a post-hole digger.

I saw some boys set a house on fire one time, an old pine cabin swallowed up by kudzu. They lit a pile of newspapers by one wall and raced out the front door, and the house just went off like a bomb. This tall witch of fire jumped through the roof and stuck her jagged fingers up into all the chinaberry trees and laughed crazy and scorched the leaves.

I saw that fire woman now.

But some way she changed and turned soft, and I knew it was Cissy, last night, holding me. She kissed my lips, and vines of pure fire crawled my throat and leaped out of my mouth and nose.

After that, a bell rang again and everything disappeared, this time fading to black.

SICK, SICK, SICK.

I thought of a cat we used to see at the boys' home.

One time it got hold of a dying rat, a rat that was poisoned and slow. After that little treat, the kitty spent a whole day hunched up on the lawn, gagging. Between the heaves, it ate grass like a little lawn mower.

I laid there on my side in a different hole now, a deeper, wetter one, and felt the way that cat felt. A vomit ocean rolled inside of me, thick black waves and sticky cold.

There *was* one thing good. The feeling gradually came back to my legs and feet. My toes twitched at first, like jumping beans. I've seen little puppies herk and jerk in their sleep that same way. I guess they dream of hunting, running free.

Maybe my feet dreamed too, of running away. But I had no place to run now. Just deep, smothery mud.

After a long time, I tried to stand up. It took me a minute. My weak legs and a swimmy head made it tough. Sour stuff came up my throat while I stood there, trying to catch my balance.

I know that in the Bible, Daniel got thrown down in a pit of lions. I wonder how that fellow would have done here, pitched into deep cool muck that smelled like something dead. Shot and kicked and clubbed with a gun butt too.

I reckon this was more like what old Jonah felt inside of that whale. Chewed up and spit out. Waiting in the wet nasty dark for whatever happens next. Anything.

The walls of this new foxhole went straight up ten or twelve feet, deep as a well. I could stretch out my arms and almost touch both slimy sides of the shaft. *Could* have touched them, with all my fingers still on. Puddles of black water stood around my ankles.

Straight up, though, was better. I could see the sky. The blue, blue sky with green tree leaves flanked all around it like designs around a bowl. One big sweet gum grew close enough so that a squirrel actually saw me from a branch and panicked off into the woods. Once, a hawk turned in a beautiful circle right overhead.

I wished right then that I could climb like that squirrel or fly like that hawk. But it didn't do any good to wish.

Right now, I was just old stick-in-the-mud Buddy.

*

The sun burned directly over me, high noon, and the light in the hole got better.

I made myself be brave and look again at my fingers. A wet leaf, soaked through with blood, stuck to the nubs. My poor hand, under the soppy bandage, throbbed every time my heart hit a lick.

Careful as I could, I lifted off the leaf. It stuck for a second in the mess around that second knuckle. Of course there was a bate of blood, dried and new. You could see a knob of gristle too.

I wiggled the little cutoff things. They hurt like fire. But something else hurt even worse.

Lightning struck inside of me, to realize my hand would always be this way. It was just an unbelievable thought. Me this way from now on. An injured person nothing could ever fix.

You could show fingers like these to people for the rest of your life. You could wave them in front of doctors, or tell preachers how you got that way, or carry the hurt hand up and put it on the fat knee of The Father himself, who caused all this mess. It wouldn't matter. What's gone is gone in this old world.

You think the flesh-and-blood of a man is so great. But a frog can get a leg cut off and—presto!—just grow another one in nothing flat. You tug a lizard's tail and it'll come off, wiggling in your hand. Old Mr. Lizard just gallops on off and grows a new one, good as the first, maybe even better.

Nothing can make a person's fingers come back.

I thought about that till I got sick. Sick, for real. Up came pieces of the last four hours, I reckon. And I hurt inside after that.

Easy does it, I told myself. Be like Sack. Things fell off Sack all the time, but he never grumbled.

I slid down and had a seat, put my back against the slimy foxhole walls. The water puddled around my ankles.

It was bound to happen someday. Life ain't always no sunny day at the beach. You get cut up and banged around and learn from all of those sharp edges and hard knocks.

Out here in the woods, too many things crawl and fly and fall and grow and rattle to ever let you have a beauty parlor life. I reckon it's always been like that. In Bible times, folks had to fight the monkeys for peaches off the trees and work hard to make sure the wolves and lions didn't belch them up.

Still, The Secret Place, rough as it is, never took away my fingers.

A man did that. A man who might do even worse. Because he was cruel.

That afternoon, he showed just how cruel. He came to the edge of the new hole, Jeeter the Giant, taller than ever now, and me in deeper. Of course, he spit tobacco down at me. It went over my arm and splashed in the cold water by my bare feet. Then he yelled, in a scary voice.

"You left something over in the other hole, parachute boy!"

He threw things down the foxhole. They came straight at my face. I jerked so they wouldn't hit me, and heard them land—*ploop! ploop!*—in the water.

There.

They wiggled like two fat white worms in the black water.

Like they were still part of me.

*

Maybe I went to sleep. Or worse.

Anyway, I had the shivers when I woke up. I couldn't stop for nothing. It was pitch-dark. The end of a whole day. Or a hole day, if you got to be a smart aleck.

My hurt fingers. I couldn't see them now in the dark. But nothing good was going on with my injured hand. It throbbed to beat the fanciest band in the world.

This hole was no fun. It didn't even have fox fire. Too deep. Standing water at the bottom.

I tried to find a bright side to look on. And I did come up with one thing.

At least no water rattlers beat their tails in this mudhole.

This would actually be the perfect spot for a ball of water rattlers to turn up. Down in a place where you couldn't get away.

In these parts, water rattlers rolled along the bottoms of rivers in snaky knots, glowing orange at night like those witch hats by the highways where convicts work. You might see water rattlers tumbling around in the muck any time of the year. They don't hibernate like most snakes.

Randy said the bite from a water rattler was so poison that you could eat a fig off a tree where one shed its skin and sweated five years ago, and if the sweat made it into the tree roots and up to the leaves and into the fig, it would still kill you dead as a doornail.

At least no water rattlers lived in this hole. But I did find some betsy bugs crawling around, and little mosquito babies, wiggletails, doing tricks in the water.

I spotted those mosquitoes in the afternoon after Jeeter came to the edge of the hole and peed in on me.

What could I do? I just put my hands over my head and squatted down and put up with it. Right under my nose, I saw all the little wiggletails. They tumbled around in the water like school was out for the summer.

The ones that hatched made dentist-drill noises in the dark all around my head.

It struck me, though, that except for those mosquitoes and the sound of my feet sucking when I moved, this new world was a quiet, sort of peaceful, place.

I even thought about being dead down here.

I reckoned a hole was a better place to die than lots of other places. A hole would be fitting, since holes always worried me.

Most folks, standing out scratching their balls by a fence or leaning over to rag off a dipstick under a car hood, never think twice about your average, ordinary hole.

Oh, they might watch a chipmunk get sucked down one. Or see some poor little girl fall down a well somewhere with the National Guard standing by, ready to dig her right out after the TV cameras set up.

But holes know something. They always go as deep as they have to go, then just stop. You find bones in holes. Worst of all, holes are always there, just waiting for something to get in them.

Now I ain't saying they're not useful. Ask old Sky King about that. All I'm saying is they make me uncomfortable.

When I was little, I heard about a man who died in a hole. He was a farmer, picking collards one day, when a funny little brown dog came down a row and nipped his ankle. It chilled the farmer's heart to see that dog trot off. It followed a straight line, not looking right nor left. It slobbered a trail of white saliva.

This farmer knew rabies, and he knew this was how he would die.

He hobbled into the house, fetched a rifle, and made an end of the dog. He burned its shaggy body on a hot fire set with fat lighter. Then, as soon as the last ashes settled, he went straight to the barn, and took out his pick and shovel.

Right in front of the barn door, he started to dig a hole. He worked all day and night, pouring sweat in the sun, pouring sweat in the moonlight. He dug deeper and deeper, and by and by, sank clear out of sight. One shovelful at a time.

He dug himself a prison. Like the one I was stuck in.

Love was his reason. This farmer had a faithful wife and three children. He feared he might do just like a mad dog himself, when the disease came, and bite everybody in the world he loved. His beautiful wife, with that cool white skin. His little children asleep in their beds.

He stopped pitching out dirt when the hole got too deep to climb out of. Then, work all done, he sat down to wait.

For twelve days, his wife stood up on the dirt mound in her calico dress and cried, and the kids came and peeked down with scared faces at their daddy. He sat on a milking stool at the bottom of that red clay hole and never said a cross word to them.

His wife passed down his fiddle, and the family heard him scraping out tunes at night, under the ground, while they stared out the windows at a full moon and a sky full of shining awful stars.

Finally, the rabies did come. And that man went mad, running around and around and around the hole, snarling, foaming at the mouth, yelling and howling and biting the skin off the back of his own hands. He scraped off all his fingernails trying to climb out of the pit and tear the whole world to shreds. And then he passed out of suffering.

A neighbor came and shoveled the dirt over him and filled up the hole.

"He must have wanted to see what it was like," the neighbor said, tapping a cross into the fresh earth. "The rabies. Else he'd of shot himself dead right off."

They said not one twig of grass ever grew again where that hole had been. Not one flower and not one weed.

There's too many stories like that for me to love holes.

*

I must have gone to sleep, because when I noticed things again, the sun was coming up.

The man with the black beard stood at the edge of the pit and stared in, tall as God. His eyes looked like he'd never slept once since the world was made.

I stared right back at him until he went away.

About an hour later, I got a surprise.

He threw something new down the hole. When I wasn't looking.

I glanced up, quick, to see him.

Too late. He was gone.

I picked a wild apple out of the mud.

A wild apple, ripe and sweet.

The green leaves of the big sweet gum tree tossed in a morning breeze overhead. I stood up and stretched and ate my gift fruit.

A sweet apple. Delicious.

What got into that Jeeter?

THREE DAYS DEEP

FIVE MORE APPLES in the next two days.

A handful of wood-ear mushrooms, the kind you can eat.

A few black walnuts, just dropped in now and then, like they fell natural. But it was impossible. No walnut trees grew anywhere near the foxhole. I could see the big sweet-gum, plus the green crowns of an oak and a wild cherry and a big sourwood. Not a walnut tree in sight.

It didn't make sense.

First, Jeeter the Giant tried to kill me. Then he threw food down to me.

What in the world did it mean?

Was he keeping me alive so the torture could go on?

I just scratched my head.

Next, a plum. A plum so ripe it tasted purple in the twilight.

*

The fruit was good, but not the rest of the news.

When the sun got high over the hole the third day, I saw how my arm had gone snakebite black, from the blown-off fingers up to the elbow. A fever throbbed up and down it, and I felt so weak I could barely stand up anymore.

But that hurt wasn't nothing compared to the ache I felt for Cissy.

It came to me that she could be close by, out in the woods, waiting on a time when she could try to save me. Part of me believed it, down in the dell like this.

See, maybe she threw down the apple and the nuts and the plum. Oh, but it was risky business. If a man like Jeeter caught sweet young Cissy Barber . . .

It could be Jeeter and that Derl already caught her. Maybe she never made it out of the woods that first morning.

But if those two *did* catch her, they sure didn't brag and go on about it. They seemed like the type to tell every awful thing they did to girls. And not just girls.

All I could do was hope and pray Cissy got up and sleep-walked away before the two devil soldiers came. She talked about that tingle she always had. I reckon stranger things have saved a person's life.

And if she escaped, likely Cissy went flying clear on out of the deep woods. Maybe she found a road to somewhere far beyond the Wiregrass. Out of Goshen and off to some far place, maybe without people like these. A new land, free and easy.

I hoped it for her. More than I hoped for help and rescue.

I got down on my knees in the slop at the bottom of the foxhole and asked a prayer for Cissy.

I prayed it to the God who loves everybody and everything.

*

One night, after the moon rolled over the hole like a big broke cemetery stone, a bunch of stars came out up there.

I felt like I was looking up a chimney. Or peeping up through the barrel of the biggest cannon ever made on this earth.

I imagined other folks out there somewhere, looking right back at me out of holes on their weird worlds.

"Here! Here I am!" I surprised even myself. "I'm down here!"

I called out loud. My voice sounded ugly, the way a crow sounds. So I didn't say anything after that.

But I prayed again. I got down on my knees, dizzy in the head, and squenched my eyes shut and talked to old God.

I promised God if I got out of this hole alive, I would build a fort in the woods where people could always come and be at peace. Just the way those Indians built that mound nested in among those red trees, way back in their time. I told God I would put treasure things in the fort. Turtle shells I found in the woods, and some necklaces made out of locust hulls picked off the trees, and dogwood limbs carved in the shape of wild animals.

Cissy too. I prayed so hard for her again. I asked God to look after her and give her some boy and new family that would be good to her. I remembered how her pretty white hair smelled in the sun. I thought how soft she felt to me.

I guess I prayed and prayed because I knew what would happen now. It was as clear as clear could be.

I would pass beyond this vale of tears at the bottom of a foxhole. Out in the woods where nobody would ever know. Curled up with my hands around my knees. Starved. Or dead from the fever in my arm. Then Jeeter the Giant, if he was still up there, would pitch in leaves and limbs till I was covered up forever. My bones would turn into coal down here.

My arm was turning to coal already. Black up to the elbow. Bad to smell. Hurting.

The hurt got clear up to my heart, too. Nothing ever felt so bad.

*

That night, an angel.

I squatted against the wall of the hole, while the water slopped over my ankles. My feet squelched every time I moved to get comfortable.

This angel came right through the wall of the hole and stood at the bottom by me. The angel reminded me of a bear, the way it stepped slow and careful, sniffing and poking around. It finally came right up close.

I raised my head, squinted to see.

It wasn't like you'd think an angel would be, all fog lights and pretty singing and sharp gold claws and sparks of fire, like loose feathers, sizzling off the pure white wings. This angel had shaggy black hair, thick as wires, all over. It hunkered down and wiped a clear spot on one wall. It wrote something right on the dirt wall, in burning letters.

"Buddy," it said out loud. "I'm an angel. Here to show you something. You watch close. People don't get this kind of personal attention much nowadays."

I pulled myself over on one arm and leaned my cheek against the mud wall, watching over the angel's rough shoulder. I could feel a fever fire burn inside my hurt arm. I knew I could write in flames too, if I had to.

"You got to go here," the angel said. "That's the way out of this hole."

I had to make my eyes focus. I could make out a capital U at the first. I squinted and leaned closer. *Up.*

"It's the only way out."

"Okay," I said. My tongue felt like a shoe. "I believe you. Up."

I heard a weird little laugh and sparks filled up my head.

When I looked again, instead of an angel, a live skunk stared at me. It stood on its tiptoes with its tail hiked. Its mean eyes burned, black little oil drops.

It made up its mind.

It sprayed.

I finally drowned the stinking thing, after lots of clumsy kicks that missed. Got a bare foot on it, blind and gagging, and held it under till the bubbles stopped. Before it died, the skunk like to have torn my whole foot off.

After the splashing stopped, way up the hole, up there where the first morning light came in, hard big laughs fell in on me like black rocks.

*

I ate the skunk the best way I could, with no skinning tools and just one hand to work with.

I've tasted better things.

The shiny skunk hair stuck all in my teeth, and the oily meat tasted like a skunk smells. But I would have eaten the dirt off the walls if nothing else came my way.

It was hungry down in that hole.

*

The fevers came and went. It rained some that day and the hole turned more miserable than ever, then the sun flumed out and made a show, then there was some weather I couldn't remember. But no matter what the weather did, the temperature in my head climbed like a bottle rocket four or five times a day.

I burned so hot, my brain felt like a melted ice-cream

sandwich lying in the blacktop parking lot of some Piggly Wiggly in the middle of August. Heatwaves and broken glass and sandspurs stuck in every thought.

I learned something in that hole, though.

You can beat a fever.

You can sweat it out. You can lie in the cool deep of the world and look up at the blue sky, blue as somebody's eyes when they tell a lie, and directly you'll feel what's still alive about you. It'll push out the fever. You'll see the fever bleed into the wall around you like a red shadow.

You'll be too tired to even move. Maybe even feel a little sick. But everything will be better after that.

*

I changed some ways down there.

I didn't really hate the whole world now. I didn't want to ruin everything I ever saw for everybody, just so they'd be like me. Just so they'd be miserable and lost, with nothing to believe in, not even a pipe dream.

A voice inside my head sobbed and sobbed, when I thought about all that I did up there, in that world where I used to live.

One time, I heard Sack's voice in that same place inside me. Sack, raging at the world, growling and roaring like a lion. But the new voice, the sad hurt, took over. Sack was drowning out.

I looked down at my hand, black and stiff. On the end, I saw a monkey's paw, with the fingers seized up.

It was hard to look at that.

But I forgave myself. I forgave Buddy for that.

I forgave Buddy for killing a man, even if it was self-defense and the man deserved to die ugly.

I forgave the world for everything.

Now I was ready.

I lay down in the water and waited and watched the far-away stars.

THE VOICE FLOATED down, heavy as a bumblebee.

"You play your cards right, you might get out of that hole after all."

Jeeter squinted into the hole at me. His black beard hung down and flapped when his mouth moved.

"Hey! Flyboy! You there?"

He knew the answer to that.

"I seen some of your Christian Soldiers on patrol this morning. Reckon they're searchin' the woods to find where you floated down."

Over to one side, in the gray water, a fat black betsy bug took a nap in the leftover skunk bones. I thought of poor Sky King, sleeping among those honey-colored Indian skeletons. That boy died for nothing. Now somebody wanted me dead for nothing too.

Maybe it was the morning air. Or maybe it was the skunk meat. Whatever, I felt my hot fever rush back in, and I got mad. Buddy wasn't no pile of bones yet.

"Hey! Soldier boy!" Jeeter hollered. "You alive?"

"Damn sure am!" I yelled back. "Full of skunk meat and gully water. Better'n I been in a long, long time."

My voice surprised me. It sounded like somebody I never met in my whole life.

The giant whistled low.

"Well, if that don't beat all. Sassy. 'At's good. Well don't you run off, FlyBoy. I might need to swap you for a get-out-of-jail card here in a minute. Your friends might make a deal, they want you bad enough."

Was it true?

Was there a chance to get out after all?

Inside me, something with feathers tried to fly all of a sudden. It tried to flutter right up that hole to the blue sky.

*

I had to believe that, sooner or later, all the chances that ever let me down in this world got together for one long guilty look in a mirror somewhere. They shook their shaggy old heads and just had to say it. Old Buddy's got enough bad luck for one lifetime. Let's give him a break.

Maybe it was my birthday today. Whatever, I believed I could feel luck in the air. I might still find a way up those wet black walls.

"You got more wild apples?" I yelled up the pipe. "Hey, Jeeter!"

Jeeter looked confused by that. He frowned, and then he went away.

Let him go on thinking I'm the parachute man, I thought. Shoot, I'll *be* the parachute man. I'll quote Bible verses and march in place till the green grass is tramped down. I'll salute till my arm falls off—*that* shouldn't take long.

Whatever it takes to get out of this pinch, I'll do it. I'll be the best Christian Soldier that ever prayed to the Christian flag. Till I get free and clear.

Someone leaned over the hole, and the light faded. Jeeter again. Eyes like double buttholes. That awful mouth.

"They're close by now, Flyboy. Hey, I about decided you wouldn't ever talk again," he said. "You ain't said four words in four days."

Not to you, I thought. *But I talked more to God down here than old Job in the Bible, fussing about his boils and risens.*

Jeeter grinned. I thought the whole inside of his head might fall out through his rotten yellow teeth.

"Old Derl, he's your neighbor now, son. Put him in the next hole over." Jeeter grinned even bigger. "Thought about killing you for what you done to him. but then I got to figurin'."

He talked in this I've-got-a-secret voice.

"Woulda killed the stupid son of a bitch my own self, you hadn't. He bugged the daylights out of me."

I had a vision right then.

While Jeeter yakked on, it flew to my eyes.

A hand peeled tinfoil back off a big aluminum pie plate. The plate nearly buckled in half with the weight of the food heaped up high. A baked cornbread pone. A sweet potato. A whole fresh sliced tomato, an ear of white corn sopped in melted butter, butter beans steaming in a green pile, fried okra, and side meat.

Buddy wanted to live.

Here's the lesson you learn at the bottom of a hole. Sad sorrow can't kill you, if you don't let it.

"There's a horse pear tree up past that big poplar tree with the lightning scar!" I yelled. "You could throw me down a pear or two. I'm starving slap to death."

He talked on, sort of crazy, too loud for a man trying to

hide from Christian Soldiers. Maybe the heat and the woods finally drove him crazy.

"Hey!" I hollered up there, louder now. "I can't hardly stand up, I'm so hungry. You can't swap me for nothing if I'm starved to death."

It got quiet up there. I heard a mockingbird sing.

Another flash of a vision.

I imagined a soft braid of Cissy's hair spilling down the foxhole, long as a ladder. I dreamed it took me round the waist and lifted me up. I felt like Jesus rising into the clouds.

All of a sudden green pears splashed down around me like hand grenades. They scared the vision out of me. Those rotten laughs tumbled down among them.

"Go on and eat 'em, Flyboy," Jeeter yelled. "Get good and fat. I want 'em to know I took real good care of you."

I ripped at a pear. It was so hard my tooth came out. My own front tooth. But I ate the pear anyway, fast, and felt it, right then and there, start to turn to flesh and blood in my own stomach.

God sent that pear to me.

I ate three, crouched in the mud with a grin on my face.

*

The Christian Soldiers finally found their way into this part of the deep woods. It was late in the day, a big storm on the way. The woods are tough even when it's seventy degrees and not a cloud. In a gully-washing rain, things can happen out of the ordinary.

I saw and heard little snatches when the soldiers arrived. Along with what I learned later on, I have a clear picture of what happened to Jeeter. And a clear picture of all that led up to a great miracle.

First, Jeeter shinnied up the big sweet-gum tree over my

hole to scout out the situation. I could see him plain against the late sky, right above me, like a cow caught in wind-tossed branches. He wedged his big belly hard into the V of the tree trunk, got a death grip with one hand, and kept the other hand free to work a pair of binoculars. It was late in the day now, blue o'clock. Jeeter peeped through his spyglasses and licked his lips, over and over, the most nervous man you ever saw.

A squad of sweat-soaked men approached, worn out and a little careless. They tramped through the blowing dry leaves with their eyes raised no higher than their shoe tops. Searching the ground. Looking for clues left by a downed pilot. On the watch for trip wires too.

Sure enough, these were Christian Soldiers, with the gold cross on one sleeve. Usually, they were good fighters, maybe not as good as the world's best SWAT team, but loaded with guns and not scared of a little killing.

The leader was seriously big, a black man. Thick black-rimmed glasses perched on his nose. Sweat glistened on his thick arms, and his face shined like an eggplant. He carried an automatic rifle on a strap around his rocky shoulders. Like the blaze on a thoroughbred horse's face, a gold captain's cross dressed the front of his helmet.

He led eleven men, who straggled through the woods in ones and twos. Tired soldiers. Disciplined or not, they sounded as loud as a cattle drive. I reckon they didn't worry about canteens clanking against the bushes when the rushing wind and snapping limbs made such a big noise.

Near the sweet gum tree where Jeeter hung on for dear life, the leader raised his hand and the group fell out. Three or four flopped to the ground, three or four others put their backs against tree trunks. Some guzzled water from their canteens, their heads thrown back and their eyes closed. You could see their Adam's apples go fast, up and down.

"Ten minutes," the black commander said, his voice stern like he was talking to bad dogs. "Cornelius, Crow, Baker. You, Martin, Hutchinson. Secure the perimeter. Do it *now*. Watch for the damned Devils."

Those five unlucky men groaned and heaved up their heavy packs and limped off in different directions. One gave a look back at the captain that said as much as any cussword you can think of.

The rest of the squad relaxed now. One man tugged free a boot and rubbed his foot with both hands. Beside him, a Latin boy struck a match for a cigarette, but the wind blew it out. Another soldier peed off to the side, downwind, looking absentmindedly at what he held in his hands.

A message floated down from the tree.

"Could shoot the head off that little pecker from here," said Jeeter the Giant. He raised up in the crotch of the tree and showed both his hands clearly, without a weapon.

Oh, it caused panic on the ground. Those soldiers might have been clowns at a circus. Guns rattled and combat boots tore up the ground and people rolled over and over to hide back of trees. The man caught peeing danced off crazy and fell down a little hill.

"Whoa now!" Jeeter announced, holding his hands even higher. "Ain't got a gun!"

The black captain fixed his sweaty face back of his rifle sights. Six other weapons leveled on Jeeter now.

"Identify yourself, soldier."

"Jeeter. Terse Jeeter. Pascagoula, Mississippi. I ain't got no gun. But I got something you want. A downed pilot."

The leader of the Christian Soldiers kept his automatic rifle trained, his finger straining on the trigger.

"You one of the Devils?"

Jeeter grinned real broad.

"Does it matter? You looking for a flyboy, ain't you,

Cap? Shot down and parachuted in here. He's alive. You can have him. Thanks to me."

The black captain lowered his gun now, but his face didn't show kindness.

"Keep talking."

Down scrambled Jeeter, about as agile as a sandbag, jumping free the last few feet from a low branch to the ground. He rolled when he landed, and the nest of guns covered him.

Jeeter stood up and brushed leaves off his filthy uniform. They flew off in the wind.

"You make me nervous, boys." Jeeter chuckled, and he did sound nervous. "It don't take but one of you to kill me. Why don't the rest of you just point those weapons somewhere else?"

Instead, the captain jammed the muzzle of a big automatic rifle hard into Jeeter's ribs.

"Tell us about our missing jet pilot, Devil. That's all I want to hear right now. My mission is to bring him back alive. I'm ordered to kill anybody that delays us."

Jeeter saw it was time to play at least one of his cards.

"I saved his life, Cap. He's in a safe place. Close by. You got me to thank."

It turned out Jeeter was a pure midget, compared to the black captain. That soldier towered to a height of six feet seven or eight, at least. He glared down at Jeeter out of thick glasses, through bloodshot eyes.

His finger twitched on his weapon, like he didn't really care to see what came down from any tree in these parts. Especially this wee little black-bearded man like Zacchaeus in the Bible.

"You've got about three heartbeats to show me where this pilot is, Devil. Talk, or you join a lot of other sorry rebel bastards in hell."

Give him credit. Jeeter didn't bluff so easy. That smile

oozed out again, followed by a spit of tobacco off to one side. He hadn't meant to, but a gust of wind carried it extra far, and it splattered a Christian Soldier's rolled-to-one-side helmet, bull's-eye.

Jeeter knew he better keep talking.

"Seems to me you'd want to be a little more patient than you are, Cap. The flyboy's a little piece through the woods, is all. You'll find him. If you make me a deal, I mean."

The captain listened, with the sweat pouring off him, Jeeter dead in his rifle sights.

"A deal," said the captain with a sour look.

"That's right. A deal. Your Bible oath to take me back safe and sound as a POW and get me the hell out of this war. I'm done with killing. I'm a good man at heart. I've had enough of this awful butchering."

The captain's nostrils flared.

"You admit you *are* a soldier then? A Devil?"

Jeeter grinned. *"Was* a soldier, Cap. But not no Devil. That's *your* word. Just a man who fought—"

Jeeter never told why it was he fought.

The captain opened fire.

His white teeth gritted and his face turned into a black mask with fangs. The burst of hot automatic-rifle fire ripped seven or eight bubbling holes in Jeeter's body, climbing from the belt on one side clear to the other shoulder.

"Devil!" screamed the captain, spit flying. "Die, you enemy of God and The Father almighty!"

Jeeter stepped back with this surprised look.

Seven other soldiers opened up on him then.

The roar of gunfire spooked every bird out of every tossing tree for two miles around. The mess that used to be Jeeter the Giant spattered thirty or forty feet away into the bushes.

A cloud of gunsmoke hid things for a minute.

The black captain stepped forward as the smoke blew off and stood where Jeeter bargained for his soul just a second ago. Jeeter's big hand lay on the ground, dirty under the fingernails. The captain kicked it off into the trees.

"God and The Father have mercy on your soul, you Devil bastard. Mercy ain't left up to me."

After a long moment, the captain ordered the squad to search the woods. The dark closed in fast now. So did a thunderstorm.

I didn't call out to them right at first.

I decided it might be a better idea to wait until after it got good and wet and dark.

$\mathcal{T}$HE LIGHT AT
THE TOP OF THE TUNNEL

ONE TIME A bad dog fell out of the sky.

It killed some people, and got killed its own self.

One of the boys in the orphans' home told this. It was all about how his family, his momma and daddy and him, had a nice pickup truck they took to town on Saturday nights, away back when. They lived in the country, not quite to where the railroad track cut through the thick trees at Big Head Gully and, after that, fed into a trestle over the Chattahoochee.

One Saturday, long before The New Times trouble, the family drove to Goshen and had a fine afternoon. They went to a movie and shopped in some toy stores. Drank milk shakes and just got giddy in the head with all the fun. When they started on back home, it was way past dark.

Where Highway 27 ducked under an overpass, all the life went right out of that trip.

Here's why.

The country around Goshen has some mean people. Folks that shoot and cut their own selves or their families if they can't find any strangers to shoot and cut. Folks born bad, like rotten eggs that hatched and grew up life-sized.

Some such mean so-and-so stood on top of the overpass that night. Smoking a cigarette, watching the road with snake-slit eyes. Waiting under the moon and stars for a car to come along, it didn't matter who.

My friend's family crested the hill in their pickup truck, all the windows down and the radio playing loud music. The momma had her hand out in the breeze, playing watch-the-fish-swim.

Oh, that sight must have brought a nasty smile.

When the truck got near, the man on the overpass reached behind him. He grabbed a big half-breed yellow dog by the scruff of the neck. He swung it up with a grunt and flung it, yelping and pedaling the air, right over the guardrail.

What did that dog think, on the way down? Why, oh why, wasn't I a bird dog, so I could fly on off from here?

What did Daddy think, when he saw a human being pitch a huge dog off the bridge, and it was too late to put on brakes and miss it? Lord, why me, why now, why this night, why my family.

That bad dog crushed the front windshield.

The boy in the orphan's home, who lived through it all, told every detail. How one minute the world out the truck windshield was black and headlight green. Then the world busted to pieces and something more awful than death got loose in the cab.

The dog snapped and squirted blood and hurt and howled. It mauled and yelped and snarled and bit anything it saw, including itself. Blinded by glass, with its broke ribs stuck through its fur, the pure torment made it rip off fingers and faces and buck up against the roof and dent it out, it hit so hard.

A real nightmare came true. Like so many did around here.

It wasn't any wonder that the daddy ran off the road and flipped the truck. It wasn't any wonder that the ugly wreck killed the momma and daddy. Or maybe the dog got them, before the wreck killed Old Yeller too.

The little boy graduated to the orphans' home, naturally. Somebody has to be an orphan, I reckon, to fill up such places.

Anyway, I got a reason for telling this story. Here it is.

That night, I waited for the soldiers to find me. The weather got as bad as I've ever seen. Then, something fell out of the sky on me too.

*

The cyclone rose just after dark. It hit like Noah's flood.

Lightning cinched the sky-high thunderheads in white-hot barbed wire. Tree limbs over the foxhole clawed at the clouds, and rain fell straight down the hole hard as eight-penny nails. I heard branches snap in half and crash to the ground all over the woods. Once, some dirt gave way from the wall of my prison, and I got scared of a cave-in.

Or drowning, if the water rose that high.

But those weren't the real worry that night.

Bigger things fell out of the sky.

A Christian Soldier.

Here he came from out of nowhere, right down the hole, steel-toed boots kicking and hands flying—*crash! splash! help!*

He hit me like a sack of corn chunked off the top of a barn. Knocked me flat down in the gravy water. It hurt so

bad, I couldn't even look. I tried one time, and the ice needles out of the sky nearly blinded me.

What would happen to old Buddy now?

Tweetie birds chirped in my ears, and soda water bubbles went popping off behind my eyes. Oh, I was scared. At
first, I knew it was a wampus cat, or maybe a bear, blinded
by rain and lightning. Then, a lighter clicked, fished out of
some pocket, and I could see everything.

I knew who he was.

The black captain. Boss of the Christian Soldiers.

Jeeter the Giant killer.

I bet there never lived two people more surprised to be
stuck in the same hole. That captain's chin dropped down
to about where the mud started. My eyes bugged out on
stalks like a scared snail's.

Before I could move, he snatched a nasty-looking pistol
out of some hiding place and pointed it straight at my face.

"One move, Devil, and you're dead meat. You got
that?"

The spinning wheel in my brain rattled, turning fast as it
could turn. Then the little silver roulette ball landed on an
idea.

"Thank the Lord," I told him, sitting back kind of
relaxed. "I've prayed and prayed. You're finally here."

"One more word, Devil," he growled, "I'll blow your
damn brains out all over this hole."

I stopped relaxing, and didn't move. Not one gnat muscle.

"Who are you?" he wanted to know. The gun jerked in
his big hand.

"I can't hurt you," I whispered, my voice still husky, un-
familiar. "Look. My arm got messed up bad in the plane
crash."

His eyes flickered, quick as a flash, down to my hurt,

back to my eyes. I saw the surprise on his face. My arm had turned as black as a rotten banana.

"You the Air Force boy?" he asked me. "State name, rank, and serial number."

Truth or dare. Big time.

I remembered the name stenciled on one scorched pocket of Sky King's uniform.

"Jellico," I told the captain. I made up more. "Air Force unit at Tyndal, Panama City. Don't remember my numbers, Captain. I've burned a fever and starved four days, and you just knocked me silly in the head on top of that."

I could have been dead and gone. Except for one thing.

He bought it.

"Excuse me if I don't shake your hand for savin' me," I tacked on fast. "You can see mine ain't fit for shakin' anymore."

We sat together in the dark mud at the bottom of a hellhole. That pistol fixed on me a second longer. Maybe he thought I seemed mighty young to be flying airplanes. Thank goodness for the hellacious rain and the mud and a sick cigarette lighter and my bad black eye and his fifteen-foot fall in the dark. Plus one other thing.

His glasses. Gone. Lost in the fall.

Directly, a relaxed look came to his face. Not a smile, exactly. He didn't look like a man who knew how to do that anymore. But what he said next made a horse leap a happy fence inside me.

"Glad to find you, Airman." That's what he said, even though there wasn't any glad sound in his voice. "I hope you're worth the trouble. I lost four soldiers out in these woods looking for you. I hope you're worth four dead Christian Soldiers."

"Four soldiers? Killed?"

"Devils loose all through these woods after we saw you

parachute in here. They're thick as fleas on a dog, looking for you. Just like us. You'd be a valuable prisoner, see? Oh, we did some killin' too. More than our four, I promise you that."

"I knew you'd make it," I told him.

Jeeter came back to life now.

I told the captain how that Devil with a black beard threw me down this hole and starved me. I told how he found me tangled in the trees in my parachute and planned at first to use me, like bait, to lure other good men. He'd blow them to kingdom come, one squad at a time, he said. Finally, though, I convinced him I'd be a good prisoner swap. Maybe get him into a country-club POW camp or something.

The captain nodded, his eyes lit.

"Devil we killed just now said he throwed you in a hole. None of us believed that, but I see now he told the truth." The cross on the captain's helmet caught the light. "Well, it's too bad. After two ambushes and four dead soldiers, we don't take chances."

He studied me a second, dark as it was, and added, "One thing, Jellico. Just between us."

"Sir?" Oh, didn't I play it cool and lay it on thick?

"You *smell* like you been down here rotting four days. Worse'n a skunk. That arm must have gangrene or something."

I played along, didn't take it personal. Mouth, don't fail me now.

But Mr. Mouth let loose a bad one.

BOOM!!! A lightning whip cracked the hide of those bull-black clouds up above and electricity leaped everywhere, the brightest flash I ever saw. Thunder rippled the water all the way down where we stood.

"Jesus!" I said.

Oh, it hung in the air.

I wished I'd said anything else right then—even "nigger."

But good luck fell on Buddy this time.

Thunder shook down a smothering load of dirt, one whole wall of the foxhole. The avalanche buried us to our knees.

The captain wanted to get back up to the world again. Quick.

"Stand back, Airman. Got to get their attention."

He hoisted his pistol, held it steady, jerked the trigger. Five times it kicked his hand down and a louder thunder than before rolled through my head. Oh, it was stupid. *More* dirt fell on us.

Out of the thick, oily gunsmoke and gritty cave-in dust, I heard him growl. "Man can't even step out in the woods and take a leak, he's gotta worry with falling down a hole in this Devil country."

Boom! Boom! The gun kicked his hand sideways twice more.

Somebody came running. A commotion up top.

"Hey!" yelled the captain. "You men get a rope down this hole! That's an order. Found Jellico down here. Our pilot's bad hurt!"

Things happened fast now. Strong lights caught us, me and the captain, so strong we had to cover our eyes. Loud voices after that, then the lights zoomed and swung and wild shadows yawed all around us.

Up top, I could see green wet shining men in the dark, hunched over like those famous picture-book dudes raising the flag on that Jap mountain in World War II. Lightning seared the air, and my mind took a photograph.

I felt something tickle my face. My head jerked back before I could make out a skinny nylon rope, green as a snake. It startled me so bad I sat flat down on my butt in the goop.

"Grab it, Airman, it's just a rope," the captain growled. Then he saw the obvious problem. My hand.

"Okay, here, give the rope to me."

Even stuck in gummy mud to his ankles, he did fine soldier work. He tied me into some kind of cat's cradle and jerked the slack out of the rope.

On his signal, I rose off the ground. Higher and higher, kicking at the walls to keep me free. I held on with my left arm, turned, spun in crazy circles the higher I got.

"Watch his arm," I heard the captain yell to his men. "He's hurt bad!"

Hauled on a nylon rope right up out of my own grave, I overflowed with love and gratefulness. Up and up went the rope swing, bumping through the dark, one strong tug at a time.

I felt fresh air and hard rain and rough hands, under my arms. Lightning ripped the sky like old cloth. Excited voices, like doctors with a new baby.

The soldiers hauled me free. The rain felt wonderful now, air fresh, air sweet. Two men carried me in a fireman's sling away from the lip of the hole. They ran. I was lighter than Styrofoam.

"Thank you. Thank you," I said. "Thank all of you Christian men."

I should have saved the thank you's.

The eyes in those battle-fired faces burned red. Something was wrong with that. Wrong here at the end of my rescue.

"Hold him! Get him down!"

The voices hard. Cruel hands. Sneering faces. Another rope wound around me. My feet fixed, hands hog-tied back of me.

What on earth? Something awful and wrong. Oh, this might be the end. How much more could a boy stand?

My eyes found a knot of men standing around the hole, looking down into it. A rescue rope lay snarled beside them on the ground.

"You hurt?" This sour voice grunted near my ear. "I'm your medic, son. I got to get you patched up. You worth a pretty penny if we deliver you to those Devils, flyboy."

My arm hair stood up all over, like I'd been hit by lightning.

These men too!

Traitors everywhere!

I watched the Christian Soldiers over the hole. They huddled and mumbled among themselves in the rain. Plotting. Finally, each one of four plucked a grenade off his belt.

Someone in the group counted:

"One, two . . ."

"Hey!" I heard a muffled voice from down in the hole. "Send down the rope! Sanders, you there? Jones? Soldier, that's an *order!*"

One of the Christian Soldiers smiled. You could see teeth as big as marble tombstones in the dark. He leaned over the hole, megaphoned his hand over his mouth and shouted.

"Ease up on your almighty orders now, Captain. Nobody's listening to your crap anymore. You got four of us killed today, and not one of them had to die. Now go to hell and explain it."

Horror. You could feel it well up and overflow the lip of the foxhole, cold and black and as heavy as smoke from a burning tire. Dimly, way off like dice rolling, you could hear the captain jam bullets into his pistol as fast as he could manage.

"Get it over with," somebody up top said.

". . . three, four. Boom."

The soldiers dropped all the grenades at once, then doubletimed back from the hole.

I imagined Mighty Danny Dynamite, so long ago, hugging that stick of TNT to his skinny fish-white chest.

A muffled explosion down the foxhole sent pieces up into the air, a mud geyser. Heavy things landed here and there in the woods.

Horror came again. But only over me. The Christian Soldiers traded smiles. One of them made a filthy sign, with both hands, at the curl of smoke drifting out of the hole in the storm.

I felt a sting in the muscle of my good arm. "Antibacterial," said a voice. "Hope it's not too late. I can smell the infection in that hand without even looking . . ."

Dear God, I thought.

Bad angels save men too.

*F*REE AT LAST

THOSE SOLDIERS STOOD over me, breathing hard, their faces smeared with bootblack and their mean eyes glittering.

Then, if things weren't bad enough, a face came down out of the dark, and my heart fell off a table.

"Hey! What have we got here!" His voice made my stomach hurt. "Buddy Butthole! Hey, butthole boy, remember me?"

I remembered Harvey Lee Lipp. Mr. Red, White, and Blue from the Bob-A-Lu. Cissy's friend, if a friend locks you in a car trunk. The big-time bullyboy.

Buddy. Buddy. Buddy. How did you get in this mess?

I got the same feeling in my stomach right then as one time when I ate a hornet nest on a dare, and the baby hornets hatched out inside of my stomach and stung me till I nearly died.

The mean old man who ran the orphans' home wouldn't

even let me go to the hospital. He said I "deserved it." All the kids at school were glad I got sick too.

That bunch of Christian Soldiers looked at me that way, listening to Harvey Lee.

"Hoo!" he was saying. "Ain't he *ugly* nekkid? Buddy Butthole, you hear? You *ugly. U-G-L-Y, you ain't got no alibi.* Yewww! And you smell bad."

Harvey Lee elbowed the soldier next to him.

"Guys, this here is pure gutter trash from Goshen, Alabama, you looking at. Ain't even got no mama and daddy. He's no shot-down jet pilot. In his mind, maybe."

Why didn't I just go on and pass away from those wasp stings way back when? I asked that, and I was serious.

I got to thinking that way.

Harvey Lee, Mr. Blue-eyed All-American Boy, he hollered the whole story about meeting me and the night at the Bob-A-Lu. With the rain dripping off the rim of his helmet, he told how he run me off, then single-handed fought The Wild Thing that night and scared it clear back to the hills. To hear him tell, Harvey Lee was a one-man Alamo, and he saved the Bob-A-Lu from Satan all by himself.

Harvey Lee still carried a big ugly scab on his chin, where he nosedived into the oyster shells out front of Bob-A-Lu that very same night. I knew his behind had some nice little corners too. But he never mentioned that part of the story.

The sergeant who was now in command listened to Harvey Lee, then looked at me, surprised. His face made a pig's seem smart.

"Private Lipp, are you *sure* this is the boy?" he kept saying. This time, all the soldiers listened while Mr. Tattletale told it over again.

Surprise left the sergeant's face, and something else, something bad, came back in its place.

It wasn't any use to pretend, so I didn't. I was too tired now.

In the cold rain, a mad-hornet swarm of Christian Soldiers gathered round. They all talked at once. Too much. I hadn't heard more than one human voice, hardly, in so many days. I couldn't understand a word. It sounded like they all hollered "rutabagas and potatoes" while they shoved one another to get to me.

That's when Harvey Lee waded right in, this awful light in his eyes, to show the rest how it's done.

"Buddy Butthole, you stink like shit," he gritted his teeth and said. "I'll have to take me a bath after I finish kicking and stomping you."

His first kick got me clean, right in the ribs. It knocked the breath right out of me.

"You ain't a durned orphan," Harvey Lee snarled. "You're a bastard. Your old lady gave you away. Everybody knows your story."

I just tried to shut down my ears and eyes and nerves and hopes and dreams and see way past those hard boots and knees, out through the trees, up the roads, up into the hills, where the cool green pines whispered in the distance, forever and ever amen.

And way out there, I saw my miracle.

Off in the distance.

Lightning flashed. A figure in the woods glided between two dark trees. It slipped across a little low run, and up the other side.

Two hundred yards, and coming hard.

The boots and gunstocks came hard too. Hard and fast. Mean. I only saw a now-and-then pale flicker of a face, like the underside of a barn owl flashing by.

Hurry. Better hurry, Sack. There won't be no Buddy left.

One man—Harvey Lee?—got down on his knees in the

mud, laughing, and he pounded my face—*bam! bam! bam!*—with his fists.

It didn't matter. After two or three hard haymakers, a man can't feel pain any worse.

See, Buddy had eyes they can't ever hit or bruise or swell shut. And these eyes watched that minute for something wonderful and terrible at once. Coming for to carry me home.

One hundred yards now, moving fast as it could in this dark and this rain and this wilderness.

A miracle.

It was a miracle covered with snakeskins, ugly as Nebuchadnezzar, and scarier than any sin you ever knew.

Oh, my hair stood up. I tell you. Just like any person in the whole world who saw that thing, I sat up straight with fear. The Christian Soldiers kicked me flat again. But I didn't care.

I didn't have to be afraid anymore.

Sack was here.

Like the cavalry. Like Mighty Mouse. Just in time.

*

Take your average bunch of hate-filled, hopping-mad, grown-up soldiers in steel-toed combat boots. They can work over a tied-up fourteen-year-old boy with a gimpy arm pretty doggone good.

Near as I could figure, here's why they bothered: It must be frustrating when you plot to swap your own shot-down pilot to your enemy for gold and riches, then he turns out counterfeit.

The Christian Soldiers took it hard, and they let me know. They hurt me so bad at the end I had to yell.

"Sack! Help!"

"Go on and holler," somebody growled. "It makes us like it more."

"Please! Please hurry! Sack!"

Then Sack did.

That horrible woman with snakes in her hair in those old picture books, she would have turned to stone her own self with just one look at Sack on this rainy night.

It was clobbering time.

*

Rain washed the hurt places on my face.

I lay on my side, spitting broken things out of my mouth. My side was killing me.

I ached bad, but I could still see the whole scene play out, herky-jerky, like in an old movie. The Keystone Kops, where everybody runs twice as fast as they can and people fall down and their hats blow off and funny piano music plays.

Sack first stepped out of the woods, raised clawed hands over his gnarly head and snapped his mighty tushes, sharp enough to bite any man's backbone right in half.

A Christian Soldier stood in back, a boy not much older than me. This boy hadn't even hit me. He had a face too sweet for what was going on.

After Sack, his face might never smile sweet again. Or even smile.

A steel-clawed hand grabbed that boy's shoulder—youch! The hand whirled him around, face-to-face with Mr. Bad Dream himself. I could see the light go out in that boy's eyes just like somebody sneezed on a candle. He crumpled up at the knees and melted.

That's when Sack let go a roar! So loud! Loud as the shout at the end of the world!

A mighty war cry!

Aaaaaaaaaaaaaaaarrrrrrrrrrrrrrrrrrrrggggggggghhhhh!

I'm the Wild Thing!

Aaaaaaaaaaaaaarrrrrrrrrgggghhhhh!

Hot flashes and cold chills scooted up and down me all at once. They traveled so fast my skin nearly crawled off and ran lickety-split out into the woods to save itself.

Oh, they did me wrong. But the worst man in the world would still pity those Christian Soldiers right then.

They about-faced, these hard-fighting, hard-hearted killers with knives in their eyes. They all turned around and saw You-Know-Who and that was just all she wrote.

Sack hit like a hundred sticks of dynamite, a runaway train with five hot engines and a brimstone tornado at a fireworks factory. All at once.

Aaaaaaaaaaaarrrrrrrrrrrrrrrgggggggggghhhhhhhh!

One little soldier spun his wheels so fast that he bogged up to his knees in the mud before he could move an inch.

Sack jumped on that one's back and snapped with his iron fangs, and the boy fainted dead away.

Two more little soldiers shinnied the first tree they came to and climbed so high, so fast, that they ran out of tree before they stopped climbing and then crashed down in the dark and bounced two feet high when they whammed against the ground.

Sack put a hairy foot on top of each one and bellowed mighty.

Three little soldiers just crawled around on the ground, dragging their hind legs like seals, barking, gone plumb out of their minds.

Sack just let 'em bark and crawl.

Four little soldiers flew fast, out into the wet dark woods like blinded goatsuckers. You could probably come back in a week and still hear screaming out there.

And that left one little Christian Soldier. Harvey Lee Lipp. He could have gotten clean away like the last four scared-blind rabbits, but he hesitated just one second too long.

Sack caught him.

If anybody had told me what that meeting would be like, I would have shaken my head. No way.

But I saw it myself.

Harvey Lee on the right. Sack on the left. A Dodge City showdown, high midnight.

It didn't last long.

Sack walked right up and looked Harvey Lee in the face. Guess which one's knees knocked like a washing machine full of baseballs?

Sack reached out, real calm, and made a little *X*, with one big hairy thumb, right on Harvey Lee's chin. It looked like a preacher putting a blessing on somebody's troubled head.

Then Sack rared back a giant fist and threw a windmill of an uppercut that knocked Harvey Lee clean out of his boots. He landed with a splash over yonder somewhere.

Then Sack tore two big clots of hair out of his own chest and stood on his tiptoes and bellowed and raged.

"I'm The Wild Thang and *I know where you live, Harvey Lee Lipp.* Aaaarrrrggggggghhhhh!"

He was clobbered. Sack knocked him blind and barefoot. Harvey Lee crawled off, heading for the hills, on his all fours.

Too bad his directions weren't better.

He crawled right over the edge of the foxhole where I'd been trapped for the last four days of my life. Whatever was left of the black captain still smoldered down there.

I heard a splash.

Sack snarled above that hole and thumped a mighty chest like King Kong.

Nobody in The Father's army even fired a shot. Nobody could, scary as it was.

Nobody ever will, when bullets are so terrified they whine and whimper in the gun and won't come out.

*

I couldn't move fast, but I got to my feet.

A big red fireball came out of the woods and rolled around and around me, in among the foxholes and pine trees. It scared me some. It tumbled big and hot and loud and fast, raising a ruckus like a roller-coaster wreck.

Lucky for me, my time hadn't come. I spoke to the fireball, two mean words—"Git on!" Then off it went, wobbling on through the trees till it splashed into Old Mercy River and sizzled out in the black water.

It was gone, and I was safe. Sack found me.

Even for Buddy, it took a lot of courage to just stand there by Sack.

"Lordy," I said. "Lordamighty. It's a miracle. Thank you."

Sack stared at me. Sack dripped in that dark rainy night like something dredged out of a pond.

Then Sack reached out those arms with that spray of sharp claws on the end and threw them around me in the hardest hug ever.

"I knew you would come," I managed to say, my mouth hurt, everything hurt. "I missed you. Bad."

Sack shook that mighty head up and down once, real solemn. I knew those eyes.

"Scared I might go on and die down in that hole," I said. "Believe this arm"—I held out the poor thing—"I believe it went and died anyway."

I heard a heavy sigh. Sack again.

"You pitched apples down the hole," I said. "That was you, weren't it?"

Sack nodded.

"You helped me," I said. "You saved my life."

That's when Sack lifted off the head, struggling with its weight a little. A gush of steam rose up and blew away in the misty night air.

A damp blond top appeared underneath, like a flower opening.

"Man," Cissy said. "This thing smells the worst."

I fell down on my knees, and hugged her waist so hard with my good arm that she couldn't talk anymore. Tears burned out through my sore eyelids and scalded their way down my cheeks, and I pulled in deep breaths.

"Thank you, Cissy," I whispered. "You just don't know."

Cissy fell down on her knees in the mud that way too. "Poor baby. I do know too. I watched what you were going through. With no way I could figure out to help."

"I thought I would die for sure," I told her. "I thought I lost once and for all this time."

"No, no, poor Buddy," she went. "Here I am."

She ran her steel claw through my hair.

"I got scareder than you," she said. "I sleepwalked, and when I woke up that morning, I was all the way over to Old Mercy River, out to my knees, and I woke up looking at my reflection in the water. Still aglowing with the fox fire. Time I got back to you, those men had you down that hole and everything raged out of control. I didn't know what to do."

"You should have just left," I told her. "It was dangerous."

"No way, Buddy. I never even thought of leaving. I got real scared, was all. I kept hoping those creeps would just go on off and leave you long enough for me to drop down some parachute cords or something. You could just climb right out and we'd be gone—*whhhttt!*—like that."

My brain wheeled around, remembering, and I felt sick and held tight to Cissy. That didn't help much. Sack smelled like rotten buzzard eggs left three days in a hot diaper pail. Cissy was right.

"I knew when those last Christian Soldiers showed up out here, there was no more waiting for the safest time," she said finally. "So I went and dug out old Sack. We were going to save you or die trying."

"You got to be Sack and Sack got to be you," I told her, and it broke my heart someway.

One of those ruined soldiers crawled through between us then, honking like a goose, dragging his legs, every now and again bucking up and kicking at the air with his heels like a stung mule.

Cissy patted my back and tried to lift me.

"Buddy, pull yourself together now. We've got to go. You didn't get out of that hole just to sit here and squawl. There's fighting men all over these woods. Devils *and* Christian Soldiers. I've been hiding out from one bunch after another. You can't trust anybody. It's pure crazy. None of it makes sense."

"You're right." I wiped my nose on Sack's knee. I got up and fought off the black bats that thumped into my face for just a second. Then I was ready, more or less.

"Let's go," I said. "It's travelin' time."

But I just stood there.

So did Cissy. We both looked out into the dark woods, this direction and that, wondering.

Cissy took my good hand and looked at me. She stood so close and pretty. The cool rain fell on her flushed face. I saw myself like a mirror in her green eyes when lightning went.

"Buddy, you know what? You smell like a skunk, boy."

After she said it, she laughed. Hard. Like a goon on the

moon. So hard and so deep in the belly it made me wonder.

Maybe Jeeter didn't throw a skunk down anybody's fox-hole after all.

*

In its weird way, the woods help you understand what you already knew all your life.

Lightning hit in the top of a tree way over there. It took me a minute to realize it was one of the red trees at The Secret Place. The tallest trees in the woods.

Every limb shot fiery sap out the tips, and the tree threw off blazing cinders of bark in all directions, like a hell-hound shaking dry after a hot bath. You could smell the scorched sap strong.

Right after that, out past any place I'd ever been, out in the deepest woods of all, I heard something else.

A sign.

The screamy-dreamy yell of a wampus cat.

Cissy heard it too. She grabbed my hand.

We took an achy step, straight toward that hollering. Me and Cissy together went toward the scary cry in the deepest woods of all.

Oh, I've moved faster. I've been in better shape. But this limp would get me there. Sooner or later.

Old Moses moved slow like this. It took him forty years in the wilderness before he finally laid eyes on the Land of Goshen. And what happened when he did?

The Israelites went there and fought with everybody they ever met. Wars from then till now.

Some promised land.

I ain't but fourteen. Maybe fifteen by now, I don't know.

But I'm way ahead of Moses. 'Cause I know the way to a promised land that's just my own.

I got a clear sign to go there too.

The Bible says Moses saw a burning bush.

Tonight, me and Cissy and Sack saw a whole burning tree.

That's the way to the Land O' Goshen.